THE PRETEND FRIEND ASSOCIATION

© *Copyright 2013 Hannah Reimers*

The PFA
Part 1: Stories
© Copyright 2012 Hannah Reimers

The PFA
Part 2: Diagnostics
© Copyright 2013 Hannah Reimers

The PFA
Part 3: Seasons
© Copyright 2013 Hannah Reimers

The PFA
Part 4: Decisions
© Copyright 2014 Hannah Reimers

Table of Contents

The PFA
Part 1: Stories

Introduction:

Monday, June 21, 2010

It was nearly impossible to stand, but I forced myself to peer into my bedroom. I clutched the doorframe, lightheaded, as my eyes glazed over. It was necessary to focus on breathing.

In and out, I told myself. *Come on, Anna Grace, don't stop.*

God, I prayed, *please don't let me stop breathing.*

Something had happened in the previous few days. We'll never know whether it was a relapse of that pesky staph infection or something else, but I believed there was a possibility my kidney disease would win.

Walking to my bed stole the last bit of my stamina, but I had to make sure my purple folder was safely tucked underneath the decorative pillows.

Think, for a moment, of what people have to keep of their childhood and teen-year pastimes. Some have incredible knowledge of sci-fi stories or "mad skills" on a skateboard. Others have high scores on a video game memory card or an array of homemade movies on the Internet. Well, I had a thick purple binder literally filled with hundreds of single-spaced, 8-point font pages about the imaginary characters of my childhood... and the secret "confidants" of my struggles to survive a debilitating kidney disease.

Twenty hours before major surgery, most people would be worrying about dozens of things. I'd act like a normal person later, but not yet. During my last minutes at home, I had to thank God for one of the many gifts that had gotten me thus far: my amazing imagination.

There are so many fears that come with being a chronically ill teenager. My most irrational fear was that if I died, my characters would die, too.

Saturday, June 21, 2003

<u>A Really Cool Adventure</u>
<u>By: Anna Grace Shramere, Age 11</u>

Jobelle woke up. She felt the ground rumbling beneath her.

"It's happening," she whispered, terrified. The people of Mara had talked about it for years, but it was finally coming true. ~~There~~ their world was ending. Jobelle's mom had talked about it before she had died during that awful miniature earthquake...

"What're you doing?" Todd asked.

I stopped writing mid-sentence and quickly covered the paper with my left hand. "Nothing," I replied.

"Okay," Todd said understandingly. While most little brothers would pester their sisters about a secret, Todd respected my privacy.

"Alright," I said, as if I was giving in after a ten-minute disagreement. "You know how you have your 'imagination'?" I asked. He nodded, likely thinking about his complex group of imaginary friends and stuffed animals.

"Well, I have one, too... except I call it the 'Pretend Friend Association'..."

I thought he'd laugh. I mean, it's fine to have pretend friends when you're in the second grade, but as an eleven-year-old?

"Cool!" He said, thoroughly interested. I felt ashamed for even thinking he'd make fun of me. He was too sweet for that.

"Pepper's one of them, right?"

Grabbing my favorite plush kitten from the top of my stuffed animal bin, I nodded. Todd gently held the hideous tabby, complete with oversized head and beady glass eyes.

~~~

Two days later, Todd and I were hanging out at the local amusement park, which was only a ten-minute drive from our house. We were in line for the mild "runaway mine train" coaster when Todd whispered to me, "Bubba's in the last car. Rochi was riding with him, too, but Bubba threw him out in the tunnel. Now he has to walk to the exit."

I giggled. Nothing new there- Bubba was always pestering his little brother, at least in our imaginations.

Todd was describing his stuffed animal parrot beating up one of his characters, a genius three-year-old toddler lovingly dubbed Rochi. Both existed in actual bean-filled plush toys; however, just as Pepper could, they had the ability to turn invisible. This way, they could "go" where we could.

As the previous riders got out, I glanced back at the last car. "Todd!" I said quietly. "Bubba couldn't have been in the back car! There were two little girls in there!" He looked at me, puzzled. "So?" he asked as our safety bars came down. He was only eight; who cared if the imaginary world our pretend friends lived in didn't match the real world?

As an eleven-year-old, I did.

The ride started, and as we careened up and down hills, I wondered why I cared. It shouldn't matter. It _didn't_ matter- in the words of Todd, "so?" But even so, I began thinking about how my imaginary friends were surviving in the real world. I mean, how did Bubba and Rochi get into the park? Did they jump the fence, or crawl under the turnstiles, or maybe Bubba carried Rochi, or maybe Rochi built a jet pack, and they flew in...

I felt very silly pondering over such a nonsensical thought and even wondered if I might be crazy. But then I thought about my favorite literary characters. Those "people"... or animals or things... weren't any more real than Bubba, Rochi, or Pepper, but their creators, as authors, had given them a world in which to live. Those characters were nothing without an atmosphere, whether it was based on reality or completely made up, such as an alternate dimension or far away planet. I realized writers must spend a lot of time thinking about how their worlds worked, but they weren't crazy. In fact, they were respected for creating incredible stories that many people cherished.

I had no desire to share my stories, but I was interested in goofing around with my pretend friends just for fun. I'd already been interacting with my cast of characters with or without Todd for years. Why not try to perfect their world- the ins and outs of how they lived, the way books and movies explained everything? After all, not only did I want to have "companions" to keep me entertained when I was bored; I also wanted to have imaginary adventures in places I created.

By the time we were getting off the ride, I decided that as long as it didn't interfere with my real life, it was okay to go on fantasy escapades whenever I got bored. To be a little less weird, I decided to occasionally write down my stories, as if I wasn't actually imagining them in the spare moments of my everyday life, which I secretly was. I had already written a few details and back stories mainly so I wouldn't forget them, but now I also had the ulterior motive of trying to feel like less of a freak.

Wednesday, January 10, 2008

Prayers for the Kidneys that Hate Me

By: Anna Grace

Dear God, please heal me completely...

1. Let me not need chemotherapy
2. Please don't let all my hair fall out
3. Take away the acne on my face and legs and arms... it hurts and makes me feel ugly
4. Please take away the swelling in my stomach so it doesn't feel like I'm being beat up all the time
5. Help my nose, cheeks, and eyelids not be puffy
6. Let my throat not burn anymore
7. Let the confusion go away- it's scary
8. Please fix my kidneys without more medicine
9. Allow me to stop taking prednisone
10. Please give me energy

"Amen," I whispered sincerely, looking up as I finished scrawling in the back of my previously abandoned diary. "Nothing You can't handle, huh? Well, it's a good thing, 'cause there's nothing on this list that I can!"

You'd think I was eighty or something, but nope- sweet sixteen with a special acronym.

FSGS.

Who knew four little letters could change a life?

Never heard of it? No problem- I hadn't either, and certainly couldn't pronounce the mouthful it stood for. Focal segmental glomerulosclerosis means that some of the kidney's filtering parts, the glomeruli, are scarred. This unlucky phenomenon causes nephrotic syndrome: more or less, doctor-speak for "protein in the urine."

Nephrotic syndrome in itself is an awful condition. If a kidney biopsy shows the cause to be FSGS, you're considered especially unlucky. In a bad case of the disease, its process is a vicious cycle. The mysterious FSGS scars the glomeruli, allowing protein to "leak through" into the urine. Our kidneys weren't made for these large protein molecules to slip past the glomeruli, so this intrusion can lead to end stage renal (kidney) failure if left unchecked for long periods of time. Thankfully, I had been told we had caught my case early.

In July 2007, a routine blood test revealed my cholesterol was 410. There was also protein in my urine. I was referred to the local nephrologists' clinic. In August, I met Dr. Jones for the first time.

"You're amazing," he told me after shaking my hand. "You're losing one-hundred times the amount of protein you should."

Cool, I thought, thankful that I didn't have cancer. My mom and I had breathed in relief at that. In the months that followed, I had wondered why Dr. Jones didn't join in our celebration.

As bright and kind-hearted as he was, I had believed Dr. Jones was the worst-scenario type of guy. In retrospect, I simply *was* the worst-case scenario. With that much protein in my urine, I should have been in kidney failure. For reasons medically unexplainable, I'd baffled everyone with disease presentation without kidney damage. Without the urinalysis, there was no indication that I had CKD, or chronic kidney disease, but I certainly did.

The human body is supposed to lose, at the very most, a trace of 0.02 grams of protein per day through the urine. My kidneys were leaking at least 24 grams. To compensate for the lack of protein in my body, my liver was desperately trying to make protein itself. Without that capability, it was making cholesterol.

A corticosteroid called prednisone is the only well-known "treatment" for this monster. There's no cure, and it isn't like prednisone works in every case. If it fails to stop the protein loss, which it does in many FSGS cases, the next treatment steps are completely experimental. My doctor had talked about cyclophosphamide, a chemotherapy drug used to treat a variety of cancers including leukemia.

I don't remember the day I started taking prednisone, but it was sometime during the last week of September. Despite the steroid horror stories you hear, the first month and a half wasn't that bad. My biggest side effects were euphoria, difficulty concentrating, and mild migraines. None of those bothered me too much; what I really hated was the how disgusting the medicine tasted.

I had never learned how to swallow pills, but even if I had, I don't think it would have helped much. Ever bit into an ibuprofen pill and tasted that bitter, metallic flavor? Well, I love that taste compared to prednisone. It isn't coated, so the moment you put it on your tongue, it begins to dissolve.

We tried several methods to hide the appalling flavor. One technique involved crushing the pills into powder and mixing it in orange sherbet or peppermint ice cream, two foods I can hardly look at to this day. It was so bad that simply the words "prednisone" or "ice cream" could make me feel extremely nauseous. Sometimes it took me as long as three hours to swallow all of the medicine. My record was ten minutes, but that had been toward the beginning, before the side effects began.

The week of Thanksgiving, I started swelling. It sounds crazy, but my entire body felt as if there was someone under my skin trying to burst through. My feet inflated like balloons, and my stomach bloated as if pregnant. To get around, I waddled like a penguin; hence my nickname "penguin" was coined. I became obsessed with the flightless birds of Antarctica.

Eating was difficult, because it only took two bites to make me feel full. I ate less but still gained weight, so my mom called the doctor... daily. Each time, the same nurse would pick up the phone and claim it was "just the prednisone, honey. It makes them hungry."

I started hating the medicine.

Life got worse in December. My original impressions of this "little kidney condition" changed. I knew it could be dangerous without treatment, but I thought that as long as I took the prednisone, I'd be cured within a few months. As my blood pressure rose along with my weight, I experienced a strange body-wide pain. My heart pounded on a regular basis, and I wondered if this thing could be fatal. I mentioned death here and there, but very few people took me seriously, so I tried to push the thought aside.

I went to school as often as possible, but it was very painful. Sometimes I forgot where I was or how to get around. This wouldn't have been abnormal, except the junior and senior high building was made up of one short corridor.

After Christmas break, I was determined to stop missing class. I had a waiver from my doctor that granted me leeway from the typical attendance rules, but I believed it was easier to go to school- no matter how agonizing and bewildering- than to stay home. So far, that plan had failed miserably. I did manage to attend on a Monday, but my feet were almost too swollen to walk. When I arrived home that afternoon, I waddled around as little as possible, rising only to go to the bathroom or rotate between my bed and the living room couch.

Writing in my journal was a rare break from the monotony

of my new normal. One day, as I pushed my diary back under my bed, I heard the rustling of papers and pulled them into sight. When I saw a familiar name scribbled in my handwriting, I immediately recognized the long-forgotten stack. I grabbed every sheet I could find and headed to our living room couch.

Monday, June 23, 2003

I was always a "big ideas" type of person, but usually, the big ideas were forgotten by the next day. Not so the PFA!

I had the opportunity to create a country in fifth grade, and I'll never forget the mix of fun and stress that team project yielded. The good thing about the PFA was it was all mine. No one would see it, except for maybe Todd, so I could do whatever I wanted without grades, deadlines, and teammates to worry about.

Who did I have already? Well, my precious big headed kitten Pepper, of course. Pepper's personality was set in stone to me. She was curious, had a low voice, loved math, and didn't love reading. Pepper had some human-like qualities: she spoke English (to an extent), could walk on her hind legs (but usually didn't), went to "doll school", and was talented in gymnastics and tap dance. Of course, she had mostly feline instincts. She asked for a specific brand of canned cat food, even though she was capable of eating "human food." She had learned how to pounce, climb trees, play with yarn, and scratch furniture by watching the real cats of the neighborhood. Dot and Tabby, two more of my stuffed animal cats, had also taught Pepper how to hunt. Being only four or five inches long, Pepper was much smaller than a real cat, so she was limited to game such as imaginary grasshoppers, which she always let go.

With a character in place, Pepper "came to life." Yes, she may have been faux fur, stuffing, and glass beads, but for a few wonderful minutes, I could escape to my own world, where she was a silly, kooky kitten.

Anna Grace put a bowl on the floor in front of the little kitten. Pepper shouted in a low tone, licking her lips in anticipation of dinner. "Pepper loves food," the kitten growled, eating sloppily while purring like a lawn mower.

Pepper finished within seconds. She leapt up onto Anna Grace's dresser, using the different drawers as stairs. When she got to the top, Pepper looked out the window and spotted the real family feline outside.

"Hi, Brownie," Pepper yelled through the glass. "Pepper wishes Pepper was real like you."

I stopped for a minute. Hmm... that wasn't a bad idea! I decided right then to let my characters know they were pretend. But in that case, what would their lives be like? Would they resent being imaginary, or would they like it? It was a mystery I was willing and delighted to explore. I snatched another sheet of paper and began making a list of "rules" that would serve as a guideline for how my imaginary characters would live.

PFA (Pretend Friend Association) Rules
By: Anna Grace Shramere

Introduction: The PFA is my version of an imaginary world. Everyone's imagination is different, so there could be a lot of differences between how my pretend world and someone else's works. To keep things easy for me, I'm going to pretend everyone uses this list, even though they probably do not.

1. It's all pretend! (If you start to think it's actually real, you should probably tell someone because that's not good!)
2. Even if I'm not playing with an imaginary friend at the moment, they are still "living". (I'm not always going to create every moment of their day, but I'll pretend their lives are taking place anyway.)
3. Everyone's imaginary worlds combine. (I know this isn't really true, but this way, I can pretend there are hundreds of imaginary "people" out there without making them all up.)
4. Imaginary people ("imaginaries") can be invisible pretend friends, stuffed animals, dolls, and the like. It doesn't matter.
5. Imaginaries know they aren't real. Grown-ups and even kids my age think pretend friends are weird or crazy, so

imaginaries know they must stay out of the knowledge of the real world.

6. Imaginaries can't be in the same place as a real person at the same time. If they are sitting in a real empty bench but someone comes and sits down, they must move so they don't get squished!

7. For every edible real thing in the world (like a can of food), there is an equal imaginary duplicate.

8. Most imaginary humans age normally (if they don't, it must be mentioned in their introduction.) Stuffed animals have a general age range they stay in permanently; for example, these may include baby, toddler, preschooler, elementary school, preteen, young teen, older teen, college student, young adult, forties, fifties, and so on. (Pepper will permanently be an elementary school-aged kitten.) Todd's stuffed animals are the exception; Bubba will always be the same age as Todd.

9. Use your imagination! If something doesn't make sense, you can try to make up a theory, but you don't have to! It's just pretend, so everything is possible.

With "rules" in place, I looked at the plush version of Pepper and switched back into make-believe mode.

Pepper went invisible so she could leap through the glass of Anna Grace's windows. She began hunting, but it wasn't much fun. The real grasshoppers ignored her, and the imaginary ones stayed far away.

Suddenly, Pepper heard something from inside a tree. It didn't sound real, like the wind or the birds. This sounded imaginary- and it was the imaginary things that could hurt Pepper.

Crunch, crunch, crunch...

"AAAAAAHHHHHHHHHHH!" Pepper screamed at the top of her lungs. She leapt back through the window and turned back into her stuffed animal form. "THERE ARE PEOPLE COMING OUT OF THE TREES!"

Wednesday, January 10, 2008 (Continued)

A lot of people think if you distract yourself from sickness, you'll feel better. It may be true for some people, but for me, no distraction- no matter how exciting- could take away the pain of kidney disease. However, if I was totally focused on something, I would forget that I was sick. The symptoms stayed, but I actually would wonder *why* I hurt.

This was one of those moments. My joints ached as I hurried down the hallway, but I forgot why for a split second. I was holding priceless childhood memories in my hands.

I hadn't written in so long. Life got in the way... high school, band, boys, friends, my hobbies... I remember deciding I had to give it up someday. Sorrowfully, I had stopped towards the end of eighth grade. The PFA had disappeared into the abyss of my room and the depths of my mind. Pepper was the only remaining trace that stayed in my every-day life. She was travel-sized and could come with me everywhere, from school and football games to the nephrology clinic and hospital.

I collapsed on our old red couch and pulled out a couple pages of drawing paper that had been stapled together. The "front cover", so to speak, had a picture of a little girl in a purple shirt looking out a window. Outside, there was a silly-looking circle with whiskers, eyes, and ears – Pepper as she was depicted way back when – standing next to a tree. I examined my artwork closely and smiled. I couldn't have been older than eleven or twelve when I made this. I opened it and read...

"AAAAAAHHHHHHHHHHHH!" Pepper screamed at the top of her lungs, running inside and turning into a stuffed animal again. "THERE ARE PEOPLE COMING OUT OF THE TREES!"

Dot- one of Pepper's guardians- ran outside when she heard Pepper yell. "Pepper," Dot said. "There aren't people coming out of the trees!"

"YES THERE ARE! THERE ARE PEOPLE COMING OUT OF THE TREES! THEY'RE COMING TO SEAM-RIP US!"

I laughed, feeling somewhere between amused and embarrassed. I'd read a lot of children's fantasy books around the time I wrote this, so of course, Pepper was right: people *were* coming out the trees in my story.

One of my favorite children's books was about another dimension- another world you couldn't get to except through a special portal or something similar. It was no surprise my first characters came from another dimension, too, but this was my own dimension, nothing like the ones other people had already created.

I continued to read as a young woman, a baby, and a preteen girl descended down a tree and into my backyard. (Pepper ran in a circle, shrieking about "gruesome" ways a stuffed animal could die.) These three characters had escaped from their world, Mara, which was dying. My prednisone mind throbbed as I tried to remember the details of Mara and its circumstances, but I could not. I continued reading as Anna Grace- myself, as strange as it was- invited the group inside through the fantastical window. (Seeing she wasn't going to be murdered, Pepper got rather bored and left to go destroy a ball of yarn.)

As the woman and Dot talked, Anna Grace observed the three newcomers.

The barefoot toddler wore a puffy yellow dress with lilacs embroidered into the fabric. She had short brown hair pulled into dozens of tiny pigtails all over her head.

Anna Grace then met eyes with a frightened human girl. Somewhat petite for her age and very slender, she wore a sleeveless, pastel-orange dress that looked elegant enough to be worn at a fancy wedding. While she kept most of her long brown hair loose, there were two thin sections behind each ear that had been braided and brought together in the middle of the back of

THE PRETEND FRIEND ASSOCIATION - PARTS ONE TO FOUR

her head.

"I'm Ariella Newbrey," the young woman explained. "This is my little sister, Jobelle, and our next door neighbors' daughter, Leah. When everything started falling apart, Belle and I ran. Our neighbor's house had been demolished when the earthquake knocked over a tree..."

"They were dead, and Leah was on the floor crying," Jobelle said in a voice just above the whisper.

"We couldn't leave her," Ariella explained, lovingly bouncing the little girl in her arms. "I grabbed her and we continued. Dad was following us..." She trailed off.

"Dad's probably dead. If for some amazing reason he's not, we're never going to see him again. He won't find us," Jobelle stated, appearing to be in a state of shock. She spoke about death, but it was as if her mind didn't really make sense of what she was saying. Through her expressionless face, Anna Grace could somehow tell Jobelle was very sad and very scared.

Oh, Belle, my foggy brain thought as I remembered my creation. Jobelle had been my favorite imaginary friend. She was an amazing playmate, despite the fact she wasn't real.

In third grade, I had switched schools. Although I loved my teacher and classmates, it had been a struggle. I was good at making friends, but the dynamic at the school was different. I didn't have any close friends, so I did the logical thing: I made my own. Jobelle and I were similar, but I purposefully made us a little different as well. She lived through all my biggest dreams... and all my worst nightmares. She had to evacuate her home and lost everything, including both parents, which was something I feared more than anything. At the same time, she could do things I'd only dreamt about. For example, I loved dancing and gymnastics, but wasn't very good and eventually gave up. Jobelle, however, was a protégé at both. When I was alone, Jobelle was there- to read with me, talk to me, play dolls with me... she liked what I liked, for the most part, but even when she liked something I didn't, I was in full

21

control. It wasn't until the summer I was between fifth and sixth grade that I really decided to develop Jobelle's imaginary world. I gave her a back story, friends, family, and even tried to develop her personality, like an author or screenwriter would.

It was strange I'd felt the need to escape from reality as a child, because my life had been good. I had a seemingly perfect family. Although all families have their issues, I had it a lot better than most of the kids at my school. Regardless, for some unknown reason, I had created this alternate universe in my head, and years later, it had come back to help me.

Now, as a very ill teenager, it was therapeutic to relive what could only have happened in my imagination.

Thursday, January 11, 2008

The next morning, I continued reading.

Monday, June 23, 2003: The Marans Arrive
By: Anna Grace Shramere, 11

"There is plenty of room in the Underground City…" Dot said. She and Ariella talked endlessly. Baby Leah was asleep in her new parent's arms. Cautiously, Jobelle caught Anna Grace's attention by stepping forward.

"What's the Underground City?" Jobelle asked, nearly inaudibly.

"It's a pretend metropolis," Anna Grace replied, a little unsure of talking to this stranger.

"My brother and I created it as a place for all of our imaginary friends to live. The main entrance is just over there by the little apple tree," Anna Grace explained. "I'm Anna Grace, by the way. This is Nectarwood, Arkansas. It's about a thirty minute drive west from Hot Springs. The state's capitol city, Little Rock, is about an hour and a half away."

"I'm Jobelle Newbrey," the girl stated timidly. "I live in Mara, or I used to. It's… gone now." Her eyes fell downcast. "I don't know where we're going to go now. I mean, this place is real. In Mara, everyone and everything is imaginary, but here… you're real, aren't you?"

Anna Grace nodded. "I know it's kind of funny to have imaginary friends when you're eleven, but…"

"No, that's okay," Jobelle interrupted. "I mean, I'd rather have someone my age dictate my life than a five-year-old."

"Wait… you're eleven?"

Jobelle shook her head. "No, twelve; my birthday was in April. When's yours?"

23

"October, but hey- what did you mean by me dictating your life?" Anna Grace asked. "Like, control you?"

"Of course, Anna Grace- that is your name, right?" She asked, not unkindly but visibly upset. "Think about it: I'm imaginary, you're real... I'm a fake, you're alive... God made you, you made me..."

"I guess, but... I don't get it."

Jobelle shrugged. "I don't, either, but like I said, at least you're not a little kid. It's not your fault that you're real and I'm not. I'm glad you're here, because if you weren't, I don't know what we'd do. Who would show us where to go?"

"You don't have to go anywhere. You can stay here," Anna Grace suggested. Without any warning, tears began to flood Jobelle's eyes and spill down her cheeks. "Oh, Belle," Ariella said as she stopped talking mid-sentence as she reached out to embrace her little sister.

"It's okay; we're going to be okay. These are nice people; there's an older girl here who can help us survive..." Ariella quieted, battling her own feelings. She, too, was devastated from all of the loss that had occurred on one unfortunate day.

Talk about unfortunate, I thought, suddenly feeling a lot like poor Jobelle in my story. I hadn't seen my kidney doctor since before Thanksgiving, and I had a feeling I was quite a bit sicker now than I had been then, despite what the nurses believed. I had an appointment scheduled for Monday, January 14th, but it had been pushed to the 27th for some weird reason. This particular morning, when I weighed in seven pounds heavier than I had yesterday, my mom told me she was going to beg someone to get me in as originally planned. I assured her I was fine, even though I knew I wasn't.

Only four days into the new school semester, I was totally caught up on my homework and had nothing better to do, so I continued reading my story. In the next passage, I had switched from third person limited to Jobelle's first-person "POV," or "point of view." Vaguely, I remembered this had been my favorite and most commonly used writing technique. Although our personalities were different, Jobelle's 'voice' was very similar to my own. Her reactions to the world around her were usually completely opposite of what my own would be, but our ways of thinking were virtually the same.

Monday, June 23, 2003 Continued: Jobelle's POV
By: Anna Grace Shramere, Age 11

When Anna Grace first told me about the Underground City, I expected it to be simply hidden. I was surprised to find an imaginary, sprawling metropolis literally underneath the backyard.

In real life, the city's construction would have been impossible. Without the freedom of a child's imagination, the walls and ceilings would have caved in long before it was finished. Thankfully, a genius species of Todd's making had known exactly what to do. Not even a huge earthquake or giant flood would ever be able to seriously damage the magnificent structure.

Despite the strange location, a giant screen on the ceiling projected live footage of the sky. It showcased the beauty of weather without the wetness of rain, cold of winter, or heat of the summer. There were hundreds of apartment buildings with dozens of businesses, several schools, and even a family-friendly entertainment district.

As I stood in amazement, Anna Grace rattled on about herself. Being a theme park junkie, she had created a vacation resort destination in the city, using her favorite attractions from various theme parks. "My favorite company has real locations all over the world," Anna Grace explained to me as we walked to the city's transportation center. "Awesome Happy Fun World has all of my favorite things from real parks, but there's stuff Todd and I made up, too. I'll take you there while Dot helps your sister. Come on! You'll love it!"

She pulled me into a vehicle they called a "car". We had similar modes of getting around back home, but this was different.

"Do all cars float like this?" I asked as we lifted about eight feet off the ground.

"No," Anna Grace laughed. "Real cars can't fly! I saw it in a movie once, and I thought it would be a good idea for my imaginary world."

"It's made quite the improvement in our lives," Dot added. "You see, in the world you used to live in, everything was pretend. Reality didn't matter. As imaginary creations living among real people, there are rules of survival. For example, we have to stay out of the way of real life. Our cars can drive on the pavement, but they can also fly to keep out of actual traffic."

Dot would not stop talking. "Here in the UC, where everyone is imaginary, we can choose to fly or drive because it keeps travel time to a minimum..."

Hoping no one would notice, I zoned out.

While Dot took Ariella and the baby to our new apartment, Anna Grace and I were dropped off at the Awesome Happy Fun World campus. We bypassed the artistic hotel and manmade lake and walked to ticket booth in front of the entranceway gates. Anna Grace was handed two tickets without needing to pay, of course, and we skipped the short line to enter the park.

Oh, wow, I wished Awesome Happy Fun World was really underneath my backyard! *Oh well*, I thought sadly. *Maybe it's a good thing it isn't real; there's no way I'd be able to walk around it anyway!* I kept reading as the details of my imaginary world came back to me.

We walked to the center of the park, Happy Landings, where there were fifteen marked trails leading to the different areas of the park.

"So, where do you want to go?" Anna Grace asked. "There's Western Village, Movie Mania, Todd Land (my brother designed that), Kiddy Circus, Fairytale Forest, Parrot Lagoon…"

I was far too upset to care about this stupid amusement park. My parents were dead. My home was destroyed. Everything I knew was gone, from the saltwater lakes to the orange sunsets…

"That restaurant over there is called the Purple Palace," Anna stated, motioning toward a violet castle-shaped building. "It's my favorite color. What about you?"

"Sky blue," I answered vaguely. A sign reading "Fairytale Forest" pointed me toward the right. I entered the enchanting area, not really caring whether or not the real girl followed me. She did, of course. A carousel played tunes from what Anna Grace called "classic animated movies", but I didn't recognize any of them. The rides were about characters almost every American child- real or imaginary- would have known, but it was all foreign to me.

I wandered aimlessly. We passed by Anna Grace's "perfect" replica of a very famous ride. I could care less. Tears flooded my eyes, but I kept walking, hoping to lose the girl behind me. Unfortunately, she kept up. I finally saw a show going on at the border of Fairytale Forest and Kiddy Circus. I stopped short to watch.

"They're *excellent* dancers," I commented, not taking my eyes off of the dancing actresses dressed as princesses.

"You can dance?"

"Since I was two," I answered to get her to stop asking me questions.

Of course I can dance, I thought, refraining from rolling my watery eyes. As a toddler, every month or two, my parents signed me up for a playgroup that focused on a specific activity, such as art or swimming. It was simply for fun, but I quickly found three favorites. I loved water, but besides learning to float for survival, my swimming skills were less than good. Gymnastics and dance, however, came naturally to me. I began at age two and never stopped.

The pirouetting princesses made me forget my problems for a split second, but as they skipped off the informal stage, my heart fell.

"It's over?" I asked.

Anna Grace shrugged carelessly. "I guess we caught the end. Do you want to stay for the next one? It starts in 45 minutes."

I nodded silently, making eye contact with Anna Grace for only the second or third time that day.

"Why don't we go to the little kids' circus thing for a few minutes and come back when it's about to start? One of my favorites is over there."

Fear overtook me. This was the worst day of my life, and I wouldn't have anything else go wrong. Maybe it was silly to care so much about a dumb show, but I did. I planted my feet firmly on the floor and gave her a challenging look.

"Okay, but I thought you might be hungry..."

I was afraid to move, but at the same time, I didn't want to starve to death. For the last week or so, there had been many small earthquakes and not enough food. I hadn't eaten for three days, so I decided not to risk it.

I shifted my weight and quickly advanced toward the circus-themed décor. Anna Grace ran to catch up to me. She took the lead and guided me to building that looked like a giant tent. Inside there was a gift shop, food court, small toddler playground, and children's ride. The amazing attraction reminded me of the playgrounds my dad had designed for the structures he had helped to build.

"I'm guessing you like little kids," I commented as I spun

around, taking in the sight of robotic circus animals.

"I love preschoolers. I think I want to be a teacher someday."

"I've known Leah since before she was born," I said. "I felt her kick against her mother's belly. Earlier today, when I saw her parents, then I saw her... I'm so glad we could save her. Actually..." I trailed off. Anna Grace looked at me, as if to encourage me to continue, but I quickly turned my attention toward the vendors.

"We have... *had*... poultry, beef, and pork on Mara. I'm really glad it isn't all different. But what are french fries?"

"They're just potatoes... but they're sliced thin, deep-fried in oil, and pretty much drowned in salt."

"I love potatoes!" I exclaimed, *really* smiling for the first time since Anna Grace met me. Of course, it was very short lived as I realized what I had done.

You stupid girl! I scolded myself. *Your entire family is dead and you're happy about food!* Without any warning, I broke into tears and hugged Anna Grace, for lack of any other place to find comfort.

"I don't believe it happened," I said truthfully. "It didn't really happen," I tried to convince myself. Strangely, I forced myself to believe my lie. I don't know how I did it, but it was as if distracting myself from the grief helped me deny the facts about what had happened. At the moment, it was all I could do.

For the next few days, my sister and I stayed in our apartment in order to mourn dad. Thanks to the PFA, we were allowed to live free of charge in the Pretend Friend Association building. Besides the many amenities including a neighborhood swimming pool, we had our own kitchen/dining room, living room, two bathrooms, and four miniature bedrooms.

The Underground City had two main groups of inhabitants. Todd had a group called the Fictional Alliance in which there were two groups- the civilians, who were the 97%

majority of the population, and Todd's guys, a family of about fifty young stuffed animals. Todd might have been the sweetest real kid on the planet, but most of his "guys" were rowdy, even on their best behavior. They rough housed, enjoyed pranks, and tormented small children on a regular basis. It's interesting, how a little boy would create a world that was the polar opposite of his own!

I was in Anna Grace's PFA- the Pretend Friend Association. We were less than one percent of the City's population.

It was quite a weird dynamic in which to be thrown, as if being twelve wasn't bad enough. I felt such a wide range of emotions. I blamed my hatred of our new "home" on everything imaginable. In truth, I missed my *real* home, especially our backyard with its sandy beach and saltwater lake.

Leah was certainly a blessing. She was too young to understand what had happened, although she had moments where she seemed to be upset. I could spend hours with that toddler, even if it meant playing pointless games, such as 'wave the socks in the air' or 'let's stack empty cereal boxes and knock them down'.

Ariella began to slowly integrate into the local social world, dragging Leah and me along with her. I hated it! There was no one my age in the PFA... except for Anna Grace. We hung out together to keep from getting bored, and before long, we knew quite a bit about each other.

My first Independence Day was exciting. "It's awesome," Anna Grace exclaimed that morning. "Every year we go to my grandparents' house on the lake. The fireworks are launched just across the water. We sit on my grandma and grandpa's back porch. And this year... before it gets dark... Todd, my cousin, and I are going to put on a show. We're singing three songs, leading the Pledge of Alliance, and doing a flag march."

"Um..." I stammered.

"You don't know what I'm talking about, do you?"

"No clue," I said with a small smile. Anna Grace tried to explain how the American Revolution had worked, but failed miserably within five minutes. She ended up pulling out her collection of children's books about fictional girls who lived at key times in American history.

"Here," my new friend said, handing me a stack of illustrated chapter books about a 1770s kid. Each book was only around 50 pages long, so we read the first couple together before Anna Grace got up.

"My mom's calling me," Anna Grace said, grabbing stuffed animal Pepper, who shrieked, "YES! Happy Birthday to Pepper and America, and maybe Jesus, because no one knows when He was born and it probably wasn't in December because the shepherds wouldn't be out in the coldness…"

"It's your birthday, Pepper?" I asked.

"Observed," Pepper answered solemnly.

"I have no clue when she was manufactured, and I don't know when I got her, so we just celebrate on July 4. It's easy to remember," Anna Grace whispered, pointing out that Pepper didn't actually know what the word 'observed' meant.

Later in the afternoon, Anna Grace left me alone like an abandoned kitten to go to the family event. I had lost so much that this should have been no big deal, but it really bothered me. I finally had a friend, and we were at the opposite ends of reality. It was very saddening.

Pouting, I fell asleep on Anna Grace's bed.

When I woke up, I was staring into a starry sky, resting in a soft patch of grass near a lake. It reminded me a little of my backyard at home. Was I dreaming?

Suddenly, a tiny but ferocious little animal attacked me.

"Pepper?" I asked.

"YES! That's me. Pepper the Cat. How is you?" Her grammar was terrible, but I was so happy to be… wherever I was.

"Where am I?" I asked.

"We're at the lake," Ariella explained. "This spot is about a five-minute drive from where Anna Grace is right now."

I sat up and saw her sprawled out on some sort of beach towel only about two yards away from me. Little Leah was on the grass close by, mesmerized by these amazing little flies. Their backs lit up every few seconds. I tried to get one to land on my hand, but it disregarded my presence. I suppose it made sense. Like all real things, the bugs were by far more incredible than anything a mere human mind could imagine.

"Why are we here?" I asked dreamily. The sun had just set, and I heard several real children talking about how the fireworks would start any second now.

"Anna Grace was worried about us," my sister told me. "She contacted some guys in her brother's imaginary ensemble, Todd's Fictional Alliance. They were heading out here with a bus load and had extra room. I wanted to let you sleep until we got here."

The fireworks show began across the lake. If there was music playing, we couldn't hear it, but that didn't matter. Many shades of white, blue, and red flashed brilliantly through the sky. I wondered if these colors had any significance.

I hadn't been so happy for months. If I had to belong to a real person, I suppose I'd choose someone with a wild imagination who had the potential to be a friend. After so many hardships, I finally felt lucky.

The phone rang. As much as I wanted to stay with Jobelle and... well, myself, I guess... I had to get up.

Several hours later, I was sitting on a couch in the nephrology clinic, leaning against my mom's shoulder. I did not feel good whatsoever. Somehow, my mom had gotten me an appointment for tomorrow, so I had to come in for lab today.

A nurse stuck her head through the door and called me back. Because a world-class children's hospital was less than two hours away, I was one of the youngest patients treated in Nectarwood. Usually, this particular nurse would literally sing my name when she called me, but today, she was quiet.

Everyone was, and when I about cried at seeing my weight, they assured me it would be okay, but this time, they didn't blame the prednisone. If I had been eating, I don't think my weight gain would have bothered me much; I was scared at the fact I had pretty much stopped eating altogether and still managed to gain close to fifty pounds in three months.

After my incredible phlebotomist drew my blood for lab work, we went home by way of a Chinese take-out restaurant. The only things I even felt like attempting to eat were cream cheese wontons and egg rolls.

Once at home, I collapsed onto my bed. I could feel my heart racing inside my chest. I grabbed my unorganized assortment of papers and continued reading.

New Beginnings– Jobelle's POV
Takes Place: August through December 2003

It took me a while to get used to being imaginary while Anna Grace was real. My world was simply a hobby to her, so I learned to spend time on my own. Ariella became a secretary at the huge Anna Grace Room Church in the Underground City, so Leah and I spent a lot of time in their indoor and outdoor playgrounds. I also enrolled for gymnastics and dance classes at a special extracurricular facility a block away from our house.

I missed my dad a lot. Staying active distracted me from my grief, but if I got bored even for a moment, sadness overwhelmed me. Even on the best days, there were times when I never thought I'd ever be happy again.

"Do you remember our baby brother?" Ariella asked me one night when I couldn't stop crying.

"We had a baby brother?" I asked, shocked enough to

wipe away a few tears. She nodded.

"Little Tayoe was born with severe heart disease in December 1992. I wish I still had the pictures of him. Tay was the most beautiful baby in the land."

"What happened?" I asked.

"He died a few hours after an unsuccessful surgery in March 1993. It was awful. Dad told me that the bad things that happen to us are like cuts. Everyone gets them, but some people's cuts are deeper than others. All injuries sting at first, but with time, they heal. Even though the scar a cut leaves may never go away completely, it will fade with time."

Ariella took my hands in hers. "You know, dad's not here anymore, but his theory has been proven true. I did adjust to life without mom, and so did you. We'll get through these rough times. We still have each other, and we have new friends as well."

She was right. Different though we were, my friendship with Anna Grace grew. Our nicknames for each other quickly became 'Belle' and 'Annie'. We played videos games and read books together. She introduced me to American movies, stories, and fairytales while helping me learn the basic history of the real world. We spent hours on end at Awesome Happy Fun World. My favorite attractions included the rocket-themed roller coaster and an indoor log flume adventure, but nothing beat taking little Leah to Kiddy Circus.

"Do you know what this place needs?" I asked Anna Grace one day while exiting the park's animal safari ride.

"More rides?" She asked with a smile, as if having 127 wasn't enough.

"No! It needs a new name!" I stated.

"What's wrong with Awesome Happy Fun World?" She asked stubbornly. I sighed. The theme park's cheesy name was my pet peeve, but unfortunately, it was the one disagreement I never stood a chance of winning.

Our hangout place at Anna Grace's house was her bed. As

the ceiling fan spun above us, we became best friends. Sometimes, we did something together, like talking or playing a game, while other times, we wrote and drew separately, Anna Grace acting as an author while I was an artist.

Our strengths and weaknesses were almost exact opposites of one another. That being the case, we had small spats over stupid things occasionally. I don't know what her motivations were, but mine were usually jealousies. It sounds dumb, but I was envious of Anna Grace a lot. She had a mom and dad while I was an orphan. She did great in school without trying while I had to work much harder for Bs. I loved the real world and would give anything to be a part of it. She was real, I wasn't, and that alone was enough to create tension, but I loved her enough to ignore that most of the time.

I dreaded Wednesday, August 20. I would start seventh grade at an imaginary, private K-8 "doll school" in Anna Grace's room. Anna Grace would begin sixth grade in a real elementary school. We'd be separated for most of the time now, and I feared she'd forget about me.

That morning, we met in her bedroom doorway at 6:55 AM to say goodbye, even though we'd see each other later in the day.

"The imaginary schools in the city are huge," Anna Grace told me before we parted. "In ninth grade, you'll have to go to East Tunnel High School. For now, Closet Doll School is so much smaller. Every young stuffed animal I have goes to Closet…"

"… INCLUDING PEPPER!" The kitten shrieked. She appeared out of nowhere and began gnawing on my new pink-and-white tennis shoes.

"Pepper!" Anna Grace scolded. "Stop chewing on Belle's shoes!"

"Dis is so COOL! We go to school to-get-her!" Pepper hugged me around the ankles with her retracted claws.

"Are you sure I can't just stow away in your family's car

and hang out in the back of your real classroom?" I asked as Anna Grace pried the overactive feline off of my foot.

Anna Grace smiled but shook her head. "Trust me; you'll be better off here."

"I <u>do</u> trust you," I answered truthfully, missing summer break already. We hugged and parted ways reluctantly.

Pepper led the way to a makeshift schoolhouse filled with around forty students. So began a daily routine. Closet Doll School had only one huge classroom which twelve teachers and forty elementary and middle school students shared.

School was okay. It was entirely run by Anna Grace and obviously made for the PFA and younger Fictional Alliance kids. I was certainly one of the older kids, which was a mix of a great privilege and an annoying nuisance, depending on the circumstance. Class lasted from 7:00 in the morning until 2:00 in the afternoon, so I continued to take gymnastics and dance after school. I got used to running from Anna Grace's room to the UC and vice-versa several times a day.

After dance and gymnastics, Anna Grace and I often "hung out" together. We drank soda, ate candy, giggled, and talked about school.

"Ugh! I can't wait for Bubba to turn nine years old in January!" I complained to Anna Grace once as I aggressively bit the head off of a red gummy bear.

"Oh, yeah, he'll finally qualify for Beebe Defensive Arts and Training Academy. I'm excited for him."

"I'm excited for the younger Closet kids!" I exclaimed through a mouthful of popcorn. "That plush parrot is the most obnoxious child in the world, but he can be downright mean, too! There's this beanbag kid with a plastic baby doll head…"

"Todd's Rochi?"

"I think so. Anyway, Bubba poked him in the eye with his beak! Can you believe that?"

Anna Grace nodded and laughed despite her mouthful of

fizzy, lemon-lime liquid. "You have to remember why Bubba and the others are the way they are," she explained after swallowing. "Todd is the kindest kid in the world. Bubba is his alter-ego. He does things Todd would only dream of doing. I know it's aggravating for us bystanders and the suffering kids, but there's not much we can do."

Anna Grace was wrong on that one. Bubba was my first and only "archenemy". I didn't find little kids half as adorable as Anna Grace did, but I didn't like to see them hurt, either. Discreetly, I began to protect them in ways I hoped Bubba wouldn't notice. Usually, I'd start a conversation with Bubba's next target before he had a chance to throw a punch.

On a lazy Saturday afternoon, Bubba "kidnapped" Pepper and threw her into a fish-filled fountain in the Underground City. In two seconds, Pepper was on dry land. Bubba, on the other hand, was "somehow" submerged before he could react. By the time the pathetic, wet mess of red, green, and yellow down surfaced, I was carefully hidden out-of-sight with a soaked fur ball cradled in my arms. Unfortunately, my joy was short-lived when Bubba grabbed innocent Rochi and threw him into the fountain.

"Stay here!" I told Pepper.

In a flash, I snatched Rochi from the cold water with one hand and trapped Bubba in the other. The squawking parrot broke free and flew wildly at my face. Before any bystanders could react, I had Bubba trapped among the fish with my wet foot. My intention was to merely scare the bully- not drown or torture him- but I got carried away and kept him under longer than I should have. I'm embarrassed to say that, somehow, the six-inch bird knocked me down, face-first, into the shallow fountain. The next thing I knew, someone had a tight grip on my shoulder. Revenge was sweet until remorse set in, and I immediately began crying.

Even though they appeared to be fine, the three stuffed

animals were taken to the Underground City's Medical Center emergency room for a "just-in-case" onceover.

When they were gone, a kind policeman handed me a tissue, gave me a hug, and let me tell my side of the story. "Jobelle," the officer said after my explanation. "I've seen you around, and I know you're a sweet girl and a wonderful person. I'm proud of you for protecting the younger children, but you can't just torture someone, even if it seems deserved. You aren't in trouble with the city, but I need to take you home and tell your parents what happened."

"It's just my sister. She's eighteen," I stated quietly. The officer's look grew even more compassionate, and I got to sit in the front seat of the police car rather than in the back.

Thirty minutes later, our home was silent. Little Leah was asleep upstairs while Ariella and I sat opposite of each other on two recliners.

"Sweetheart, what I am supposed to do with you?"

I didn't know anything except that I was guilty and couldn't stop crying.

She sighed and laughed at the same time while putting her face in her hands. "You don't know how hard it is to be a sister *and* a mom simultaneously." Her grief came back suddenly, and we cried together for a long time.

She did manage to punish me. I was completely terrified at the mere thought of apologizing to Bubba at school, so the entire weekend was torture. When Monday finally came, Bubba was absent.

"Where's Bubba?" I asked Rochi.

"He's fighting in the battle," the kindergartener responded. The second to fourth grade teacher overheard. "Todd loves science fiction, so his imaginary friends often have cartoonish battles. Bubba was called to the front."

I felt my heart sink as I suddenly understood. When he returned on Friday, we sat together at lunch silently.

"I'm sorry,"

Somehow, Bubba and I had a silent understanding after that incident. He still picked on whomever he could, but there was something less malicious about it from that point on.

Autumn brought crisp, cool weather and beautiful fall leaves. Leah's second birthday party was a blast, regardless how irritating Awesome Happy Fun World's Kiddy Circus could get after ten hours straight. And no matter how hard Ariella tried to prevent the typical hands-in-the-cake toddler moment, frosting still managed to get everywhere. After watching some acrobats during the hour-long line for Flight of the Pachyderm, Pepper tried to do a flip of her own. Unfortunately, she miscalculated the landing and ended up in the cake.

No one cared. Gourmet ice cream is better than birthday cake.

I was in awe of Thanksgiving and Christmas, two holidays I'd never celebrated back home. On New Year's Eve, I spent the night in Anna Grace's room, anxiously awaiting 2004's arrival. Anna Grace fell asleep but awoke seconds before midnight as I heard fireworks explode outside.

"Anna Grace!" I whispered excitedly. "If you get the windows open soon, maybe we can watch the show!"

Anna Grace rolled out of bed and sighed. "They're just on the ground, Belle," she said. "You can't see them…"

When Anna Grace spread the blinds apart, she was right. The black night was cloudy and starless. There was a flash of lightning and roll of thunder about thirty seconds apart. With a storm on the way, the popping sounds stopped. I let out a slow breath.

"Sorry," I apologized. "I love fireworks. When I first came here, I hated everything. I was too upset to think about anything but my dad. For whatever reason, when I saw those fireworks on the fourth of July, everything changed a little. I don't know why. Maybe I realized… that maybe it's not so bad to be imaginary.

It's a little disappointing to be made by a person, but... I guess it's not so bad to be created by your best friend."

Suddenly bright hues illuminated the sky. Fireworks of all colors lit up the night.

Friday, January 12, 2008

My mom and I sat together in an exam room at the nephrology clinic. There was a commotion in the hall. Usually, Dr. Jones knocked before coming in, but the nurse who had recorded my 210/120 blood pressure had left the door ajar. Dr. Jones pushed the door open and immediately said sympathetically, "Oh, yeah, that's not steroids."

It was one of those moments where you want to ask 'really' in the most sarcastic tone possible, but it was also a huge relief. As silly as it sounded, I had believed the nurses that it was "just the prednisone," even though I knew deep inside there was something more serious going on.

Dr. Jones began speaking of the experimental "next step". Because too little was known about FSGS, there was no protocol beyond the three months of steroid treatment. Originally, he had talked about cyclophosphamide, a chemotherapy medicine usually used to treat cancers like leukemia. I did not want my hair to fall out, but I especially didn't want to deal with daily vomiting. Thankfully, Dr. Jones said he had thought it over, and I agreed to begin a different drug, cyclosporine, that night.

Cyclosporine is a powerful anti-rejection agent used in organ transplants. Its purpose is to weaken a person's immune system so the body isn't able to attack the foreign organ, like it would a germ. No one knew for sure, but FSGS was thought to be caused by an autoimmune response. Something told my body to attack my poor kidneys as if they were foreign contaminants, even though they had been mine since before I was born. The hope was that cyclosporine would stop whatever was attacking my kidneys by weakening my defenses.

Dr. Jones then explained why I was puffing out like a blowfish. I had lost so much protein through my urine that my body's albumin count was only 1. Normal was at least 4. Protein acts as a sponge to pull the extra fluids out of tissues and into the bloodstream. No matter how well your kidneys are working, if you don't have protein in your body, the fluid will stay trapped in your tissues, out of your bloodstream, and away from even the best-functioning kidneys.

After explaining this, Dr. Jones asked me to do him a favor, even though I wouldn't like it.

"What?" I asked.

"I want you to stay in the hospital for a day or two." He explained that they'd give me intravenous albumin, a type of protein. The albumin would replace what my body had lost, at least for a little while. It would help me get rid of the water weight.

Call me weird, but I would have been ecstatic any other weekend because we only had twenty cable TV channels at home compared to the hospital's sixty. However, I was concerned about getting out in time for honors band try-outs on Monday. Dr. Jones promised he'd do his best to get me out by Monday morning at the very latest.

They called the hospital and said I should show up at admissions either that night or the next morning. We chose to come in that night after running home to eat and get some supplies; I figured the earlier I started, the earlier I'd finish.

We showed up at 6:30 that evening. The admissions desk was closed, so we had to go in through the emergency room. When I got into my room, it was time for the 7:00 shift switch.

Just goes to show you how little I knew about hospitals!

I was very weak, so someone found a wheelchair to take me up to my room. It felt a little strange; I had never been in a wheelchair before, except after my biopsy when I was transferred from post-op to a private room. This was the first time I needed one because I felt so... sick.

I guess everything was kind of becoming clear. Sometimes, FSGS isn't so bad. Some people get into remission without a problem and never relapse again. I'd assumed, even though I felt I might die during treatment, that if I made it through those three months of prednisone, I would be okay. I was slowly realizing that I wasn't in that percentage of patients. I had steroid-resistant FSGS, which is something you don't want to have.

They wheeled me up to my room and helped me get into

the hospital bed. I immediately began posing Pepper on my nifty remote control and taking several crazy photos, not that you needed or wanted to know that...

It was about 7:15 on a Friday evening, which is arguably the worst time to attempt to get admitted to hospitals in Nectarwood. Not only are nurses switching shifts for the next twelve hours, a whole new group of weekend personnel is taking over. In other words, it's somewhat organized chaos; the nurses of both shifts have to switch off and inform each other what is happening with each patient.

I can't imagine how frustrating that must be as a nurse, so I give them all the credit, but it's pretty darn annoying for patients, too. I wanted someone to put in my IV, bring in the "human albumin," and get this thing over with so I could bust out of this place by Monday for honor band tryouts!

While the nurses had their meeting, the nursing assistants did the basic housekeeping jobs, like bringing everyone cold water and changing sheets. There was this one guy, Larry, who was really nice. He looked all over the floor (and maybe then some) to find my mom a reclining chair for the night.

Larry was funny. He felt bad that I was sixteen and in the hospital, especially over the weekend, so he tried to crack as many jokes as possible. He had to check my blood pressure, but the only machine he could find was old.

One of the biggest dangers of being very swollen was the high blood pressure it caused. When the machine registered 197/121, my mom and I weren't surprised. After all, I had been in Dr. Jones's office only three hours ago, and my 210/120 reading hadn't seemed to alarm him.

"This machine's ancient," Larry said jovially as he took the cuff off my arm. "If that were true, we'd be calling a code blue! You'd be dead!" He laughed as he went to put away the 'World War II-era' monitor.

"It might be that high," my mom told Larry, but he was already rolling the equipment away. I heard him tell one of the busy nurses the machine was out-of-order. He came back in a few minutes with another machine.

Larry took my blood pressure again, and it had risen significantly! I usually panicked over things like this, but here I was, laughing. I don't think I was nervous, although that's what Larry attributed the reading to. He somewhat jokingly told me to meditate, which I don't, but I did pray.

On the third try, the machine beeped at virtually the same numbers it had before. Larry's face was priceless. Have you ever seen someone smile really big, then move their hand over their face, and totally change their expression? It was kind of like that- from joking to dead serious- except he wasn't playing around.

I can't tell you how hard it was to not burst into laughter. You know someone thinks it's serious when they start using the term 'sweetheart'. I suppose it *was* serious, but it was hilarious at the same time.

"It's okay," Larry assured me. "You're in a hospital, and if this is going to happen, this is the perfect place."

He left quickly, probably to go tell a nurse. My mom and I started laughing.

I was <u>so</u> glad Larry had considered me an emergency- maybe a nurse would hurry up and put in an IV!

Friday, August 19, 2005

I rummaged through an ever-growing array of notebooks filled with the adventures of the past two years. My name was scribbled at least once on every page.

A lot had happened since 2003. Over the past year specifically, I had matured from a little preteen to a young adolescent.

These notebooks, however, didn't detail the real events that took place in my life, such as our trip to Orlando in the early summer of 2004 or my performance in a local young people's theater production. My family had hundreds of pictures and videos that kept those memories alive. In contrast, my notebooks were of my imaginary stories- the many things my brother and I had created together, and the even more numerous stories I had invented by myself. I quickly read the pretend happenings of 2004.

I loved my imaginary universe. It was always growing and changing. I stopped actually acting out the adventures around the time I turned thirteen. As much as I still loved my characters and their entire world, I finally gave in to the "fact" that being as old as I was and still having pretend friends was "weird."

So I did the most logical thing I could do. I gave it up and started writing a "normal" story with non-PFA "people".

It didn't get far. I couldn't come up with anything remotely interesting. No matter how I tried, my mind kept drifting back to the PFA. I thought about what the imaginary "members" of the organization would be doing if I had continued writing.

Before long, I began writing the "could-have-been" stories of the PFA, leaving myself in the picture. It was easier than it had been, of course, because it took half the time. Now I wrote as I made stuff up, rather than waiting until I had "acted it out."

It wasn't weird.

Right?

Or what is?

I flipped through a few more pages, and began wondering:

If someone found this- like my mom or dad- would they

think something was wrong with me? Would they believe that I still acted out make-believe stuff... just like a preschooler? If it wasn't freaky enough for a fifth grader to "play pretend", it certainly was for an eighth grader to act the same way.

Did this mean I had to give it up altogether?

No, I told myself. *I can take myself out, and the PFA can continue without me.*

That idea lasted about two seconds. I smiled at the reason. Sure, everything about the PFA lived only in my imagination- but like real people, there was a dynamic.

There was no way Jobelle could survive without "me" in the PFA.

I quickly thought through numerous alternatives until I came up with a reasonable solution. It was actually simple.

I thought about Anna Grace and Jobelle's tight-knit friendship, and the first thing I noticed was the way I phrased my own thoughts. I said "Jobelle and Anna Grace", not "Jobelle and I." Now that I didn't actually playact anymore, I called Jobelle's best friend Anna Grace, but I didn't quite see her as myself. As personal as the PFA was, my character Anna Grace only *represented* me. She did everything I did in real life, but she wasn't really <u>me</u>.

I decided to take my name out of any future PFA documents, but leave myself in through a parallel character- someone who represented me and did everything I did, but without putting my name directly into an imaginary world. My "parallel" would be the imaginary version of me, and in a way, the part of me that still "escaped" to this imaginary world whenever possible. I named my imaginary self Annie. No one I knew would ever call me that in real life; in fact, I think I'd hate it if someone tried. However, Annie was imaginary- she could be a little different than me.

I ran to my family's computer and did a search of every PFA document. *Oh boy*, I thought as I swapped out every mention of "Anna Grace" with the name "Annie."

I really <u>am</u> crazy now.

Saturday, January 13, 2008

I woke up at around 6:00 AM and had to go to the bathroom... again. It had been about eight hours since my nurse, Stella, had first come to my room.

My first IV experience in September 2007 had been terrible. This time, I was pleasantly surprised I couldn't feel this one at all, except during an intravenous bumetanide push.

A lot of people are familiar with the term 'intravenous,' meaning through the vein. If you've ever visited anyone in a hospital, you've likely seen a bag or two hung above the bed. A line sends the necessary medications or fluids directly into the patient's bloodstream using an intravenous tube, or IV. Usually, the fluid or medicine is 'dripped' slowly. However, there are times it is important for medicine to be 'pushed' into the person's body quickly. It's similar to a shot, utilizing a syringe with a needle. Unlike a regular injection, the needle is inserted into the person's IV, rather than through the skin. With no poke, you'd think an IV push is painless, and I've been told it usually is. However, with bumetanide, I felt nauseous and lightheaded, even though it was injected very slowly. I could imagine this would bother a lot of people, especially considering it caused that similar burn you'd feel after getting a vaccination, only this was slightly more severe.

The main reason I was in the hospital was for an albumin drip. The albumin was a dark yellow. It reminded me of egg whites. Several bags hung over my bed, which meant I had to drag an IV pole with me to the bathroom. Thankfully, the albumin drip didn't hurt at all.

The effect of the combined high-dose diuretic and intravenous protein was remarkable. It was as if the fluid was melting off of me. I was urinating about a liter an hour, and I had lost about ten pounds of pure fluid since I had fallen asleep around midnight.

Unfortunately, I could tell the albumin wasn't staying in my body. Straight albumin is foamy and frothy, so when protein is in your urine, it tends to be bubbly. I had to catch and count everything I voided, and the huge bubbles in my urine matched those in the albumin bag that hung above my head.

The good news was the water weight was coming off. I could breathe comfortably again and some of the bloated-body pain was fading. At the moment, that was all I cared about, even if the disease was still running rampant and it would take a harsh drug to bring it into check.

God had taken me this far, and I knew He wouldn't let me go.

The next few days were filled with adventure, for lack of another word. Dr. Jones added a ton of medicines to my list. While he decreased my prednisone dose from 50 to 30 mg, he added cyclosporine, my newest defense and a somewhat experimental strategy. Better than the chemo that I had thought would be the next "step" in my adventure, cyclosporine was still harsh, especially those first couple days. I also had a fistful of cholesterol-lowering medications, blood pressure drugs, aspirin, supplements, and more diuretics. My magnesium levels had plummeted so much that I needed two high-dose supplement shots. There was still a lot of water in my body tissues; so much, in fact, that the tiny holes in my skin where the magnesium injection needles had poked actually leaked a clear fluid.

Between the prednisone and cyclosporine, my mind was very foggy by Monday morning. Sitting in my hospital bed proved to be exhausting and confusing.

Dr. Jones was wonderful as far as getting me out of the hospital in time to get to clarinet auditions, but after the entire weekend, I could care less. It scared me a little to think that, after all of the work I had done in preparing for All-Region honor band, I readily decided to skip the event in order to go home and sleep.

We celebrated my brother's thirteen birthday that night. While I taped Todd's reaction to his new trombone, I noticed my body's reactions to the new drug. My hands were uncontrollably shaking, my vision was blurry, and my throat stung. The next evening, I was watching a movie with my family when I tasted blood. My gums had started bleeding spontaneously - a trademark side effect of cyclosporine.

Cyclosporine was a weird drug, to say the least. Even within the first couple days, it gave me tremors, made painful acne break out everywhere from my head to ankles, and put my mind in a short of dreamlike state constantly. Even so, I felt so much better than I had on prednisone alone. I still had to force a ton of prednisone down my throat daily, but I my life seemed hundreds of times better than it had for the past two months.

On January 21, I woke up feeling different. It's difficult to describe. I felt sick, similar to how you might feel if you have an awful case of strep throat, but I could breathe again! My feet weren't balloons anymore, and my bulgy stomach was non-existent. I went to the doctor that day for a routine check-up. While I wasn't in remission, I was quite a bit better, with my protein loss down to "only" 11 grams. For anyone else in the world, 11 grams of protein loss would be very bad news, but for me, it meant hope.

Wednesday, October 5, 2005

My brother watched goofy videos after school, but I had another way of relaxing after a hard day. I wrote about the entirely fictional world of pretend playmates, which usually made me feel like either the most immature eighth grader in the state or most insane person in the world. It varied from day to day.

You can only do so much with a few main characters... so I decided to add two more teenagers to the PFA. As I worked through a character development process, it became obvious to me that I should fashion the new arrivals as siblings with a very troubled past.

At first glance, the imaginary world I had created seemed perfect. When I really thought about it, I realized the imageries' lives would be chaotic if they were an actual society. How would the government work? Well, it wouldn't. Everyone would have their own cities, but most would be ruled by preschoolers. While some people would live in marshmallow castles, others would be faced with starvation, violence, and who-knows-what else as they were neglected by their creators when the preschoolers grew up. *That's because everyone else is sane!* I argued with myself in a joking manner.

Anyway, the newest members of my creative cast were sixteen-year-old twins, Bethany and Graham Rodgers. From an imaginary city somewhere near Nashville, the kids' parents had been divorced for three years. The parents had had joint custody until their father was convicted of an unknown crime. For the most part, everything was fine until their mom was diagnosed with terminal cancer. Thrust into a muddled foster system, Bethany especially was struggling. The PFA offered to take them into Underground City's foster system, which wasn't ideal but better than the alternative.

Annie and Jobelle had been growing apart slightly due to different interests and personalities. Bethany brought them closer together as the three formed a close-knit trio. She was a unique mix of both girls, being athletic like Jobelle but musically inclined like Annie.

Graham was Beth's kind and soft spoken yet goofy brother who was always overprotective of his twin. Originally, he was an afterthought type of background character, solely written to be a comfort to his sister, as Ariella was for Jobelle.

Todd and I didn't work together as much anymore on our "imaginations," but we did read each other's stuff to provide often-silly "commentaries." When I asked Todd who his favorite was in a short story I had written, he replied, "Graham! Duh!" Wanting to please my audience, I found a way to make Graham a little more central, and without meaning to, I had changed the dynamic of the PFA.

I Hate You More- Jobelle's POV
Takes Place: August through November 2005

School started in August. Since I had "graduated" from eighth grade in May, I was forced to attend the large high school in the Underground City.

"I hate you!" I screamed as I jumped off the bus after the first day.

Graham Rodger's voice echoed from one of the yellow vehicle's windows. "I hate you more," he shrieked, sounding somewhat like a girl.

"Hey, Belle," Ariella said cheerfully as I entered our house. Little Leah waved as she attempted to pirouette on her tiptoes. Too angry to acknowledge either of them, I threw a pink wad of paper at the table and ran to my room. I figured I had about ten seconds until my sister showed up in my room.

Ten... nine... eight... seven... six... five... four... three... two...

"Jobelle Newbrey!" Ariella scolded as she threw open the door.

With one second to spare, I thought, sitting up on my bed.

"How in the world did you manage to get a pink slip in eight hours? Don't you know it's a very bad idea to start off with that kind of reputation on your first day of high school?"

"Graham Rodgers is a loser," I commented.

"What does Graham Rodgers have to do with anything?"

"I told him my dad was dead. The ungrateful lunatic said I was lucky! I don't care how neglectful someone is, how can he say that?"

Ariella shook her head. "Apparently you took some kind of action."

"Uh, yeah! I punched him as hard as I could. He yelled at me so loudly the driver had to pull over, then Beth and I got into a fistfight. Graham grabbed me off of her and I kicked him."

"Jobelle!"

"What? Like you wouldn't have done the same thing?"

She would have and she knew it, but Ariella dismissed the thought. She knew my blood was boiling.

"Cool down, Belle," she instructed in a gentle tone as she gave me a fluffy pillow to keep my angry hands busy. If the pillow had to breathe, it would have suffocated.

"I want to talk to Annie," I mumbled after a silent minute.

"I'll call her for you. Are you ready to talk now?"

I nodded and set the pillow on my lap. "I know what I did was wrong..."

Ariella cut me off quickly.

"I know you do, Belle. I'm not going to lecture you. In fact, I shouldn't even punish you."

Ugh! She knew me too well. While most kids would whine and gripe their way out of getting in trouble, my guilty conscious was never worth 'going free.'

Ariella laughed as she left my room. "Alright, you're grounded for a month."

I assessed the numerous bruises on my arms, legs, and face

while wondering where Bethany learned how to fight so well. Within a few minutes, Annie was in my room.

"Ouch," I moaned with a wince as she carefully placed an ice pack on my left shiner. I told her what had happened, and she slapped my wrist.

"You know why they're in the foster system, right?" she asked me.

"Neglect," I stated, suddenly feeling worse for a reason I couldn't put my finger on.

"Their mom is dying of cancer, Belle," she told me quietly. I felt my heart drop, but that still didn't excuse Graham's horrendous statement. "Why can't they be with their dad?"

Annie sighed. "I don't know the details or to what extent, but he's abusive. He'll be in prison for a long time."

My heart began racing. "Why didn't you tell me?"

"Beth wanted as few people as possible to know. With your mom and dad being gone... she didn't want you to feel bad, I guess."

Graham, Bethany, and I were forced to sit together on the bus the next morning. The silence was deafening.

"I'm sorry," I finally whispered. "I had no idea."

Bethany rolled her brown eyes and looked out the window, but Graham turned to me.

"I forgive you," he said quietly. "I'm sorry, too. You didn't get in trouble, did you?"

Bethany's head whirled around, smacking her curly brown hair against the back of our seat as she glared at her twin. Graham ignored her.

"I'm grounded for a month," I admitted. To my surprise, the rather handsome boy shook his head.

"That's not fair! I got a week, and Beth got two. Shouldn't we all be punished equally?"

"Life's not fair," I commented to shut him up. I wasn't used to having boys- especially very cute boys- notice me.

For the next couple weeks, Graham and I didn't talk much, but a silent friendship formed. It took Bethany a while to forgive me. She never said the actual words. Instead, the day after I was 'un-grounded,' she began talking to me as if nothing had happened.

By the end of September, Bethany, Graham, Annie, and I were known as the "Fearsome Foursome". We often hung out at the Annie Room Church of the Underground City. On Sunday mornings, we stuck together in the service. On Wednesday afternoons after school, we got to church early and worked as a part of the praise team. I quickly learned that both twins had amazing vocal and instrumental skills. Bethany tried to teach me how to play guitar to no avail. Graham tried to teach me how to crash symbols, but because I either jumped at the noise or caused the symbols to miss each other, he ended up putting a triangle in my hand.

"Hold it by the string!" He'd have to remind me. Annie would always giggle. "You know," she'd say after an amazing run on her clarinet, "For being the best fourteen-year-old ballerina in the city, you sure don't have a clue when it comes to music."

One Friday night, I slept over in Annie's room. "Do you like Graham?" she asked suddenly. "I mean, it's obvious you two are becoming close friends, but do you *like him* like him?"

That was a good question, because I really didn't know. It would be a lie to say he wasn't cute, but like him like that? Before I could respond, a flashlight shined on my face.

"Hey! What are you…?" I began to whisper through tightly squinted eyes. The light went dark again, and all I could see were various shades of red, green, and orange fogging my vision.

"You aren't blushing," Annie told me. "So you don't have a crush on him… yet."

Halloween night was so much fun. Imaginaries from the PFA, the Fictional Alliance, and other imaginary organizations met at the Annie Room Church for an incredible fall festival. I showed up as myself in my full ballet getup while Annie donned a fifties poodle skirt outfit. Little Leah was the cutest pumpkin in the world. In contrast, Pepper ran around trying to disappear as she portrayed her hero, the Cheshire Cat.

Annie and I took Leah from one decorated car's trunk to another. Her favorite, ironically, was the Todd's Guys sci-fi trunk. We spent way too much time playing with a remote-control robot. When I finally picked up my niece and headed to the next trunk, my life turned upside-down yet again.

Tuesday, February 11, 2008

I had spent the past month at home, trying to adjust to my temporary new life. Try as I might, I'd only made it to school once since January 11, and it was only for thirty minutes before the first bell rang.

School was impossible. Even if I could walk without feeling like an elephant was standing on my lungs, the logistics were an issue. With my family's schedule, I'd have to be ready to leave our house by 6:55 in the morning. It took me two hours to take my medicine, meaning I would have had to get up around 4:55 at the latest. Side effects often woke me up for two or three hours every night.

In the morning, I was nauseous until around noon. The pain, exhaustion, and breathing issues began around 1:00. Things often got very blurry as well, and everything turned into a dreamlike state. My best time of day was between three and five in the afternoon. Sometimes, I felt almost normal, but by six, I had a hard time moving.

For better or worse, my doctor appointments were always around 4:00 pm. I always saw Dr. Jones himself during my absolute best moments, meaning he never saw my true suffering. I also believed that it was best to not let him know everything that was going on, unless I thought it was a life-and-death issue. Maybe it didn't make a lot of sense for me to not mention how uncomfortable I was all the time, or how difficult life in general was, but I did. *What difference would it make?* I thought. *When I complained about prednisone in December, despite the fact my mom called the nurses daily, they didn't do anything. If Dr. Jones knows all this stuff, what's he gonna do about it?* I was still trying to convince myself I wasn't really sick; I wouldn't admit even to myself that, yeah, I was chronically ill, and probably *severely* ill as well.

Every day, I clung to my faith to survive. My mom and I made a game of purposefully looking for *why* God had allowed me to get sick. We knew there was a reason for my diagnosis, because all things work together for the good of those who love the Lord. I took this a little bit farther, also looking for the "weapons" God had given me to endure this thing. Besides my family and friends, I was so thankful I was born with an incredible imagination.

I smiled as I read about Jobelle's reunion with her father, Dale. There was a long, poorly written page on how Mr. Newbrey had survived the end of his world. He had escaped while helping the orphanage's children exit through another portal from Mara to earth. Together, he and the adult leaders of the orphanage found an imaginary city. Mr. Newbrey helped design and build a home for the escapee children and others being bounced around in the foster system. He quickly rose to a top position on the city's Imaginary Board for Child Welfare. When he somehow discovered his daughters were alive in Arkansas, he quit his job to find them.

Mr. Newbrey never imagined his family was alive. On that life-changing October night, he had two big surprises in store.

The moment I let go of my dad, he turned and motioned to two little kids, a boy and a girl, probably around nine or ten years old. The little boy had short, light brown hair while the girl's hair was long, blonde, and beautiful.

I wish I had looked like that when I was her age.

They had the same bright blue eyes, perfect noses, and precious shy smiles as if they were right out of a Christmas card. There was something innocent about them, but I couldn't place what.

Suddenly, I recognized the girl's hairstyle to be Maran.

"Jobelle," my dad said. "This is Tayoe and Kittina."

The boy studied me with curious eyes, but the girl- Kittina- smiled and attempted a curtsy, which is also a very Maran custom.

"We're twins," Kittina stated quietly. It made sense; most kids their age wouldn't dare to stand near a peer of the opposite gender, and never so close in physical proximity.

"We were dropped off on the orphanage doorstep as

babies," Tayoe explained. "No one knows our real birthday, so we estimated it to be December 24, 1994. Your dad's been really nice to us."

"I adopted them two years ago. We were living in an imaginary organization near Nashville when someone- a Gwen, I believe- from the PFA told me she knew you. The minute I knew you were alive…"

What? Why the heck did he adopt kids? Out of all of the orphans who escaped Mara, why would he suddenly pick these two?

Then it hit me. The little boy's name was Tayoe, just like my deceased younger brother.

He continued talking, but I zoned out. The twins and I stared curiously at each other, and I tried to comprehend the fact that I suddenly had two younger siblings.

I don't remember where I had gotten the idea for what I had just read, but I was excited to "see" Kitti and Tayoe again. Goofy and funny yet gentle and kind, Tayoe had been purely inspired by my little brother. Kitti was what I imagined Todd would have been like if he had been a girl.

I continued reading.

My Little Siblings- Jobelle's POV
Takes Place: November 2005 through June 2006

My life changed again on November 1, 2005, but it was for the better. The best part was that my dad was alive. He and our newest two family members moved in with me, Leah, and Ariella.

Kittina and Tayoe were precious kids. Even so, when your family doubles in size overnight, you can't escape without conflict. I'd be lying if I said I didn't feel jealous or angry for a while, but with lots of love from my family and friends, I managed to adjust. Besides, with the Christmas ballet approaching, all of my free time was spent perfecting the lead role. I danced constantly, even during the rare time I had to spend with my friends.

All six performances were crammed into the three days after Thanksgiving. Needless to say, I went to bed late at night on Sunday and basically slept until Tuesday evening. On Wednesday, it was so nice to be able to go to school and not have to think about rehearsals from four to six o'clock.

I hadn't been to church on a Wednesday night since before Annie's fourteenth birthday, but I hadn't been there at all since the Christmas decorations had been put up. It was only 3:30, so I skipped to the children's ministry wing to wait for Annie. Surprisingly, someone had beaten me to the large group room. Little Kittina sat quietly at one of the many activity stations scattered throughout the area. She looked so tiny in the huge, basketball court-sized space.

"Hi, Jobelle," she said timidly when I sat beside her. She was at a table littered with crayons and a couple dozen rubbing plates and stencils. Using a pink oil pastel, Kittina was rubbing a butterfly print onto dark purple construction paper.

"You can call me Belle, you know," I told her.

"Well, you can call me Kitti," she replied with a smile, looking up for only a moment. I admired her amazing hairdo and wondered out loud, "Has Ariella been doing your hair for you?"

Kitti finished her artwork. "No," she said nonchalantly. "I have." She handed me her completed work, but I was too flabbergasted at her hairstyling talent.

"You did your own hair?"

Kitti nodded as she grabbed a much thinner sheet of pink paper.

"How?"

"Well," she began as her delicate fingers diligently folded

the paper this way and that. "I used to do almost everyone's hair back home in the orphanage. An older girl taught me when I was four."

I briefly reminisced the day when our world had ended. Ariella had taken both me and little Leah as her own. If she hadn't done that, where would I have gone?

"What was it like living in an orphanage?" I asked.

She shrugged. "Our nannies and uncles- the people who ran the place-were very kind. They loved us and cared about what happened to us. The government didn't bother, though. There was never enough food, clothing, or space. It was okay, though, because Tayoe and I had each other."

"Did you ever get scared?"

She smiled, pulling out an Origami-style butterfly with flapping wings. "No. Tay and I promised we'd never let anything bad happen to each other. Oh!" She looked across the room. "Stay here! I want to show you something!"

As she darted to the makeshift stage area to find a certain CD, I looked down at the butterfly rubbing she made for me. In cursive, she wrote: "To: Belle- I'm sorry about everything Love: Kitti".

"Kittina," I called, walking to the stage. I handed the paper back to her.

"This is beautiful," I said softly, "but what could you possibly be sorry about?"

Kitti's inquisitive eyes searched the room, as if she was trying not to cry. "Everything," she answered. "I guess for ruining your life."

This was so much more shocking than the elegant braids had been. I put my arm around her shoulder and led her back to the table.

"Talk to me," I whispered when we were sitting again.

"I know you've been upset lately," she stated correctly. "I can't imagine how hard your life's been. Tay and I don't remember our parents. Things weren't great at the orphanage, but we were loved and treated as well as possible. You were eight years old when your mom died, right? Four years later, when Mara was destroyed, you lost everything you had- including your pet horse Midnight- and you thought your dad was gone, too. A couple years later, your dad shows up out of nowhere with two kids. When we had to evacuate, everyone from the orphanage got out safely. Tay and I even had the few things we owned in the backpacks we brought. It was traumatic, but we didn't really lose anything. You've been through so much more…"

Her little lip quivered. I gently took her hand and pulled her into a hug. "Kitti," I said gently as she wept into my shoulder. "How in the world did you know all of that?" I was taken aback at the mention of my beloved Midnight- I wasn't sure if even Annie knew about that.

She pulled back, wiping the tears from her eyes with the back of her hand. "It was easy," she sniffed. "I've read kids' mystery books since I was six. I've overheard a bunch of things about you over the past month. There were a lot of other things, too, like pictures. I had a list of questions about you, and I'd carefully ask different people when no one else was around. Once I had information, it wasn't hard to put two-and-two together. I told Tay you must hate us…"

I put my index finger gently on her lips to hush her. "Kitti, I don't hate you. I've been mad at the situation, but it isn't your fault. I'm just amazed you figured all of that out. I love you, Kitti."

We clung to each other until Annie arrived. Those minutes were when Kitti and I actually became sisters.

Everyone bonded with my new little siblings, especially my three closest friends. Kitti and Tayoe adored Annie, who headed up the children's ministry programs at the ARC (Annie Room Church). There was the instant "twin" camaraderie between Bethany and Graham and Kitti and Tayoe, too. Graham,

Bethany, Annie, and I were still the Fearsome Foursome, but we didn't mind the two preteens joining us at times.

We celebrated Kitti and Tayoe's eleventh birthdays on December 19. Everyone pitched in to get Kitti an art set and Tayoe a hand-held video game system, and dad gave them both one-time-use cameras. Rather than yell with excitement from receiving a Game-Guy console, Tayoe immediately took pictures of everyone and everything, using all 28 exposures within five minutes. The next day, dad found a Christmas wish list on the refrigerator listing "disposable camera" around fifty times in messy handwriting.

On Christmas Eve's "Eve", my whole family, Annie, and I took the Rodger twins and Pepper to Awesome Happy Fun World. Besides the park's ever-annoying name and the fact some dummy from school loaned Tayoe a digital camera, the 23rd might have been the best day of the year. When Kitti, Bethany, and I saw the recently opened indoor roller coaster, we begged Graham to ride it with us.

"I'm too young to die!" Graham exclaimed. "Can't I just find Tay and Mr. Newbrey over in the space arcade ride? Crud, I'd even go to the princess dress-up shop with Ariella, Annie, Pepper, and Leah to get out of this!"

"Oh, come on!" Bethany pleaded. "You wouldn't have decided to split into our group unless you weren't interested in *something*." She exchanged an odd glance with Kitti, who giggled for some unknown reason.

Graham crossed his arms over his chest and pouted. Even I couldn't help but giggle at that!

"Please," I asked through laughter.

"No," Graham said. "I told you, I don't ride roller coasters."

"It goes in and around the faux mountain," I explained. "It's not like it's the track and sky. You can't really tell how high up you are."

"Beth and I will buy you the huge Awesome Happy chocolate cupcake later!" Kitti suggested.

"I won't be alive to eat chocolate later," Graham said. "And if I do survive, I'll be throwing up."

"It's not that bad," Kitti said. "I read it goes upside down three times. I've seen you play football. Isn't running through a bunch of scary guys who are trying to pummel you a lot more dangerous than a ride that's been tested over and over?"

"Okay," Graham sighed reluctantly. "But I'm not riding by Beth! She'd probably unbuckle my seatbelt or something.

"_I'm_ sitting by Bethany," Kitti suggested in an authoritative tone, as if she had thought this whole thing out. "_You_ can sit by Jobelle."

Forty-five minutes later, we were finally at the front of the line. "It's our turn to go 'mountain climbing'!" Kitti exclaimed as the empty Mount Fuji-themed train cars pulled up. As I settled in one of the seats behind Kitti and Bethany, Graham actually asked the ride attendant if anyone had fallen off yet. I laughed slightly.

"You don't have to ride this," I told him with a smile. Without thinking, I took his hand, and my heart fluttered a bit. He only shrugged. I screamed, laughed, and enjoyed the amazing coaster... and the fact that I was holding hands with a very sweet boy I was starting to have a "crush on".

On the first day of the semester, I got called to the office during fourth period. Ariella met me at the door.

"Dad's at work. Leah's fine," she began quickly. "Jobelle, the Rodger twin's mother died this morning. Dot picked them up not long after school started, so they're at her house. Annie can't get out of school, so I signed you out. Do you mind?" I shook my head.

Once at their house, I ran into Bethany's room and hugged her tightly. "Help Graham," she begged me through tears. "He's in the next room."

Fear seemed to wash over me. What was I supposed to do? I took a deep breath and turned the doorknob. Graham was leaning against the wall, his back facing me. His shoulders heaved occasionally.

My fear melted, and I felt pure sympathy. Ariella had been smart to pull me out of school for the day. I still had emotional scars from my mom's death. I remembered my own grief as I neared him.

"Graham?" I attempted to whisper, but no sound came. "Graham?" I repeated. He didn't answer.

I remembered holding his hand on the roller coaster, so I very gently put my hand on his shoulder.

You can do this, I thought to him, knowing he likely didn't want to talk. *You handle this, just like I did when my mom died and when I thought my dad died.*

Graham tensed under my hand, but he got more comfortable with me as a minute or two went by. After a few minutes, he turned and locked eyes with me. I felt my heart break. Those gorgeous eyes were overflowed with tears. His pathetic face brought on a flashback of sorts, and an image of my mom flashed before my eyes. I think Graham noticed that I was zoning, because he put his hand over mine.

"I'm sorry," I whispered.

The next thing I knew, my arms were around Graham, and he was crying into my shoulder. A salty pond seemed to fill my eyes, but I refused to cry. I had to stay strong for him.

Later, at home and away from my mourning friends, I wept miserably into my dad's shoulder.

The next few weeks were tough. Graham and I held hands a lot. We weren't dating or anything; in fact, although I did have quite the crush, I highly doubted he had even an ounce of romantic interest in me. We were simply close friends, and Graham needed me. The hand-holding phased out, but our friendship remained.

"You like Graham now, right?" Annie asked once. My face flushed bright red, and she nudged me playfully.

In early May, I looked all over the church for a certain children's music CD I wanted to give to Leah. As I entered a storage closet, the walls suddenly began to shake. Some African percussion crafts left over from vacation Bible school started to rattle. My mind flashed back several years.

"Dad!" I screamed.

"I'm coming, Belle! Don't stop running!"

Ariella clutched my hand. The baby's screaming filled the air.

"Dad!" I cried out loud, dodging under a broken table. Tears streamed down my face.

What happens to imaginaries when we die? I believe in the Bible, but that applies to real people. God is real. What would he think about me? Would I be in heaven when Annie died someday, or would I cease to exist?

"Dad!" I screamed again.

The door creaked open.

"Hello?" A young male voice called. I recognized Graham.

"Jobelle?" He asked. "Hey, are you okay?"

"There's an earthquake!" I shouted through tears. Graham's face melted with compassion. He quickly took my hand and helped me stand up.

"No, Belle. Pepper's playing the drums upstairs. Listen."

Sure enough, I heard the faint crash of a symbol and a deep voice shout something about joy. I burst into tears, and until the end of the school year, we occasionally held hands again, especially if someone mentioned the word 'mom.'

Wednesday, February 27, 2008

On my worst days, everything was a struggle. Prednisone made it nearly impossible to concentrate. I had to find ways to keep myself occupied when I wasn't struggling through schoolwork. I couldn't read books or watch movies I hadn't seen before because everything new confused me. This forced me to cling to everything I already knew, especially nostalgia. I loved reminiscing about better times, before I learned about nephrotic syndrome. On many days, I'd play family videos or go through photo albums, remembering my incredible childhood.

Even more intriguing was reading about things that weren't real but equally nostalgic. The many "Pretend Friend Association" adventures had never truly happened, but they still were connected to actual memories. The later stories carried memories, such as what inspired the idea or what was happening as I wrote.

The remarkable thing about the PFA was that, no matter how complicated it was it didn't baffle me, because I knew it so well.

Not everything I found was written from Jobelle's first-person point-of-view. She was obviously my favorite character, but I remembered wanting to go places she couldn't go. I had played around with third person originally but eventually decided to expand into other character's first person worlds.

It had been a challenge, if I remembered correctly, to get inside the heads of other characters, especially males, because their perspectives were so different from mine. Although my opinions differed greatly from Jobelle's, her 'voice' was very similar to my real way of talking. Naturally, no one else's thoughts would sound alike, so it required a lot of silent dramatization. When I wrote, not only did I create another world, but I stepped into the "role" of another person.

Kitti's hard-working and optimistic nature had been a stretch. Her thoughts were cheerier than my own. She spun a positive twist on nearly everything. Not only that, she was a literal genius and mastermind mystery solver. She wasn't nearly as impulsive as her adopted sister but shared more of my opinions than Jobelle ever would.

Hi Everybody! Kitti's First-Person Point-of-View
Takes Place: January 2006 to May 2007

Hi everybody! My name is Kittina Newbrey, but pretty much everyone calls me Kitti. I was born around eleven years ago on Mara. My twin brother Tayoe and I were dropped off at an orphanage's doorsteps when we were babies. We called the people who ran the orphanage our nannies and uncles. They were very kind and loved us a lot, even though the conditions were less-than-perfect. We left that imaginary world during a big earthquake. Our daddy adopted us, and we lived in Nashville for a few years before joining the PFA.

Our apartment in the Underground City was fantastic! Tay and I each got our own room. I couldn't believe it at first! The best part was that daddy's lost daughters were both alive. I had sisters!

Ariella was great from the moment I met her. Jobelle was less-than-happy about us at first. I didn't blame her; in fact, I felt bad for her. It didn't take much investigation to unravel her past. She'd had a scary first fourteen years, and I knew suddenly inheriting two little siblings couldn't have been easy! I talked to her about that once, and things got much better.

There were tons of people in the Underground City, but there weren't a lot of PFA kids our age. We made some friends when we began going to Closet Elementary and Middle School in January 2006. It was weird to be in fifth grade again. Back in Nashville, I had tested into sixth grade after my eighth birthday. While it wasn't hard schoolwork-wise, being three years younger than everyone else had been difficult. Even Tayoe had problems with older kids, but he was lucky enough to be put in fourth grade. In Annie's Room, the teachers of Closet School 'officially' allowed me to be with kids my age, which made me very happy.

I liked "hanging out" with the "Fearsome Foursome" of

the Pretend Friend Association. Jobelle was my big sister, but Annie, Bethany, and Graham were like siblings, too. My big sister was excellent at art, which we could spend hours doing together. Annie was musically inclined enough to teach me how to play clarinet, but the real musicians of the Fearsome Foursome were the Rodger twins. Because they helped with the children's choirs at the Annie Room Church, they somehow managed to enroll Tayoe and me into the preteen group in the middle of the 2005-2006 school sessions. I was so glad they did!

After singing several solos for the children's service, I was asked to perform alone in "big church" on Palm Sunday. Originally, I was supposed to skip children's church that day, but Tayoe persuaded me to attend, because they were making pretty flower wreaths craft. About two minutes before I was supposed to sing, Annie found me and literally had to pull me away from the craft table and push me onto the "stage". First, I had managed to get the flowery wreath on my head. After the last note, I ran back to the kid's service. Someone from the tech team had to chase me to get my microphone back.

Later in the morning, Graham picked me up and spun me around.

"Hey superstar, do you want to be on the Praise Team?"

I was happily surprised. "Don't I have to audition for that?"

He shrugged. "Usually, but with a voice like yours, why? Where'd you get that cool grassy, flowery, headband thingy?"

"Oh, this wreath? I made it at children's church." I took it off and put it on Graham's head. Annie walked by.

"Hey, Annie, how do I look?" He called.

"Aw, that's beautiful, Graham," she said jokingly. "You should really keep that on and show Belle."

I laughed. Graham put me down in fake fury and placed the wreath back on my head. He was just being silly, of course, but I noticed that he truly was a little embarrassed. I giggled again.

Everyone knew that Graham and Belle had gone from foes

to friends to very best friends, but I suspected more. I knew Belle had a crush on Graham, but I had guessed Graham's feelings were mutual. My assumptions had proven true!

As a twin myself, I wondered how that affected Bethany, to no longer have her brother as a best friend. "Oh, we're *still* best friends," she assured me once when we were alone. "So are Jobelle and Annie. No one says a person can't have two best friends at once. What about your brother and his two friends? See? He has three best friends- Blue Bear, Tomes, and you. That doesn't bother you, does it?"

I told her that it didn't, but it did. At recess, I still made stuff from grass and flowers while Tayoe dug for leaf fossils nearby. Instead of talking to him, I listened silently as he told dumb jokes with his daring duo. That was hard, but I didn't want to think about the day we'd actually care about the other gender. The good news- for me, anyway- was that Tayoe claimed all girls outside of family were disgusting. I hoped that idea would never leave his head. I didn't have any impractical thoughts about boys yet, but my "boys-are-gross" attitude was long gone. I wished I could be eleven forever, because I knew it was only a matter of time until I starting acting like my silly sister.

I skipped forward to the last thing I could find: a very short blurb about the imaginary high school's class of 2007 graduation, written in my usual storytelling format, first person from Jobelle's point-of-view.

I had dreaded this night for ever. Crying can be contagious at times, and high school graduations are sob-fests. I hated crying in front of anyone, except maybe my dad or Annie. I promised myself that I'd never cry at a high school graduation-mine or otherwise- but I knew I was on the brink of tears. After all, Bethany and Graham were graduating high school, leaving me behind to enter eleventh grade alone. …

Ugh! What an awful ending, I thought. Obviously, the last few meaningless sentences hadn't been meant as the ending. For whatever reason, I wanted to know what happened next. Kooky on steroids, I briefly thought, "Hey! Who's the dummy who didn't finish this thing?"

Oh, yeah, that'd be me.

I turned on our old computer and searched through the files, trying to find anything from the PFA I hadn't printed. There were tons of files, but nothing I hadn't already read. Bored and frustrated, I opened a new word processing document and typed the first thing that popped into my mind:

Kidney disease, I hate you!

I laughed, probably psychotically, and wrote:

PEPPER HATES YOU, KIDNEY DISEASE!!!

At my own mention of Pepper, I allowed myself to turn my imaginative brain back on for a moment. A million ideas flooded my head, and for a second, my thoughts drifted back to the days of writing PFA stories.

If Annie's life is a parallel to mine, she'd have kidney disease, too, I thought. *It'd be exactly my case. There's a start.*

Wait, a start? A start to what? I wasn't even slightly interested in having actual imaginary friends like I had, but writing? I had to admit that I missed thinking like an author, even though I was far from one.

This was not the time. My brain was fried most of the time; if I couldn't understand new concepts easily, how could I possibly write?

The PFA isn't a new to me, I reminded myself. *I've done this in some form or another since I was two. I know these characters as if I've met them and this world as if I've lived in it; because in a completely fantastical way, I have.*

Well, what could it hurt? *I'll never get it published*, I

thought. I turned off our old computer and headed to our newer laptop that allowed me to do homework in a recliner rather than sitting up at a desk.

I decided to start in the present, not writing the adventures the characters could have had since 2007 but using bullets to help keep my thoughts straight.

- Bethany would have moved back to Nashville by herself to pursue an imaginary singing career. Graham would have stayed in the PFA, enrolling in the Underground City's community college.
- Everything that happened since I got sick would have happened to Annie…

I stopped short at that thought and remembered several various moments, including the first time I tasted prednisone. The word alone made me gag, but I forced myself not to vomit as I reminisced about how much I'd complained about the drug. Only when its side effects began did some people believe me, but even then, many didn't.

What would have happened to Annie in the imaginary world? My real-life best friends were incredible, so I wondered if Jobelle would act the same toward Annie. I smiled as an idea quickly came to mind: Jobelle would do something I never would do, as was often the case, and she'd pull Graham in with her. I set a date for the story- October 6, the morning of the 2007 craft fair- and began to write.

Back to the PFA-
Takes Place October 2007 in Jobelle's Point-of-View

Over the previous few weeks, my best friend Annie had been a mess. She had been diagnosed with a kidney-related condition called nephrotic syndrome and prescribed a medication called prednisone. I had researched and found a foreboding stigma surrounding the drug, but ignored every scary claim.

After finishing a science project on global warming, I believed the Internet was mostly constructed of worst-case scenario information.

My little sister was concerned for Annie, but that isn't saying much. As sweet and caring as Kitti is, she's afraid of nearly everything, especially anything remotely medical.

"Prednisone?" Kitti asked with eyes full of compassion.

Annie nodded. "How do you know about corticosteroids?"

"I had terrible allergies when I was little," Kitti explained. "I was constantly stuffed up until I turned five, when my nanny decided the inhaler and anti-histamines weren't doing any good. The only thing that worked was prednisone. I'd take it until my allergies went away, usually for a month or two, and then they'd taper me off over a couple weeks. I was on and off it for three years. There must have been an allergen solely found back home, because I tapered off when we moved here, and I haven't had a problem on earth."

"Were the side effects bad?" Annie asked.

"Not really," Kitti said, shaking her head. "I was on a fairly high dose, too- maybe about thirty milligrams? I'm not sure. I was hungrier and moodier than your average five-year-old, but it wasn't anything awful. I had more happy highs than depressed or angry lows."

"She was so fun!" Tayoe added, putting his arm around his twin. "It seemed like it gave her more energy than usual."

"That would be the euphoria, Tay, but yeah, I never had any big-deal problems on that medicine. The tablets tasted gross, but by the third or fourth course, the orphanage doctor switched me to the liquid form. It was still icky but better."

Kitti's description of prednisone's "gross" taste seemed to be an understatement, at least in Annie's mind. She complained about the prednisone all the time, and although she was my best friend, I quickly got really sick of it. How bad could it be?

I exited the apple tree entrance of the Underground City and ran towards the gate. For years, the only way to get to Annie's window was to climb over a chain-link fence, unless you wanted to pass through Todd's room, but one cannot simply walk past Bubba. After complaining forever, an imaginary gate had been installed, but by that time, I was used to taking things into my own hands.

"What do you have against the gate? It was installed so you would quit moaning." I whipped around to see Graham in the orchid, outside of the enclosure. Without a running start, I climbed back to the other side and stood on the inside of an abandoned, real tire swing that Anna Grace's dad had built for her a decade earlier.

"I wasn't moaning. I was being an active Underground City citizen. Hey, want to have some fun this morning?"

"You and your sisters are already dragging me to that stupid craft fair in Hot Springs. What's the point, anyway? There might be six imaginary vendors there, if you get lucky. If Tayoe and Ariella's boyfriend weren't coming..."

"Kit, Ariella, and I are artistic- we like window shopping. It's tradition. Anyway, I have a different idea."

"Which is?" He asked, standing next to me on the tire swing. (It's a good thing imaginary weight doesn't have any effect on real items!)

"I want to taste a little bit of Annie's prednisone powder to prove it's not gross."

"Are you mad at her for some weird reason again?"

"No!" I exclaimed truthfully, although he had a point. Annie and I were great friends, but after four years of hanging out daily, we knew each other well enough to be downright cruel if so inclined.

"Can't you just give her the benefit of the doubt?" Graham asked.

"No," I stated as I jumped off the swing.

"Why not?"

"Because I'm not an insanely nice person like you," I exclaimed, playfully shoving him. "Besides, I really _am_ curious."

Graham was too moral to take anything from Annie, even something she hated. Like an old softy, he asked Annie if we could 'steal' some of the orange steroid powder. We each took a tiny bit of residue- maybe a milligram or so. Graham gagged, but I actually threw up. Water did nothing to rid my mouth of the disgusting flavor or strange burning sensation.

"Oh my gosh!" I exclaimed, wrapping my arms around Annie's shoulders. "I will never underestimate you again!"

Later at the craft fair, I was unceasingly hungry and experienced several migraines. Graham's mellow, easygoing attitude gave way to moodiness. While it was probably just psychological, the "side effects" from "prednisone" were an unpleasant but important experience for me, because I began caring about what Annie was dealing with.

I sighed, wishing more real people knew about lesser-known chronic illnesses. If there was more awareness about kidney disease and other rare and misunderstood sicknesses, maybe I wouldn't feel so alone.

If I was mad about anything, it was the isolation this uncommon disease caused. Of course, God never left me, and my family and friends were incredible. Even so, I felt alone in this fight. No one could know exactly how I felt, except someone who also had nephrotic syndrome.

Suddenly, I got a slightly "cruel" idea.

The imaginary part of me- Annie- was dealing with everything I was. What if another person in the PFA got kidney disease, too? After all, illness is a wonderfully brutal antagonist.

Almost immediately, I determined the only imaginary person besides Annie who could handle FSGS. I opened a new word processing document and began typing.

The PFA
Part 2: Diagnostics

Introduction:

Monday, June 21, 2010

I sat on my bed and collapsed against the overstuffed pillows, breathing heavily. My eyes scanned the bedroom as I tried to memorize each detail. I wanted to remember everything, from the movie poster that had graced my wall since eighth grade to the relatively new dialysis machine that stood like a statue by my nightstand.

Once I had slowed my pulse, I used my last ounce of energy to reach into a pillowcase. My frail hand fumbled upon the worn binder. I held it gently and opened the front cover. Inside were hundreds of pages of imaginary stories and a blue gel pen. Carefully, I dislodged the pen from its spot. My hands shook with fatigue as I managed to scrawl a message on a scrap of paper.

Hey Todd,

Remember the PFA- the Pretend Friend Association thing we used to do when we were little kids? Well, I used to write that stuff down. I found about half of these papers when I first got sick; the rest I've written since. All those hours we spent making up stories turned out to be one of the precious gifts God gave me to get as far as I have with this awful disease.

Anyway, if anything ever happens to me, keep this. I don't care if you show mom or dad; if this ends up in your hands, it's your choice. Whatever you do, don't you dare let anyone bury Pepper with me- that would really freak her out. You've always been a good uncle to her, even if you did let Bubba attack from time to time, so I know I can trust you to be an even better dad.

I feel so "psycho." Of all the things I could be telling you in a letter like this, I'm telling you about something that isn't even real! But maybe that's a good way to survive a scary situation- to use your imagination to try to make sense of the chaos in the real world.

I'm sorry that this happened to you. I don't mind being sick, but I hate that my illness has made you a "sick kid sibling." You're the strongest guy in the state and the best brother in the world. I wish I knew why kidney disease struck our family, but I have to believe that God will work all of this together for good. God knows the plans He has for you. Trust Him always. I love you, mom, and dad with all my heart and defunct kidneys.

Anna Grace (6/21/10)

Wednesday, February 27, 2008

Cautiously, I stepped outside the patio door of our house and into the fenced backyard. The wind-chill had to have been below freezing, but I didn't mind a bit. Suddenly, a pair of paws bounced onto my shoulder.

"Nectar!" I half-heartedly complained, pushing our black Labrador off me. "I'm glad to see you, too. You're probably wondering what I've been doing, staying here all day almost every day," I told her. "I've been wondering the same thing."

Nectar was an old dog in her early teens. We had rescued her as a puppy on a bitterly cold Christmas Eve when Todd was a baby. Since then, she seemed to keep track of our family's routines, waking up in time to see us off to school and standing like a soldier each day at 3:45 to make sure we got home safely. My many days at home seemed to have her confused and ill at ease.

I managed to sit on the porch's cold concrete without too much trouble. While stooping this low would have been impossible three weeks ago, the medicines had sucked most of the weight- water and fat alike- from my tiny frame. I had been trim before the prednisone, but now I was skin and bones. It was better than the constant pounding sensation that came with the edema, or severe swelling, but it frightened me.

"Nectar, get off me," I moaned, pushing the large dog off of my lap. "Can't you see I'm sick?" She reluctantly flopped to the ground and looked at me with sad eyes. "Even you can tell, can't you? Then why can't everyone else? Why do people think I'm not praying hard enough, or that I'm thinking too many negative thoughts, or that I'm a making a mountain from a molehill?"

The family cat, Brownie, hopped the chain link fence that separated the front and back yards.

"Way to be Jobelle, Brownie," I told our pet as she moseyed her way over to my lap. "I write these crazy stories, and one of my characters hops that same fence all the time," I explained. "Hey, what are you doing on my lap? Didn't you just see me kick Nectar off?"

Brownie seemed to understand but ignored me. Instead, she spun in a circle several times and plopped down as if I had come outside specifically to be her bed. I tried to dump her into the grass, but she dug her sharp claws into my jeans.

"Sorry, Nectar," I apologized after giving up and letting Brownie fall asleep in my lap. "It's a double-standard."

I thought for a second. "Actually, many things have double standards," I continued randomly. "A lot of FSGS patients end up on dialysis. The five-year survival rate on dialysis is lower than the five-year survival rate for some cancers. Most people know how dangerous cancer can be, but it seems the public doesn't understand much about other illnesses. I'm glad there is public knowledge about cancer, but it's not the only very serious disease out there. Maybe I'll write a book about my illness someday."

Nectar yawned while Brownie purred in her sleep.

"I know," I told Nectar while petting her head. "No one wants to read about kidney disease."

I sighed, wishing more real people knew about lesser-known chronic illnesses. If there was more awareness about kidney disease and other rare and misunderstood sicknesses, maybe I wouldn't feel so alone.

I once again tried to kick Brownie off, but she seemed to purr louder. "So you've got Pepper's body and Jobelle's stubbornness," I told the sleeping ball of fluff. Nectar barked and rolled onto her back. "You're as smart and sweet as Kitti," I said, scratching the dog's belly.

"See that little apple tree?" I asked rhetorically, pointing across the yard. "That's where the Underground City entrance is... well, one of the entrances, anyway. There are twelve in all. Way over there, hanging from that big oak tree, is the tire swing dad made for us. It's old and worn, but it's never been taken down. That makes it a perfect candidate to be an object of the Pretend Friend Association."

The dog looked at me quizzically and barked, waking Brownie very briefly.

"I'm crazy, huh?" I asked Nectar as Brownie closed her eyes. "Besides family, friends, and faith, a fictional story I started when I was a little kid is getting me through this. It's insane! From preschool to my fourteenth birthday or so, I put an imaginary spin on almost everything real that happened. It's nice to have an excuse to do it again, because even when I forgot all about the PFA, I think I missed writing about it. Now that I'm writing again, I can't seem to stop the ideas. It's always been based on what's happening in the real world, and everything in my world is medical! The imaginary world is about to become more medical, too, so Annie isn't alone in her physical challenges."

I struggled to my feet, dropping Brownie to the ground in the process. "Sorry, Brownie," I said as the cat hissed glumly. "I'll tell you more about my imagination later!"

Once inside, I booted up the laptop, opened a new word processing document, and began typing. I took my memory back to July 2007- the month we found out something wrong- and began creating fictional happenings.

Jobelle's First-Person Perspective (POV- Point of View)
Takes Place: July 2007

"La, la, la, la, la, la, la, la, la... moving... la, la, la, la, la, la, la, la, la, la... breathing... LAAAAA..."

I tried- really, really hard- not to cringe. It was official: this would be my last year volunteering as an assistant music leader at the Annie Room Church's day camp program. I was a great dancer and didn't mind the extra chance to hang out with one of my best friends, but sometimes, it got too loud and irritating. The dancing and sign language aspects were fun, and the music was a lot better than you'd expect for a kid's program, but children's percussion instruments can be annoying.

And Pepper is very tone deaf. If that's not bad enough, she never actually learns the songs, even though she has perfect rhythm. She picks out essential- or sometimes non-essential- words and repeats them over and over and over…

Thankfully, the last song of the thirty-minute session ended. The children stampeded out the door to their group's next center with the adult leaders chasing them.

"Sorry, Graham," I said when the last kid had slammed the classroom's door closed. "But you're getting a new assistant next year. I think I'll sign up for arts and crafts or maybe even games. This is crazy! You're a musician. Doesn't this drive you insane? Most of them are *so* bad."

Graham laughed as he tossed a few lost maracas and rhythm sticks into the 'instrument box.' "Nah, I think it's great. They have to start somewhere."

"I don't think I want Pepper to start singing anywhere. She already has a hobby; she's the best tap-dancing cat I know. Isn't that enough?"

The doors flew open, and in ran the last age group of the day: the soon-to-be seventh graders. The boys were being obnoxious with whistles that someone at the video rotation center had unwisely given them. The girls, on the other hand, all huddled around my little sister, Kittina.

"What's going on?" I asked the group of eleven and twelve-year-olds.

"Kitti's dying!" One of the eleven-year-old girls shrieked. "She threw up… and, and…"

"I'm *not* dying," Kitti answered, although her freaked face could have said otherwise. It took me about two seconds to figure out what was going on and grab my little sister's hand.

"We'll be back," I told Graham.

"What?"

I shook my head. "She threw up."

"What's wrong with her?" Tayoe asked.

"Calm down," I told the group, trying to figure out what to say. "When little kids are getting taller, their legs hurt. When older girls are growing up, sometimes our hormones can make us sick. Our stomachs hurt, and sometimes, it can make us throw up. End of story."

I bolted out of the room with Kitti in tow.

"End of story?" She asked.

I cringed. Being twelve and having only a dad, chances were she didn't understand much about maturing from a little girl to a young woman.

"It's okay," Kitti assured me. "I spent the first eight years of my life in an orphanage. You catch on pretty fast when you're surrounded by teenage girls."

Once I had taken care of Kitti and asked the campus nurse to give her ibuprofen, she threw up again. She sniffed miserably as a huge tear rolled down her face. "Am I a wimp?"

Yes, I thought internally, even though I told her otherwise. "No. No one likes throwing up… or *growing* up, for that matter. Just be glad you don't need blood work. Annie called me on the imaginary cell and told me they ran a blood draw at her yearly physical. The blood sample got contaminated, so she has to do it again tomorrow."

I would never forget the real events of that day.

It had been Wednesday, July 11, 2007. My mom had taken Todd and me for routine well-child check-ups. There wasn't a specific reason why. For years, our insurance had only allowed us to go to the doctor when we were sick. This year, the coverage had changed; allowing all family members to get free annual visits to make sure all was well.

For me, it was the typical fifteen-year-old girl's well-child visit, complete with a shortened version of the abstinence and 'don't do drugs' speech, which even the doctor admitted wasn't necessary. I was an all-A student in seemingly perfect health.

Even so, my mom was curious about my thyroid. I wasn't

heavy by any means, but my mom pointed out that I weighed more than I probably should. I wasn't a big eater, and while I wasn't an athlete, I wasn't a couch potato, either. My doctor agreed it was a good idea to do a blood test and urinalysis.

Needless to say, I had been freaked. I didn't cry, pass out, or fight the phlebotomist like I'd heard some do. However, I did give her a few strange looks when she showed me to the bathroom and told me to 'pee in the cup'. For some reason, I had been very embarrassed about walking back to the lab with a container of urine.

Later in the afternoon, when the day's events were out of my mind as I played on a create-your-own-zoo computer game, the phone rang. "We have to go back to the doctor's office tomorrow to redo your urine and blood tests," my mom announced several minutes later. "It got contaminated somehow, so the results say your cholesterol is 400!"

I panicked at the idea of having to get poked and cart urine around again. I didn't want to skip breakfast and fast until after my blood was drawn, either.

A much more terrifying thought hit me.

What if my cholesterol really was that high?

"Oh, don't worry," my long-time best friend Kris consoled me over the phone. "One time they forgot to tell me to fast, and I had just been to a birthday party and eaten three cupcakes, five sodas, a bunch of candy, and a couple cups of ice cream," she told me. "Anyway, they said I was going to die because my blood sugar was so high. When we did it again fasting, it was perfect. You're fine."

That had settled me down considerably. The next morning, my blood was taken and immediately sent to the lab.

"I don't think there's anything wrong at all," my pediatrician said. "Our machines make mistakes occasionally. I just know that I'd be going crazy waiting for the results, and I don't want you to have to worry. The blood and urine is in the lab now, and it'll come back in a few minutes."

It took about an hour for the numbers to come in, so I was

"starving" by 11:00 AM because we hadn't brought anything for me to eat. The nurses gave me a glazed donut and soft drink. I was still holding the soda can when the doctor entered the room to report that the original results had been correct. In fact, the second test's results were slightly worse.

"This is so strange," my doctor said. "You appear perfectly healthy, and I know you exercise and eat right."

I was assured the bad levels were not my fault. High cholesterol ran in the family, so we assumed it was an inherited problem. I was referred to the children's hospital in Little Rock for the cholesterol.

"I hate to send you ninety minutes away to two specialists," Dr. Clair stated. "I think the cholesterol is going to be the chronic issue. There is protein in your urine, but it's likely a kidney infection. The nephrology clinic in town sees pediatric patients. I'll schedule you an appointment there soon so we can clear that up."

My appointment with the cholesterol specialist wasn't until late September, but my local kidney appointment with Dr. Jones was set for 4:00 PM after the second day of school.

My legs wobbled like gelatin as we left the office. When my mom and I got into the car, the first thing we did was pray.

At my first appointment with Dr. Jones in mid-August, I was shocked to learn that I had just one condition- nephrotic syndrome- that was causing both the high cholesterol and protein loss. Dr. Jones gave us the option of going to the children's hospital, but because my parents and I saw the disease as a "little kidney problem" and were under the impression that it would go away easily, we decided to stay with the adult facilities in town.

Dr. Jones had explained nephrotic syndrome by drawing pictures on note cards. I took them to school and drove my friends crazy with my newfound medical issues. Back then, I had no idea this kidney disease that would soon impact many areas of my life.

How would "Annie's" friends have reacted to the new information? I began typing again.

Jobelle's First-Person Perspective (POV)
Takes Place: August and September 2007

The last thing I wanted to do was start eleventh grade. With Bethany in Nashville, Graham at community college, and Annie as always at a different school, I would be the last PFA kid at the Underground City's high school.

"Swim away, fruit rings! Hurry, the metal Spoon of Doom is going to eat you! HURRY! Oh no, you're captured... and heading into the seventh grader's mouth!"

Kitti giggled as her twin, Tayoe, mocked a fake scream while shoveling a heaping spoon of kid's cereal into his mouth.

"Tay," I asked my brother. "How in the world are you so awake at 6:45 in the morning?"

"I haven't slept in all summer. Besides, school's cool. I can't wait to get back and see the guys."

"This year is going to be so much better!" Kitti said with a sweet smile. "Even though we still have to go to the little kids' school, we're *finally* in junior high! Pre-algebra, middle school science, interesting reading assignments... it's not going to be boring anymore!"

Tayoe and I exchanged exasperated looks.

"You're *such* a know-it-all," Tayoe said sarcastically, knowing his statement was anything but true. Unlike a stereotypical bookworm, Kitti never bragged about her astounding mind. The kids in her class knew she was an all-A student, but very few people knew just how easy school was for her. No one but her teachers, family members, and closest friends knew of her astronomically-high IQ.

"Ladies and gentleman!" Ariella announced from the top of the staircase. "May I present... Leah Newbrey, our big-girl kindergartener!"

Dressed in a navy-blue sailor dress, my five-year-old niece bounded through hall, down the steps, and into her "Uncle

Tayoe's" arms.

"I get to go to school with you and Pepper and Auntie Kitti!" Leah exclaimed as Tayoe spun her around. "And Auntie Jo-Jo gets to go to school with her friends, too!"

She had no idea how much I wished that were true! By the end of the day, I had a very serious case of "senior-itis", even though I had just become a junior. When my last class finished, I hurried to the dance studio for my daily two hours of training. For the first time ever, I couldn't wait for my choreography class to end. At five o'clock sharp, I raced out of the Underground City and through Annie's window.

"Belle!" Annie exclaimed, looking up from geometry homework. "How was school?"

"Awful," I said with a moan. "You?"

"Not as great as last year, but okay. Band's going to be fun. We practice during third period and afterschool on Tuesdays. I have to miss clarinet practice tomorrow for my stupid doctor's appointment."

"Oh, I forgot about that. Are you nervous?"

"Duh! There's something wrong with me! My cholesterol is 400! I saw a man on one of those weight-loss shows who weighed 600 pounds, and his cholesterol was only 280!"

"It's a unique problem to have," I admitted out loud. "But do you think it's going to be worse than strep throat or the flu? I mean, those things are bad, but they're not cancer."

She nodded. "I'm mostly scared because it's a kidney doctor. It's *so* embarrassing to pee in a cup, and what if they want me to dress in one of those ugly exam robes?" She lowered her voice to a whisper. "My doctor- Dr. Jones, I think- is a guy!"

"I know what you mean," I empathized, thinking of my many sports injuries from over a decade of advanced dance. "You *do* get used to it."

She raised her eyebrows in doubt.

I sighed. "Would it help if I came, just like in the old days?

No one would know I was there, except you."

"You'd have to skip school. My appointment is at 2:30, so you'd either have to hitch a ride or hang out in my family's car all day."

"What's wrong with skipping school?" I asked mischievously.

"Jobelle!" Annie scolded.

"I'm kidding, Annie! Well, mostly…"

She rolled her eyes. "If you can figure out how to get to downtown Nectarwood at 2:30 in the afternoon, I'd be more than happy to have you around." She paused to sign her name at the top of her math assignment. "So, have you talked to Graham lately?"

"I emailed Bethany yesterday…"

"Yeah, I know. I was there, remember? Have you talked to her brother?"

I felt my face flush but played stupid. "Why?"

"It was your first day of school without Graham. I know you missed him."

"I missed Bethany, too…"

"Of course, but you're a lot closer to Graham. You two are best friends."

"You and I are best friends, too!" I argued.

"There's a huge difference: we're both girls. Graham's a *guy.*"

"Are you saying that you think I have a crush on Graham?"

Because you're absolutely right, I thought, although I was far too shy to admit it.

She raised her eyebrows again.

"Well, I don't! Just because he's a guy and we're best friends doesn't mean we're an 'item'! Haven't you ever read *Little Women?*"

"Yes, but I really don't see Kitti marrying Graham…"

I threw an imaginary pillow at her.

You're right, I thought. *I would never let Kitti marry Graham.*

"… and then Tomes hit a homerun!" Tayoe explained to our dad as I walked through the front door of my family's apartment. "Rochi was on the swings on the other side of the playground. The ball flew SO far, it hit Rochi right on the head!"

"Hey Dad," I interrupted. We talked for a few minutes until Tayoe got bored and left. I finally asked the pivotal question.

"Dad, you're awesome. Can I cut school tomorrow?"

"No," he said with a chuckle. "But thanks for asking about something before you acted on impulse again. I'm proud of you." He paused. "So, I'm guessing you offered to go with Annie to her appointment," he said knowingly. "I already called your principal. You're dismissed after fifth period tomorrow."

"Thank you!" I said genuinely, giving my dad a hug. "How am I going to get there?"

"A young man named Graham will be more than happy to take you."

I couldn't help but smile. "Thank you!" I repeated in a squeal, trying not to jump up and down too much. Dad simply smiled and kissed the top of my forehead.

"You miss having Graham at school with you, don't you, honey?"

"Dad!" I whined.

He chuckled once again.

The next day, I ran through the crowded hallway and out the door as soon as the bell rang. Graham was leaning against the bed of his green truck, looking at his watch.

"Hurry up!" He called as I skipped down the concrete steps.

"Nice to see you, too," I commented. He snatched my

backpack off my back and swung it over his shoulder.

"How's eleventh grade?"

"Stupid. How's college?"

"Stupid." He tossed my backpack into the teeny backseat and gasped.

"What?"

"Someone put a large order of cheese fries and blue coconut crushed ice on the passenger-side seat! I wonder who that could have been!"

I laughed as I climbed into the truck. "Thanks."

When we got to the kidney clinic waiting room, it took about two seconds to realize everyone was over seventy. Annie's mother was the baby of the group, and she wasn't even the patient.

The appointment itself went well. Besides the urine test and a blood draw, all they did was talk. Dr. Jones explained that nephrotic syndrome is a condition in which there is protein in the urine, usually accompanied by high cholesterol and other hidden symptoms.

Nephrotic syndrome didn't change anything at first. Dr. Jones ran a few tests to see what was causing my condition. Most were blood and urine studies, but I also had an abdominal ultrasound.

An ultrasound, sometimes called a sonogram, is a diagnostic procedure that uses high-frequency sound waves to take a picture of what's happening inside the body. It is most frequently used to see unborn babies. In a darkened room, I had to lie on an exam table next to a computer. A technician spread a medical gel over my belly and pushed a special wand over my skin. It was painless, fast, and actually kind of fun.

It's not so bad having nephrotic syndrome, I thought after those easy tests.

I had a follow-up appointment with Dr. Jones on the second Friday of the school year. Every test to show exactly what could be happening to cause nephrotic syndrome came back inconclusive. The only way to determine what was creating my condition was a moderately invasive kidney biopsy.

During a biopsy, a long needle removes a small piece of kidney which is then examined under a microscope. Dr. Jones told me I'd be given local anesthetic where the needle would penetrate. I'd also be sedated. While I wouldn't be alert enough to comprehend what was going on, I would be "awake" to hold my breath or breathe deeply if told to do so. It would take about a half-hour for the technicians to use a CT machine to find the exact spot to inject the needle, but the actual "poking" of the kidney would only take a few seconds.

It wasn't without risks. Most were minor things like mild pain and blood in the urine for a few days, but there was a one-percent chance that my kidneys would shut down altogether. I would need to stay in the hospital overnight for observation.

The procedure was scheduled for late September. I had to wait a month, and I spent a lot of that time worrying. I kept focused with school and band, but even then, nephrotic syndrome was often on my mind.

During that month, I did notice a few previously undetected symptoms. For years, I had gotten out-of-breath walking up the stairs to the front of my high school building. I always contributed it to not being a basketball or softball player.

"It's really tiring to go up these stairs, right?" I asked Kris, who was in no better shape than I. She shook her head, and I began to wonder if my protein loss could be causing my exhaustion. I assumed it was normal to sleep from 9PM to 6AM every night and still be absolutely fatigued. Could that have been my condition, too?

About two weeks before the biopsy, Dr. Jones put me on a low dose of a blood pressure medication that contained a diuretic, or water pill, to help keep the swelling down. I was also given a cholesterol-lowering pill to take each night. These medicines caused some side effects, such as sudden dizziness and nausea, but nothing was too bad.

Early in the morning on Friday, September 21, 2007, my mom and I- with Pepper in her stuffed animal form, of course- headed to the outpatient area of a local hospital. With the children's hospital only an hour and a half away, I was the youngest patient- by far- in the waiting room.

"Aren't you a little young for a biopsy?" A nurse asked rhetorically as I was led to the lab. I was a new "kidney disease adventurer" on biopsy day, so needles still made me mildly nervous. *Great,* I had thought. *As if a biopsy wasn't enough, they have to draw blood, too.*

Before my mom and I were put into a pre-procedure room, the lab technician pricked my arm to check how quickly my blood clotted. As simple as it was, I was fascinated to watch the tiny cut's bleeding slow down over the course of a few minutes.

Maybe even the things that hurt aren't so bad, I had decided. I changed my mind less than an hour later when an inexperienced nurse started my IV. I later learned that most IVs truly do "stick and sting like a bee sting" as the nurses claim, but this one felt more like someone had jabbed me with a knife.

About ninety minutes later, I was rolled into a brightly-lit room with a donut-shaped CT scan machine placed near a wall. The nurses grilled me over and over, asking continuously if I could be pregnant or if I did drugs.

"Only the medicines Dr. Jones has me take," I replied innocently.

The procedure went like clockwork. I was told to hold my breath at times, but other than that, I had no conscious thoughts during the biopsy. The medicine made me feel happy and unconcerned, and although I was technically awake, I wasn't anxious at all.

I don't remember the "stabbing" of my kidney. Some people hear a click or feel a slight pressure as if someone is pushing on their back, but I wasn't aware of anything until they lightened the sedation. I came back to normal consciousness fairly quickly. I stayed in the observation wing that night so nurses could monitor me for complications. When a phlebotomist came to draw blood at 4:00 in the morning, I couldn't help but fictionalize it. With my mind back in the present, I typed exactly what had happened, but from an imaginary character's point-of-view.

Pepper the Watch Cat (Pepper's POV)
Takes Place: September 2007

There was this day when Pepper's mommy had to go to the hospital so they could stab her in the back. So they did that and Pepper stayed with grandma. Then Uncle Todd and grandpa visited, and then they went home. And then it was nighttime.

Pepper's mommy had a tube coming out of her hand. She had to make it still, so she put it on a pillow. Then she put Pepper on the pillow next to her hand and covered us up. Good-night; Pepper is sleeping.

Then a nurse came into room to check mommy's blood. The light came on and she was all cheerful. She lifted up the sheet to get to Pepper's mommy's arm. All she saw at first was Pepper's beady eyes.

The nurse said, "Ah! What IS that thing?"

"That's Pepper," Pepper's mommy said. Everybody laughed.

The next Tuesday, Dr. Jones told me my nephrotic syndrome was caused by FSGS, meaning some of the kidneys' tiny filters- the glomeruli- were scarred. A few days later, I started high-dose prednisone with the hopes of achieving remission.

In my early days of prednisone treatment, I complained about the taste, but I didn't hate the medication. It had side effects, but nothing was awful.

In fact, not much changed. Schoolwork became more difficult, but nothing too noticeable. In history class, I had an odd habit of filling in two answers for multiple choice questions. My "band buddies" told me I was 'crazy' but that wasn't out-of-the-ordinary. The first few months helped me understand that some people with nephrotic syndrome truly can live fairly normal lives.

In mid-October, the disease began to take its toll on my energy levels. My body felt extremely heavy, and I found myself getting out of breath easily. Sometimes, it was very hard to breathe, but I attempted to ignore my symptoms.

Looking back, I realize how little I knew about the world of chronic illness. My concerns were that of a typical teenage girl's, which was exactly how it should have been. I was worried about wearing ugly hospital gowns, bleeding, and pain. While even those weren't exactly standard high school fears, they were what you'd expect of a tenth-grader in a medical environment. Back then, my stress-inducers had been normal too. Doing well at marching band competitions, trying not to be completely weird at school, getting high A's, having my hair and make-up look just right, and so on, were priorities.

In the present time, February, none of that mattered anymore. All I wanted was to pass school with C's. I didn't care what my hair looked like because I considered my swollen face to be hideous, and I could care less if people liked me or not. Only five months after my biopsy, I was in survival mode.

Fall 2007– Jobelle's POV
Takes Place: October through December 2007

"Hey, Annie," I said, peering into her bedroom window.

"I'm *fine*, Belle," she stated in an aggravated tone.

"Well, good morning to you, too," I responded, equally as aggravated. Unfortunately, she had a point. The Saturday before, I had gotten sick simply from sampling a particle of her crushed prednisone. Since then, I had been watching her health like a hawk. Obviously, I was starting to annoy.

"That's not what I came here for," I said truthfully. "I need your help with a problem." I reached back and pulled my 'problem' to the window.

"Hi, Annie," Kitti called, climbing through the window and into Annie's room. "Will you put this in my hair? Belle can't do it right." She handed a white sash to Annie, smiled, and spun around on her heels.

"Sure, but I thought you were the expert," Annie said, tying the light fabric into Kit's inverted partial ponytail.

"I'm not good at accessorizing... not yet, anyway, and all Belle can do is put on makeup. Ugh, I _hate_ makeup." Kitti folded her tongue lengthwise and stuck it out at me in her usual playful way.

"Alright, she fixed it. Now get out of here," I commanded, kissing her forehead. "Have fun at recess."

She gave me a pouty look before waving to Annie and bounding away. Because they went to a one-room school with kindergarteners through eighth graders, Kitti and Tayoe still had recess as junior high kids. Although Tayoe loved the chance to play dodge ball, Kitti wasn't the athletic type. No matter how much dad tried to interest her in something more active than music and mystery books, Kitti was more concerned with observing sports in her usual intuitive fashion.

"She's such a cutie," Annie said out loud.

I nodded in agreement. "The boys will be after her in a few years. Tay's going to go crazy. He's so protective of her."

"Speaking of protective..." Annie said, grabbing my wrist and pulling me to her bed. "You're worried about me. What's up?"

She looked at me expectantly. Kit read everyone perfectly, but Annie was a different story. Was my concern that obvious?

"I don't know," I decided. "Ever since I tasted that prednisone a few days ago, I just have this... feeling."

"What do you mean?"

I should have known it would be hard to explain.

"You've been complaining about prednisone a lot, and I thought you were just... I don't know, complaining to get attention... you do that sometimes." She didn't argue. "When I tasted that grain of crushed powder, I knew you weren't..."

"It's just a little kidney condition, Belle," Annie interrupted.

"Is it really, Annie, or is that what your doctor has told you?"

"Why would he lie?"

"I don't think he would intentionally," I agreed. "What if he's not telling you everything? You don't have Internet access here, so you wouldn't know. From what I've read, this thing- FSGS- it's a really big deal sometimes."

"The key word there is *sometimes*. Belle, I feel fine."

For the third year running, fall was marching band season for Annie...

Band. I wasn't quite as passionate about playing clarinet as Jobelle was about dance, but I still loved music enough to risk my health for it.

Before my diagnosis, I had been told I would need all four impacted wisdom teeth pulled. I had been terrified that it would mess up my mouth so I couldn't play clarinet for a week, so I convinced my parents to let me put it off until the next summer. When I found out I had a kidney problem, my first fear was that I would no longer be able to march in band. Thankfully, because I played the lightweight clarinet, Dr. Jones said it was fine.

I was so delighted to be able to participate in our fall show that I ignored every complication caused by combining nephrotic syndrome with marching band. Every time we went out to the practice field, I had difficulty breathing, but I never told a soul.

Why? Well, it was simple. What if Dr. Jones, my parents, or my band director wouldn't let me march? What if I couldn't play clarinet? It was my favorite thing to do! I suffered in silence, even when I thought I'd pass out. The only person who knew was God.

Annie was a true-blue band geek, just like Graham had been. The PFA had several up-and-coming instrumentalists. Kitti and Tayoe were natural musicians and couldn't wait to join the imaginary high school's band. And, as surprising as it was, Pepper had rhythm. Her quick feline reflexes made her a better-than-average drummer. That being the case, the PFA took a vanload to a Friday night football game to watch Annie's band perform. Todd's Fictional Alliance also brought their bus, packed with rambunctious kids. The good news was they brought imaginary concessions.

I could care less about football. Graham and Tayoe generally watched the entire game while I walked around aimlessly, dodging groups of real and imaginary people. After the second quarter, a few of us hopped the real fence and sat on the sideline for a better view of the bands.

"NACHO!" Pepper shouted while the other team's cheerleaders presented their routine. She was small enough to squeeze between two chain links, carrying a cheese-covered tortilla chip in her mouth.

"Where'd you get that, Pepper?"

"Found on ground. Yum."

"Yeah, I hope so; it'd better be good for all the germs that are on it."

Pepper shook her head. "It safe; Bubba dropped it, Pepper picked it up. Bubba don't even miss it."

"Pepper!" Bubba squawked from the stands. "Give me my nacho!"

"You got lots of nachos. Pepper only got one nacho."

"GIVE IT BACK!"

"But Pepper already ate it," the kitten said innocently while shoving the entire thing in her mouth. Before Bubba could do anything, Pepper curled up on my shoulder. Since Bubba and I made a point to avoid each other, Pepper knew Bubba wouldn't 'attack'. She was right.

"What is they doing?" Pepper asked as the band marched onto the field.

"They're marching to the beat," Graham explained. "They have to stay in step; that means that everyone has to move together, like one person."

"HI MOMMY!" Pepper shouted. She jumped from my shoulder to Graham's. "Why doesn't she answer?"

"When you're on the field, you're at attention. You have to be completely still unless you're marching. No doing your hair like that girl in the front, or wiggling around like that boy in the back."

"Oh. Pepper's mommy never moves when she's not supposed to."

"Nope," Graham answered. "She's very careful. She told me that she had a migraine once but marched through it. I've seen kids' pants drop to the ground, bugs get in girls' hair, people fall down, bats smack trombone players in the face… you name it… but a real band geek won't budge."

"Somebody hit somebody with a BASEBALL BAT! HAHAHA…"

"No, Pepper," Graham interrupted. "It was a bat, as in the animal that eats bugs, and flies around using sonar."

When the band finished, we hurried off the field to avoid getting trampled. Everyone was supposed to meet back at the van before the start of the fourth quarter. We didn't get very far into the parking lot when dad stopped us.

"The Fictional Alliance is staying here until the game is over. After the real people go home, they're going to have their own football game."

"They're inviting us?" I exclaimed in shock. While our pretend societies got along well enough, there was a sense of rivalry between the Fiction Alliance and Pretend Friend Association.

"Why not?" Dad asked, being ever the peacemaker. "We

would invite them to a social event, wouldn't we?'

I wouldn't, but of course dad would.

"Our van is still driving home in about five minutes for anyone who doesn't want to stay. Bubba's brother Gugga said that they have plenty of room on the alliance's bus to take everyone else home."

It wasn't a huge surprise to me that Kitti and I were the only ones in the van, besides the driver. We would have gone to our 'house' in the PFA's apartment complex, but because no one was home except Leah and her babysitter, we chose to spend the night in Annie's room. We'd been there for a while when we heard the infamous cry.

"HONEY! PEPPER HOME!"

I rolled my eyes when Pepper ran into the room at 10:30. She promptly collapsed where she stood, fell asleep, and began snoring.

"Oh, she does that when she's tired," Annie explained as she entered the room seconds later and put her clarinet case down. "Where is everybody?"

"Kitti fell asleep in your closet while reading again. Everybody else stayed for the Fictional Alliance's football game," I answered.

"Oh, yeah. Bubba mentioned using a pumpkin as a football. Pepper wanted to stay, but I made her come home." She picked up the sleeping lump of fur and tucked it into bed under her pillow. I went to the closet to find my sleeping sister, who had fallen over against a rack of clothing. I sighed upon seeing her puffy hands again. After years without incident, Kitti's long-forgotten allergies had returned the week before. *Could it be the fabric?* I thought.

"Kit, get up for a second. I'm going to get you into a sleeping bag.'

"Why?' She asked groggily, turning her head slightly. The side of her body that had been leaning against Annie's clothes was swollen.

"Come here, you're having another allergic reaction.'

"No epi-pen,' she begged, jolting awake. "I hate needles!"

"Dad told Tay and I you only need the shot if you can't breathe. For this, you're just supposed to take an antihistamine.'

She nodded pathetically. I found the medicine in my purse, gave one pill to Kit, and got her somewhat settled in her pink sleeping bag.

'Why does this keep happening? Kitti wondered. "I haven't had problems with my allergies since I was eight."

"The allergy test next week will tell us what's going on," I told her, leaving out the part about the allergist having to prick her skin dozens of times.

When Kitti was asleep again, Annie and I walked back to the bed. Annie plopped down heavily and pulled off her black marching shoes. I've never seen anyone's feet so swollen, not even Leah's mother at nine months pregnant. It was as if someone had taken a latex glove and blown it up until it was one puff away from popping. It was a gruesome, horrifying sight.

"Where are your ankles?"

'Somewhere in there, Belle,' Annie laughed hysterically. Then, twenty seconds later, she was sobbing that she had to switch band uniforms because her old one had become too tight. The mood swing wasn't too unusual; in fact, it was becoming the norm. Since she had started high-dose prednisone, Annie's moods were wilder than the rocking pirate ship ride at Awesome Happy Fun World. What worried me was her outrageous amount of water retention.

Around the end of marching season, Annie began showing more obvious signs of being sick. At a competition in Little Rock, I noticed her lying in the grass while waiting to tune her clarinet. During the football games, she lagged behind the other girls heading to the concession stands during the band's third quarter break.

Annie's sixteenth birthday fell on the last band competition of the year at a large high school in Hot Springs. It happened to be fall break for the imaginary schools in the city, so Graham was able to drive Kitti, Tayoe, and me to the contest, even though it took place at 1:00 in the afternoon.

We sat at the very top of the bleachers to avoid getting squashed by real people. Graham meticulously critiqued the other bands, pointing out errors and achievements to Kitti and Tayoe. Annie's band took the field at about 2:45, and I couldn't believe what I was seeing.

"Something's wrong," I told Graham.

"What?" He asked. "The kid in the front...."

"No," I interrupted. "You told Pepper a couple weeks ago that they're at attention?"

"Yeah..." He agreed.

"Annie's moving a lot."

Graham found the clarinet section, observed briefly, and shook his head. "Yeah, Belle, it's called *breathing*. They don't count off for that."

I didn't say anything. He appeared to be right until a duet piece. Everyone started marching in step- as Graham would say- but the drum line suddenly got off beat. The duettists faltered, and the entire band lost track of time. All seventy members seemed to guess when to stop.

During the fiasco, Annie's behavior suddenly changed, as if the "train wreck" had been a much-needed break. As she moved across the field, Annie walked.

It was ironic. Only a week before, I had made fun of Graham for teaching Pepper how to march. "Why do you need to know?" I had asked the kooky kitten.

"Because Pepper is bored out of Pepper's mind and wants to learn something," the cat had replied. Graham took that as a good enough answer. Apparently, there was a difference between marching and walking. Walking was how you move from one place to another every day. Marching, however, involved posture, rolling your foot from heel to toe, and holding your instrument a certain way. Annie's efforts to march perfectly were very obvious, and if she made a mistake, it was an accident.

This, however, was no accident. When chaos struck, Annie seized the opportunity to take a break from the stringent rules of marching.

The band got its footing and began to play again, but Annie still seemed dazed. "You're right," Graham said quietly. "You think she's okay?"

I shook my head.

"Annie, this is not normal," I told her that night. "You're eating almost nothing but inflating like a balloon. Sometimes, your personality is completely different than you. What are the doctors and nurses saying?"

"That it's normal," she replied weakly.

"Have they _seen_ your feet?"

She shook her head.

"Can you describe how you feel now?"

"I feel fine," she claimed, even though she was lying on her bed, gasping for air.

"What's wrong?"

"Something's always wrong. My eyelids feel really heavy, and I still have a headache from the migraine I had in eighth period."

"You said your belly is... what was that word? Stretched out? "

"Distended? It is."

"I see the stretch marks, Annie. Your skin is widening like crazy. Are you trying to tell me that this much change doesn't hurt?"

"Of course it does! I'm dizzy, nauseated, exhausted from walking, and I can't breathe... but those things go away when I'm lying down."

"That's not my definition of fine, Annie."

"It must be someone's. Everybody says it's the prednisone. This is normal. This has to be normal, doesn't it?"

I didn't know, but I doubted it.

As massive doses of steroids and the disease itself weighed her body down, she forced herself to live as normally as possible. She didn't want any accommodations, not even bathroom passes, though the medicines forced her poor kidneys to create extra urine.

I started having sleepovers with her from time to time, just like we did when we were little kids. Sleeping seemed excruciating for her. Her breaths were labored, and she never moved a muscle. One time, she stopped breathing for about three seconds.

I wish I didn't have to get used to Annie's new illness, but I did. There wasn't much of a choice, especially with the mayhem of everyday life in the Underground City. The Fictional Alliance's numerous battles against strange "bad guys" never ceased. Some fights took place in the city itself. Unlike the terrible wars the real world sees, most of the "weapons" used were greasy potato chips and messy food coloring. Even so, such things could delay your commute to work or school.

With a new concern about health flooding through the imaginary metropolis, the Annie Room Church (ARC) teamed up with the Underground City Medical Center to offer free health screenings. The day before Thanksgiving, when we were at the church for Wednesday night services, dad took Tay, Kit, and me to the gym, which was overflowing with medical personnel and equipment.

About twelve tables were scattered around the basketball court for patients to visit. Most of the stations hosted painless, familiar procedures- such as BMI screenings. When Kitti saw the needles at the center where blood was drawn, she almost passed out. This wasn't too much of a surprise, since she had cried miserably during her allergy test several weeks before. Personally, while I wasn't a fan of needles, I wasn't really afraid of having blood drawn. Graham, on the other hand, was probably more freaked than Kitti when it came to anything medical.

Speaking of Graham, he tapped me on the shoulder.

"Graham! I can't believe you're here!" I exclaimed.

"I know, but I guess it's important. It's free, so fear is a bad excuse. A blood test probably saved Annie's kidneys," he said quietly. "If my mom had had a blood test earlier, maybe…" He stopped talking and smiled sadly at me. I reached for his hand but stopped as a group of Fictional Alliance stuffed animals stampeded by.

"You'll be fine," I assured him. Graham stayed with my family as we made our rounds. I was surprised at how calm he was. Kitti, however, was a sniveling mess. She even cried when the blood pressure machine 'hugged' her arm.

"133/82," the nurse read as she ripped the cuff off of my sister's arm.

"Isn't that a little high?" Dad asked.

The nurse shook her head. "It would be, but I don't think it's too abnormal for someone so nervous."

Dad was worried about Kitti for a few minutes but relaxed when Graham's pulse was 110.

The blood draw table was next. Dad and I were probably easiest on our nurse. Tayoe wasn't scared in the least, but he had a hard time sitting still.

"Come on, Kit, it's not that bad," Tay said as the phlebotomist searched his arm. "Watch her do it to me. All she does is take the needle, stab me, and watch the blood squirt out into the little tube."

"That's disgusting!" Kitti cried, gagging.

"It's just blood," Tayoe said. "It's cool. Since we learned about the human body at school last year, you're always talking about the plasma and white blood cells and stuff. Don't you think it's awesome to see it?"

"Not if it's mine!" She managed through sobs.

Graham opted to go next for Kitti's sake. While he seemed composed, I could almost hear him screaming internally. Graham was a good enough actor that you never would have guessed he was scared stiff, unless you knew his heart rate.

I remember Annie talking about different widths of needles; the one they used on Graham was huge. When the needle penetrated his skin, he inhaled sharply.

"You're okay," the attendant said confidently. Graham looked at me and raised his eyebrows, as if to say 'yeah, right.' He held his breath until the needle was in a nearby sharps container.

"Your turn, Kit," dad said gently. She shook her head.

"It's not so bad," a familiar voice said. Annie knelt beside Kitti, her swollen legs barely letting her reach the floor.

"What are you scared of?" Annie asked soothingly. "Are you afraid of the pain or seeing your blood?"

"Both," Kitti admitted timidly.

"First of all, don't watch. We'll thumb wrestle with your free hand, and you won't see a thing. Secondly, it only hurts for a second, and it's like a bee sting. You might feel it for a moment when it slides out, but that doesn't hurt. I promise. Can she have your arm now?"

Kitti reluctantly let the attendant touch the 'bendy part' of her arm. "I've never been stung by a bee before," Kitti said through sniffles. "I've been stung by a wasp, though, and I screamed because it hurt so much."

"But you were little, right?" Annie asked.

"I guess I was about ten... ouch!" Kitti jumped. She looked down to see the tiny butterfly needle sticking out of her skin and nearly threw up. Before any blood made its way into the vial, the phlebotomist announced "it blew" and pulled the needle out of Kitti's bloodstream.

"Seriously?" Annie exclaimed.

"What does that mean?" Kitti asked as a bruise formed where the needle had been.

"I couldn't get it, sweetheart," the lady admitted. She looked up at my dad. "Maybe you guys could come back Monday to try again?"

"That'll be fine," dad agreed, although I knew he wouldn't put Kitti through that again.

"At least she got to cry," Graham whispered in my ear later. "No one thinks it's weird when a 12-year-old girl freaks over a blood test, but an 18-year-old guy bawling like that would have gotten a few strange looks."

Thursday, February 28, 2008

At noon the next day, I booted up the family computer once again. I felt terrible, but I knew I couldn't let FSGS dictate my life completely.

How far did I get yesterday? I asked myself. *I wrote through Thanksgiving. I'll start there.*

In real life, my health's downward spiral began the day following Thanksgiving. I missed five days of school because my eyes had swollen shut. Everything that happened during those several weeks was a blur. I vaguely remember that I gained seven pounds of water weight in one night and that one of my teachers suggested I go to the emergency room immediately.

There's only one story I remember very clearly. Two minutes before Christmas break, I was practicing my clarinet in the band room when I started gasping for air. A girl I had known since third grade took notice. I told her about my 210/110 blood pressure, and she looked at me with concern.

"Anna Grace," Amy asked in a surprisingly nonchalant tone, "are you going to die?"

I didn't know how to react. It was the first time anything about death had come up- outside of my brain, that is. I was relieved that someone had finally acknowledged the seriousness of what I was dealing with, so I answered honestly.

"I don't know."

"But I don't want you to die," she answered.

Without another word, she grabbed my colorful highlighters meant for marking sheet music and drew something hastily on the back of a scrap of paper.

"This is Charlie, your Christmas angel. Hope you get to feeling better soon!" The bell signaled our dismissal for winter vacation. Amy sped out of the room, having absolutely no idea what she had done. Somehow, unbeknownst to Amy, Charlie had given me hope. In January, when I had to spend the weekend in the hospital, Charlie had come with me in Pepper's duffel bag.

Thinking about Pepper reminded me of another "brilliant" prednisone-brained thing I had done. I switched to Pepper's first-person.

Pepper the Advent Cat (Pepper's POV)
Takes Place: December 2007

And now Pepper will tell you about the happiest day in Pepper's life. The happiest day in Pepper's life was when Pepper lighted-did* the third Advent candle at church. It was special. But Pepper almost dropped-did* it.

Anna Grace's Note to Self (So when I get into remission I can remember what my crazy mind was thinking when I wrote this.)

Pepper commonly says the "ed" sound twice in past tense words. Her pronunciation of "lighted" would be light-ed-ed, but it's easier to write "lighted-did". Anna Grace Shramere, 30 mg prednisone daily, 2/28/08

I laughed as I wrote that, because Pepper the Cat really had lit the third Advent candle on a Sunday morning. When we got home from church that particular day, I remember thinking I was going to die.

Snap out of it, I had told myself. *This is just a stupid kidney condition that will go away very soon! Prednisone is doing this to me, and I'll be off it soon! Nephrotic syndrome isn't that bad. I'm not sick... I'm not sick... I'm not sick... I'm not sick...*

So I did the logical thing to get my mind off of things; for being on prednisone, that is! I found four battery-operated tea lights, arranged them in a circle, found a CD with instrumental Christmas music, and video-taped myself "helping" Pepper light the Joy candle.

Unfortunately, I never destroyed the video file. It's entitled "Your Mind on Prednisone- Pepper Lights Joy Candle 2007."

I reverted to Jobelle's POV and kept typing.

Annie's health seemed to deteriorate on Christmas Day, but I didn't have time to worry. There was so much happening in the PFA, from gift exchanges and dinner to the short morning service at church. Even after the 25th, there was no time to think about what was going on. We celebrated Kitti and Tayoe's belated thirteenth birthdays, took a day trip to Hot Springs and Little Rock, and kept busy with New Year's preparations. While Annie claimed she was glad I didn't have time to fret over her, I felt bad for my lack of concern. My dad pretty much forced me to go to the PFA New Year's Eve Party at the church.

"She's fine, sweetie," he told me over and over. "It's just the medicines." Dad was only telling me what everyone else was saying, but my gut feeling was too strong to ignore.

At the party, I sat on a bleacher in the gym, absent-mindedly watching people dance to holiday music. Pepper twirled like a clumsy snowflake while Leah danced with great precision, considering she was only six. For not being biological relatives, Leah was growing up to be a lot like me.

With my peripheral vision, I saw Graham sit down beside me. I turned to give him a shy smile, which he returned. Before long, our eyes flashed back to the basketball court. As easy as it was to talk to Graham, there were suddenly butterflies in my stomach.

"So…" he said. "How's your dancing career coming?"

"Fine; it should be after rehearsing eleven hours a week.'

"Look at Leah," Graham mused, pointing at my very talented niece. "About a month ago, she showed me something she drew at school and told me, 'When I grow up, I want to be just like Auntie Jobelle.' You know, you're her hero."

"Great," I laughed sarcastically. "She's already following in my footsteps. Not a week goes by in her young life without tap dance, cheese fries, or time-outs."

Graham met my gaze and smiled. "Time outs, huh?"

I nodded. I had never been a bad kid by any means, but compared to the rest of the goody-two-shoed kids in the PFA, I was considered a trouble-magnet.

Graham randomly began stammering. "Hey… if I ask you something… no matter what… well, do you promise you won't laugh at me or hate me?"

"I'm supposed to promise not to laugh at you? Come on, we laugh at each other all the time."

"Yeah, but for fun…"

"Graham," I said seriously. "I could never hate you. *Ever*. So ask me anything, okay? Because that's what best friends are for, and with Annie sick, I need you."

He drew in a deep breath. "Okay. Um…"

"Uh-huh?"

My heart raced. I had dreamt of having this type of conversation with Graham for a while. Yes, we were best friends, but there was definitely chemistry, to say the least. I had a huge crush but had been too scared to say anything to him.

"Belle…" he said apprehensively. "Beth… well, you know how my sister gets… but, well, Beth, Beth thinks…"

I raised my eyebrows slightly.

"Beth thinks…" He looked like he was about to have a heart attack. "Beth thinks I might have a crush on you," he admitted quickly. He blushed to his hairline and stammered, "I know, we're friends and all, and sometimes I think my sister is crazy, but…"

He stopped. I wished he'd have finished his sentence! I didn't know what to say. Graham had brought the topic up through his sister, so I decided to do the same.

"Annie thinks I like you, too," I said shyly, also blushing. We both smiled, as if laughing at a funny joke. We were silent for a moment.

Say something! I scolded myself. I had thought about this scenario hundreds of times, but now that it was happening, I was drawing a blank.

He brought this up, so he must be okay with it. Maybe he wants to know what I think as much as I want to know what he thinks.

I decided to push it a little further, trusting that he'd forgive me if I said something stupid.

"Annie's pretty smart," I said quietly.

"Yup," he agreed. "Beth and I've known each other since before we were born. She can read me like a book."

We held each other's gaze for a little while. I didn't know about him, but I was at a loss for words.

"Well, my apparent 'crush'..." Graham said, standing up and holding out his hand. "...may I have this dance? I mean, if you want to, and if you're not tired or..."

"Yes," I said, rising and taking his hand. Leah stood on top of my dad's feet as he waltzed her around the room. I caught his eye for a moment, and dad winked at me. Kitti also seemed to notice and grinned from ear to ear, just like Pepper on pizza day.

I'd danced a billion times before, but this was my favorite routine of all-time, even though it was impromptu.

Later that night, everyone slept over at the church in the children's ministry wing. Ariella, Kitti, Leah, and I stayed in Leah's Sunday school classroom. While Ariella sang Leah to sleep at 1:00 in the morning, Kitti pulled her pink sleeping bag next to mine.

"So?" She whispered. "Are you dating Graham yet?"

"Kit! We just danced, that's all. Go to sleep. You look exhausted."

"I *am* exhausted, but I'm more excited." She quickly slipped on her pink kitten pajamas, yawned, and crawled into 'bed'.

"My eyelids are heavy," she announced lightheartedly.

"No kidding, Kit. You've been awake for eighteen hours."

Anything about eyelids reminded me of Annie, whose eyes would swell shut from time to time. When Annie ended up in the hospital during the second week of January, I wasn't surprised.

Pepper's Got Questions (Pepper's POV)
Takes Place: February 29, 2008

Dear Diary,

Hello. This is Pepper. How is you? Pepper not sick or nothing, but Pepper is afraided- very, very afraided. She gonna get sick soon. Everybody gonna get sick.

You see, Pepper's mommy's got this thing called nephrotic syndrome. Pepper asked some questions about nephrotic syndrome long time ago. Mommy answered questions, but one question is wrong. You try to guess what question wrong. Okay. Here we go, the answers to Pepper's questions in Pepper's own words.

1. What is nephrotic syndrome? It's sickness of kidneys. The kidneys get hurt and lose stuff they not supposed to lose.
2. Did Pepper or anybody do something bad to make mommy to get sick? Did mommy do something wrong? No. It just happen.
3. Can Pepper or anybody else get the sickness? No. It don't be contagious. You can't catch it like a cold or flu or basketball.
4. Is nephrotic syndrome going to be over soon? Don't know. Mommy's doctors working hard to make it go away forever. But it's called chronic sickness. That means it takes a long time to go away or get better. It not like cold or flu. You have it for longer than day or two.
5. Is mommy gonna die? Lots of people with kidneys that isn't working good get better. If they don't get better, then the doctors got a machine called dialysis that helps them. Some people even share their extra kidney with someone else. It called transplant. That really cool. So almost everybody get better somehow!

Look very careful at all answers. Okay, time up. Which is wrong?

Pepper think number 3 wrong! People <u>can</u> catch it like baseball. Because is contagious. Yes, must be. First, mommy gets it, now Pepper's friend gets it. She caught it like basketball. Pepper don't got it yet, but Pepper thinks she will. NEPHROTIC SYNDROME COMING!

I laughed, picked up stuffed animal Pepper, and petted her inanimate head.

"You're pretty smart, Pepper," I said out loud, as if she could hear me. "First Annie got nephrotic syndrome, and then someone else in the PFA got it. Don't worry- it's all a coincidence. You can't catch nephrotic syndrome. Every answer on your list is correct."

Monday, March 3, 2008- Jobelle's Point-of-View

Two months before, I had been sitting in a real hospital for Annie, unnoticed by the world. It was pleasant compared to what I faced this particular Monday. I was in another hospital, the Underground City Medical Center, having just been told, "at least it's not cancer..."

No, it's not cancer. It's nephrotic syndrome. No, it isn't generally a life and death danger, but it's changed my best friend. It had affected me once already... did it have to bite me in the foot a second time?

Seriously, hadn't there been enough times my life had changed in an instant?

It's important to understand what I had seen Annie endure before I go any further. Pregnant women had nothing on her edema. By Christmas, Annie's feet were as swollen as inflated latex gloves. She gained thirty pounds in two months while eating virtually nothing. I hate hospitals, but that's where Annie ended up by the second weekend of January. They gave her

112

aggressive diuretics that pulled forty pounds of fluid off her body in three weeks. Her blood pressure had a nasty habit of rocketing through the roof, causing her to gasp for air.

I'll never forget the night of February 28 and 29. I had a foreboding sense that Annie would be hospitalized before March. While that assumption fell flat, nephrotic syndrome struck again at 3:00 AM on Leap Day morning. This time, it struck my family even more directly.

With a start, I awoke to a bone-chilling, agonizing, eardrum-puncturing scream. The whole night is a blur of nightmarish memories, but I'd never seen anyone- not even Annie- as dangerously swollen as my little sister. Kitti was rushed to the emergency room by ambulance, mainly because they were afraid there was fluid on her lungs. I went back to bed, but didn't sleep.

Due to her erratic heartbeat and off-the-charts blood pressure, Kitti was in PICU for around twelve hours. Once she was stable, they sent her upstairs to the pediatric nephrology floor, nicknamed the Penguin Unit. Tayoe and I had been visiting her on and off since Saturday morning.

Kitti had looked awful. Five bags of nutrients and medicines, three I recognized to be albumin, hung above her. There was also a short strand of colorful beads draped around the metal IV pole, each bead representing a medical treatment she had already endured. She was excited about her ever-growing IV decoration, although I certainly was not. If Annie had been enrolled in a program like that, she'd have a strand of beads lined all the way down the hallway by now.

Kit's treatment plan was eerily similar to what Annie's had been, including the standard three months of high-dose oral prednisone, but there were some differences. For example, the doctor prescribed intravenous steroids to jumpstart the anti-inflammatory effect. She also decided to hold off on the biopsy, even though lab results and several ultrasounds hadn't found the cause of Kitti's condition. With her evident "nephrotic syndrome-ridden past", the healthcare professionals assumed it wasn't FSGS.

I was shocked at first. Kitti had nephrotic syndrome as a small child? Actually, according to Annie, the doctors' conclusion made sense. Tayoe described Kit's old "allergy" symptoms as puffy eyelids, congestion, general ill feeling, decreased appetite, shortness of breath, and exhaustion. Nothing worked for her mysterious sensitivities except prednisone. Prednisone treats severe allergies, but it also treats nephrotic syndrome. In reality, the symptoms were closer to that of nephrotic syndrome than allergies. It clicked.

In a way, I really hoped she'd had this monster in the past. If those symptoms were caused by nephrotic syndrome, prednisone had worked wonders for her. Surely, it would work its magic once again.

I thought about my own diagnosis. While I was eased into the world of chronic illness, a lot of people get thrown into chaos in the blink of an eye. What it would be like to appear healthy one minute and be fighting for your life the next? I switched to the perspective of a young, newly-diagnosed patient and began to write.

Kitti's Point-of-View: Takes Place February 29, 2008

When I woke up in the middle of the night, I immediately knew something was very wrong. My arms, legs, and chest felt so heavy. Breathing was hard, and everything was so dizzying. There was a strange sensation, like someone was sticking thousands of little toothpicks deep down through my leg and into my bones, and I felt like I was going to throw up.

It was the scariest thing that's ever happened to me, worse than escaping from Mara.

I remember different things, mostly watered-down

sensations and vague images. There was my dad's voice, Tayoe's hand holding mine, and someone calling 911. I had no concept of time; whether it was seconds, minutes, or hours will always be a mystery. Eventually the medical workers arrived. There were at least two, a man and a lady, but there may have been more.

"Am I going to die?" I asked daddy as they lifted me onto a different surface. He just held my hand, but the lady told me that I wouldn't. She put two little tubes in my nostrils. The air blowing into my nose smelled like plastic, but it made me less lightheaded. A kind man hooked up a couple blood pressure cuffs to my legs and put "sticky pads" on my chest. Someone tied a rubber band tightly around my upper arm. Suddenly, there was a huge sting on the bend of my elbow. I panicked.

"They're just drawing a little bit of blood, honey," my dad said in a comforting way, but the last thing I wanted to do was calm down. I managed to catch a glimpse of a needle sticking out of my arm. My vein was buzzing like a mosquito while the blood trickled into a little tube. The sight of my blood made me feel dizzy again. I could feel the needle come out, but that was the last thing I remember.

"Kittina, can you squeeze my hand?" Someone- a lady's voice- questioned me. Yes, I tried to say. No words came out, so I did as I was told. "Good girl," the person said. "Can you open your eyes?" I did so. "There you are, princess. Dad, come here and hold her hand. Look, here's your dad, sweetie. He's been here with you the whole time."

"Was I asleep?" I managed.

"You fainted," dad said.

"Don't worry, sweetheart," the nurse said. "You're okay now. We have you on oxygen. It will make you feel better."

I touched the tiny tubes that had been pushed up my nose earlier. "Is that what this is?" I asked.

"Yes," she answered.

My dreamlike state went away. I could think clearly again,

so I began assessing the situation. I was on a rolling bed in the back of a moving vehicle. There were sirens, machines beeping, red and blue lights flashing…

"Where am I?" I asked.

"We're in an ambulance, Kit," dad told me. "We're going to the hospital."

Big smiles for ambulances… if you're going to get really sick, you might as well get to cut in front of all the traffic, even though there's nobody out at 4:00 in the morning.

"What's wrong with me?" I asked suddenly.

"Your blood pressure is very high," the lady told me, "and your body is very swollen. There is a lot of fluid around your lungs, so it's making it difficult for you to breathe."

"Is that why she passed out?" dad asked.

"It seems to me it's because she saw her blood, but it's possible the edema isn't helping."

Edema? I quickly remembered that was a word Annie has used quite often when describing nephrotic syndrome.

"Kidney disease?" I asked, suddenly feeling very weak.

"We don't know yet," the woman commented. "It's a possibility, but there are dozens of things it could be."

"Can't swelling have to do with heart disease, too?" Dad asked.

"I'm not going to speculate," the woman said. "Let's just get to the hospital. Kitti, why don't we put on your music?"

"My music?" I asked when dad pulled out Tay's portable CD player and put the headphones on my ears. He must have loaded it with my favorite CD and given it to dad before we left… after all, I don't remember leaving.

"I hurt," I said as we pulled up to the hospital. Someone asked me what hurt, and then asked me to rank the pain from 0 to 10. My legs were at a two, my chest at a five, and my stomach fluctuating between seven and eight. Someone had me drink some icky cherry syrup that made me feel tired and my mind foggy. It also eased the pain, so I was happy. The same person waited a few minutes, and then stabbed the back of my hand with a needle... that didn't come out. He called it an IV and promised that the only thing in my vein was a soft plastic tube.

Inside the hospital, they rolled my bed into a big room and put me in my own little curtained-off area. I was so glad daddy got to stay with me, but I really wanted Tayoe. I didn't know where he was or if he knew that I was okay. If he had gotten sick and been taken away to the hospital, I would have been so scared. Because Tayoe's my brother, he's always had this silly idea that he had to protect me. I wondered what he was thinking, and if he was as terrified for me as I would have been for him. As I thought about those worries, the machine that sat next to me started beeping. My dad called the nearest nurse.

A kind woman around my dad's age entered my curtained "zone". She had shoulder-length red hair and wore red awareness ribbon earrings.

"Hi, princess," the woman said. "I'm Rachel."

We introduced ourselves as she hooked a bag of yellowish-brownish fluid on a metal pole above my rolling bed. I recognized it as something Annie had been given when she was in the hospital.

"Don't worry, sweetie," Rachel said. "I'm going to take good care of you. Your blood pressure and pulse are high, but we'll fix that very soon." She gave me a small handful of pills, explaining they were for my blood pressure.

She asked daddy and me a huge list of questions before we finally had time to ask questions of our own.

"Do you know what's wrong?" My dad asked right away.

"We have our suspicions," Rachel stated vaguely.

"Is it cancer?" My dad asked with a shaky voice. My heartbeat got faster, and Rachel pressed the button on my machine again to make it stop beeping.

"No promises, but we're 99.9% sure that it isn't. The

doctor on call is pretty sure it's kidney related, seeing as her cholesterol and kidney numbers are slightly elevated."

Daddy breathed a sigh of relief. Rachel then talked to me about random things, like school. In the words of Rachel, we "hung out" for a while until my medicines started working.

"Well, Miss Kittina, it seems your pulse has improved. Your oxygen is great, too. Do you think you could get up to do a really easy test?"

With Rachel's help, we went into a tiny bathroom, and she showed me how to "collect a clean-catch urine specimen."

"I know a girl, Annie, who has to do this all the time," I told Rachel. "She has this thing called nephrotic syndrome. Her actual sickness is a big long word, but it has a four letter abbreviation. It starts with an F, I think."

Rachel nodded. She seemed to be thinking about something hesitantly. Usually, I would have been better at deciphering why Rachel was upset, but I didn't feel like thinking. "What do you know about nephrotic syndrome, Kittina?"

"You can call me Kitti, Ms. Rachel."

"And you can call me Rachel without the 'ms,' dear. So, Kitti, what do you know about your friend's illness?"

Why is she asking me about nephrotic syndrome? I thought, too confused to figure out the obvious.

"Her kidney's filtering parts- I forgot what they're called- well, they're sick. Something is hurting them, and protein is leaking into her urine. The protein is damaging her kidneys."

"Well, aren't you the nurse in training?" She asked.

I shook my head. "I hate anything medical."

"Really? That surprises me. You aren't crying a bit and seem like one of our ER veterans."

"I cried when they stuck this dumb needle in me!" I held up my IV.

"Oh, grown men cry when they get IVs," Rachel comforted me.

118

"Annie didn't. She doesn't hate needles as much as I do."

"Remember, the needle only made the little hole for the little straw to go into. The needle is in a sharps container somewhere."

Rachel led me back to my zone and helped me onto my bed. "I'm going to run the urine down to the lab. Hang tight. We should have answers really soon."

I drifted in and out of sleep for a while. My dad slept in a recliner next to my roller-bed, never once letting go of my hand. One or two hours later, I woke up to Rachel pushing a syringe of something into my IV.

I panicked. Even though the needle wasn't going into my skin, the clear liquid hurt! It burned my veins and made me feel dizzy. I tried to pull away as I started to cry.

"It's okay, Kitti," Rachel said gently as she stopped for a second. "This is called bumetanide. It's a diuretic, but I usually call it a water pill…"

"It hurts!" I complained through tears. My dad woke up and tried to distract me. After about five minutes, the awful thing was over. Unfortunately, the worst was yet to come.

"Sweetie," Rachel said with sympathy in her eyes. "Your blood pressure keeps spiking. The medicine I gave you is going to help you urinate so we can get some of the swelling down. We're going to put you in PICU- the pediatric intensive care unit- for a little while. During that time, we need to be able to measure all of your urine. With your BP as high as it is, the ER doctor doesn't really want you getting up to go to the bathroom or using a bedpan, so we're going to insert a Foley catheter. It'll only be in for a few hours. Hopefully by this evening, we'll get you into a regular room. We'll pull the Foley then."

I didn't understand half of what she said, but she showed me the little tube that would go into my bladder and drain my urine into a special bag. It wasn't bad until she tried to put it in. Over the next five minutes, Rachel and dad pleaded with me to be still. I didn't care what everyone said- that it was important to me feeling better. All I cared about was that the insertion hurt. It was more uncomfortable than painful, but I didn't like the sharp pressure or the fact I wasn't wearing underwear while a bunch of people huddled around me. They finally had three nurses hold me down while I screamed, and afterwards, I cried for a while.

At the beginning of kidney disease, I had been very concerned with being clothed at all times. I wasn't comfortable with anyone but my mom seeing me naked, even though it was medically necessary at times while inpatient. Only after several internal ultrasounds did I get used to being examined in revealing gowns. I didn't want to put Kitti through that much agony- at least, not yet. Even though I heard Foley catheters were uncomfortable and could be slightly painful when inserted, it seemed like a realistic yet not too overly terrifying way to introduce Kitti to one of the realities of chronic illness.

At about 7:00 in the morning, Rachel came to say goodbye. "My shift is almost over," she explained. "They're going to send you upstairs pretty soon. We have a diagnosis, and the on-call doc said I could tell you. It's not cancer or anything you don't know about." She took my hand and looked at my dad.

"It's nephrotic syndrome."

It felt like someone had punched me in the chest. Annie had it. Just thinking about what she endured made me cry, but realizing that I'd have to somehow do the same stuff scared me to death.

"I'm sorry," Rachel said. "The good news is that it isn't cancer, and it is treatable. True, it can be a life-changing ordeal, but commonly, it's a minuscule blip on the radar."

Rachel looked at me. "I have something for you. When I came back from lab, I made a stop at the pediatric hematology and oncology ward. You'll be a nephrology patient, but I couldn't resist. I wanted to give you something for handling tonight so well, and personally, I think it's kind of silly they don't have these for kids with all kinds of chronic illnesses."

In her open palm, she held several plastic pony beads and three beautiful glass beads. "We call these 'I Can' Beads. Each bead represents a procedure or treatment you've been through. Each color means something different. I had to divert from the regular code a little, since you don't actually have cancer. Hold out your hand and I'll show you." She began placing small plastic beads into my palm, one at a time, as she explained what each one meant.

"These letter beads spell your name. It's unlucky to get sick, so here's a playing dice bead. Two clears for 'pokes,' sparkly purple for an IV push, two dark pinks for special events (the ambulance and visiting us in emergency), two hearts for spending tonight and tomorrow night in the hospital, a metallic orange for the Foley insertion, and a green for heading to PICU. Kids get to choose special beads for other things as well. I had to go fast, but I grabbed a glass bee for your first and hopefully last IV. I don't think they'll continue giving you these, so here's some for your dad to hold onto until you earn them. Here, dad- a sparkly orange for when they pull that pesky Foley, a glow-in-the-dark for tomorrow's X-ray, another glow-in-the-dark bead for tomorrow's pelvic sonogram, a white for the prednisone course she'll be on, and this special one for when she gets into remission." She gasped for air at the end of the run-on sentence. "Oh, and Kitti, I noticed when you first came in the pajamas you had on were pink. I'm hoping that means it's your favorite color?"

I nodded, and Rachel sighed in relief.

"Oh, I'm so glad! Like I said, kids officially in the program get to choose the colors of the letter, glow-in-the-dark, heart, and other special beads."

I think dad was more grateful than I was, but for the first time that night, I attempted to smile.

Rachel gave me a bubblegum lollipop and said goodbye.

"You're a very brave girl, Kitti," she assured me. "You can do this."

Within an hour, I was sent upstairs to PICU. I wasn't as sick as some of the other kids in this part of the hospital, but I still needed constant monitoring until the swelling decreased.

Being in PICU wasn't scary in itself. Everyone was very nice. A TV with hundreds of channels hung from the ceiling, and my bed moved up and down. The medicines they had given me were exhausting and the catheter was uncomfortable, but it wasn't too bad.

Around 9:00 in the morning, Dr. Emilie Ballard arrived. I liked her immediately. Probably in her early thirties, she was in the middle of a nephrology fellowship and spent time with both adult and pediatric patients.

The ER doctor hadn't even talked to me or my dad, but Dr. Emilie, as she insisted we call her, pulled a chair next to my bed and talked to us for at least forty-five minutes. While some of the conversation was about pills and nephrotic syndrome, a lot of it was practical. My dad expressed his surprise and concern when Dr. Emilie talked about the upcoming three months as if I had been diagnosed with cancer.

"Is it really that serious?" Daddy asked. "The way you talk about potential help we could get... tutoring, support groups, special events for chronically ill kids, a 24-hour hot line... it feels as if we're talking about leukemia. My daughter's best friend has nephrotic syndrome and I've never heard of these services."

"No one talked to her about such things?" Dr. Emilie asked.

He shook his head. "They acted as if she'd go into remission within three months."

"Well, it's true. Many children- and teenagers- with nephrotic syndrome *do* get into remission and never have another problem. However, nephrotic syndrome is a chronic illness. It doesn't go away overnight, and it has the potential to be quite serious. Best-case scenario, Kittina will be on high-dose steroids for about three months. No, it's not leukemia, but three months is a quarter of a year, and prednisone is not a fun drug," Dr. Emilie said as she listened to my heart and lungs with her stethoscope. "It's not bad to know about all the support available to you, even if this is just a three-month ordeal."

"Do I have to go on prednisone?" I asked, trying hard not to cry. Dr. Emilie flipped her stethoscope around her neck and sat back down.

"Yes," she told me quietly. "But you've on it before, haven't you?"

"Not on such high doses," I whispered. "Am I going to get fat and ugly?"

"Kittina, I don't think it would be possible for you to be ugly. You might gain some weight from the steroids, but you'll still be beautiful. So, here's the deal. In about an hour, we're going to start you on a steroid pulse, which means I'm going to give you very high doses of medical steroids through your IV. We'll get you into a regular room hopefully by this evening and out of the hospital altogether in a couple of days. I'm going to put you on about 50 milligrams daily of oral prednisone to start, and you'll come by my office weekly for a month or two. Hopefully, you'll get into remission soon."

We discussed a lot more, including blood test results, treatment issues, and my possible past with the condition. We talked about all the underlying things that could be causing the protein in my urine. All my lupus and reflux results were negative, whatever that meant, and I didn't have diabetes. Dr. Emilie said it could be minimal change, FSGS, or a few other diseases.

"If the prednisone doesn't work, then what happens?" I asked. "Annie did the prednisone thing, but she got sicker. I think she's on cyclosporine now." "How is she doing?" my doctor asked, honestly concerned.

"Physically, not great," daddy stated.

"But she's okay mentally," I had to say.

"How old is she?"

"Sixteen," I answered. "She's had it since at least July."

"Is it minimal change disease?"

I shook my head. "It starts with an 'F.' Usually I can think of it…"

"… But you're foggy," Dr. Emilie finished for me. "Is it FSGS?" She asked in concern. I recognized the letters and nodded.

"FSGS has a higher kidney failure rate than other causes of nephrotic syndrome," Dr. Emilie muttered in thought. "You and your friend should powwow," she continued. "We don't have a child-life specialist on our general nephrology floors- heavens know we need one. I've tried to get the hospital to get us our own child-life department, but they won't have any of it. Thankfully, there are a few specialists that work with the pre-dialysis kidney kids as much as possible."

"What are child life specialists?" Daddy asked.

Dr. Emilie seemed annoyed, although I instinctively knew it wasn't at my dad's question. Why was she mad? I wished my head didn't hurt so much.

"Child life specialists do their best to improve the quality of life of kids facing medical challenges, whether it's for an outpatient surgery or long-term care," Dr. Ballard explained. "For example, if you ever need a biopsy, they will give you a tour of the procedural room and show you how the equipment looks beforehand. We have several specialists who focus on the transplant and dialysis units- which I'll do _everything_ in my power to keep you from ever needing - but we don't have regular child life resources on our non-dialysis 'kidney kid' units. Because you won't have unlimited access to those resources like other patients, my thoughts are that maybe you and this Annie girl can work together. You could talk to each other about your experiences and give each other hints on what helps you cope."

I liked that idea, but even so, the thought of several months on high dose prednisone didn't make me very happy.

Dr. Ballard then pulled out a computer that had been hiding in the wall. "So... we've run some blood and urine tests. Tomorrow, you're scheduled for a pelvic ultrasound to look at your kidneys. I'd put you down for a biopsy, but if you really did have this as a small child and responded well to corticosteroids, maybe it won't be necessary. We'll hold off. If you don't respond to the steroids within a few months or get worse at anytime, I'll biopsy you then."

Just before she left, Dr. Ballard's eyes wandered to my IV pole. She smiled.

"Who gave you these?" She asked, eyeing my reward beads.

"An awesome nurse in the emergency room," I explained.

"Rachel," dad corrected.

Dr. Ballard nodded, as if it made sense. "You like your beads?"

"I love them," I said, watching my young doctor gently touch the glass bee.

"Well, on my lunch break later today, I'll wander up to 3C and see what I can do. I can't promise you the next few months will be fun, but I can promise to make this as easy for you as possible. When all of this is said and done, your beads will make a heck of a special necklace."

There it was again- Dr. Emilie's edginess. I knew that 'heck' wasn't a bad word. It even rolled off Graham's tongue on a semi-regular basis, but it didn't seem like something that was appropriate for a professional doctor.

"I'm sorry I'm grumpy," Dr. Emilie said as she left. "Upstairs, I'm treating a fifteen-year-old boy whose kidney transplant failed this morning. It could have been prevented if one of my colleagues had paid better attention to his patient. I'm angry at incompetent doctors, and I'm sick of these stupid kidney diseases interrupting my patients' lives."

So that was it. Dr. Emilie's agitation was fueled by passion. She was a fighter for her patients, and I couldn't help but think she was a little bit of a rebel in general, just like my sister.

The thought comforted me, and I smiled as I fell back to sleep.

The fluids seemed to drop off of me, and before we knew it, the swelling was almost gone. With no more worries about my lungs, they removed my catheter and sent me to the pediatric nephrology unit early in the evening. All of the units in the pediatric sections in the hospital were named. The nephrology areas included Eagle, Penguin, Dialysis, and Transplant. I was put in room 304 on Penguin.

Within an hour, I had a gram of corticosteroids in my body. I'm glad I don't remember what I did for the first few hours after that mega infusion. They said that I dashed around Penguin Unit in a daze of crazy happiness. After about thirty minutes of nonstop running, I started randomly yelling and stealing toys from preschoolers in the playroom, so they pretty much had to restrain me in my hospital bed. My dad went to get me dinner from a fast food restaurant at the other side of the Underground City because I had apparently demanded chicken nuggets, a cheeseburger, fries, potato tots, onion rings, a corn dog, and cheese sticks. Thankfully, I don't remember that very severe case of euphoria, but I do remember my crash into despair that occurred during the hour dad was gone. I missed Tayoe, Jobelle, and everyone else, even though it had been less than 24 hours since I had been admitted.

I huddled under my pink blanket, crying, wishing I could sleep until my illness was gone. After a little while, I heard someone walk into my bedroom. Very carefully, I peeked through a tiny hole in the fleece fabric.

It was Annie.

In some ways, I had been dying to talk to her for the past few hours. In other ways, I didn't want to see her ever again. Ignorance can be bliss, and she was a living reminder of everything ahead of me.

Annie lowered the right side rail on the bed, and sat down. I didn't move.

Go away, I thought. At the same time, I hoped she could help me somehow.

"Kit?" Annie asked, gently uncovering my head. I immediately pretended to be asleep. Having recently watched Pepper take a cat nap on the playground at recess, I figured it wouldn't be too hard to fake. It's fairly simple- slow, deep breaths in a rhythmic pattern.

"Your eyelids are flittering," Annie commented. Without thinking, I squeezed my eyes tightly shut. Annie chuckled softly.

"I know you're scared," she told me gently, brushing wisps of my hair from my face. "Nephrotic syndrome can be a really scary thing, but it isn't unbeatable. I'm sure you'll do much better than I have."

I continued my sleeping charade. I was sure that if I opened my eyes, I'd burst into tears. My nose began to run anyway, and tears seeped through my closed eyes.

What would it be like to be diagnosed with such a terrible thing? Maybe it was a strange question- coming from someone who had kidney disease- but I didn't feel like I really knew what the instant fear of a scary diagnosis was. When Dr. Jones had told me I had nephrotic syndrome and later FSGS, I didn't think much of it. Nephrotic syndrome and FSGS didn't sound like scary things. It took time for me to slowly understand that what I had was potentially serious. What would it have been like if Dr. Jones had told me I had cancer or would need an organ transplant immediately? *It would have been an entirely different experience,* I answered myself silently. *I didn't understand what I was up against. Which is best? Is it better to have a traumatic diagnosis and immediately learn the seriousness of the situation, or is it better to not understand for a while?*

"Your numbers aren't as bad as mine were," Annie said in an attempt to comfort me. "Just because you have nephrotic syndrome doesn't mean you have FSGS. There are different causes of NS. Many non-FSGS cases, and a percentage of people with FSGS, attain remission after a couple months of steroid treatment, and then the sickness is gone. Some people never relapse."

"I probably already have relapsed," I told her quietly, opening my eyes but still fighting my urge to cry. I was afraid my eyes would swell shut as Annie's often did.

"Remember how I had allergies?" I asked. "My doctor thinks it's probably been kidney disease all along."

"How..."

"My 'allergy' symptoms were puffy eyes, difficulty breathing, lethargy, and lack of appetite. The prednisone took care of it every time. Dr. Ballard says it fits; the prednisone was putting me in remission, so the 'allergy symptoms' went away." I wiped my eyes with the back of my hand. "I keep hoping they made a mistake, and that it's just allergies."

"I know," Annie answered. "But it's not. You're spilling protein. The albumin in your blood is low; your cholesterol and BUN numbers are elevated..."

"What's BUN?" I asked.

"B-U-N stands for 'blood urea nitrogen'. It's just a kidney function number."

"Kidney function number," I repeated, trying to rest my case. "Doesn't 'elevated' mean 'bad'?"

"Not necessarily..."

"But I thought the higher my numbers are, the worse my kidneys are?! Because my BUN is 47, and no one will tell me what that means!" I yelled, feeling a surge of anger and waves of fear as the tears began to flow.

"Did they give you prednisone already?" Annie asked as she hugged me. I nodded miserably. She didn't say much after that, likely because she knew I wouldn't understand anything new.

Annie left when daddy brought dinner. I stuffed myself with more food than I usually eat in an entire day and fell asleep about an hour and a half before I normally go to bed.

~~~

"Daddy!" I cried when I opened my eyes to see my strange surroundings on Saturday morning.

Carefully, my dad sat on my bed and picked me up. I felt like a big melting blob yesterday, but now I was skin and bones.

"I'm here, Kitti," he said, holding me closely.

"Daddy, I'm scared," I admitted. "I don't feel good. Make it go away."

"I wish I could, princess," he answered.

"Where am I?" I asked.

"In the hospital," was his answer, and my memory came back. Unfortunately, it hadn't been a dream. I touched my IV, the silly tube sticking out of my hand, and frowned.

"I hate it," I told daddy.

"I know, but it's to help you get your medicine."

"I don't like needles," I retorted, suddenly feeling very agitated.

"Remember what Rachel told you?" My dad asked. "The needle is in the trash somewhere…"

"Not the trash!" I barked, seething for no apparent reason. "She said sharps container!"

"You're right, sweetie. I'm sorry. Try not to yell. The steroid pulse is tricking your emotions…"

"I'M NOT YELLING!" I screamed at the top of my lungs.

He ignored my comment and took my hand. "The only thing in your hand is a little plastic tube."

"I HATE the ambulance medics! They put all these things in me!" I felt pure rage, but my dad was handling it with incredible calmness.

"Hush, sweetheart. You don't know what you're saying…"

"YES, I DO!" I shouted before bursting into tears. This mental confusion was bewildering… my emotions were running so strong, but I couldn't understand why.

"I want to wake up," I remember pouting miserably, feeling positive that everything was just a bad dream. "This can't be real. I wanna wake up, daddy."

"So do I, baby," he said sadly.

I had several visitors, including Tayoe and Jobelle. Belle came and went throughout the day. Even with what my nurse called 'predni-brain,' it was obvious to me that Belle was frightened by my stick-figure body. Apparently, I had lost close to a fourth of my bodyweight in the past few months. Nephrotic syndrome's trademark edema- the body wide swelling- had masked how thin I had become.

I stopped for a moment and thought about the real-life siblings of kids with chronic and serious illnesses. What would that be like? I thought about Todd. He was the best little brother in the world, and it was as if kidney disease hardly phased him… as far as I could tell. Were there things I wasn't seeing?

Well, yeah. Who wants to go to the hospital after school every day for a week, even if it is to visit family? What would it be like to spend the weekend before your thirteenth birthday worrying about your sister? I knew Todd had dealt with these two scenarios. How did he really feel about these things? What were his worries? What else happened when I was in the hospital?

Most people didn't consider me very sick, mainly because they didn't understand what nephrotic syndrome and FSGS were. For kids who were considered "sick"- with illnesses more widely known such as cancers- what did their siblings face? They probably had more support groups, but they also had more hardships. I wasn't in danger of immediate death, but a lot of young patients are. What would it be like, knowing your brother or sister could die while you're at school? Or, even worse, what if you weren't told what was going on? If you were like me, your imagination would go wild, and what you'd create would likely be so much worse than the real thing.

I searched our newly-connected Internet for information on siblings of the chronically ill. There wasn't nearly enough known about these incredible kids, but the range of emotions they can feel was staggering. Most websites stated guilt, anxiety, jealousy, and embarrassment, but there were darker side effects as well. Poor academic performance, severe depression, delinquency, post-traumatic stress disorder... the list went on.

Todd was one of thousands of children who spend parts of the weekend in the hospital waiting room, only to be sent back to school on Monday. So what's worse... dealing with the disease, or dealing with the person who has the disease?

Todd became my hero at that moment.

Kitti's POV Continued

My favorite visitor was Tayoe. While I knew Tay was terrified for me, he hid it well. He had way too much fun with the many TV channels and the video games in the playroom. Dr. Emilie was on-call that weekend, so she checked in on me regularly. When she couldn't find a child-life specialist to talk with Tayoe and Belle about living with a sister on high-dose steroids, she talked to them herself.

"Well," Dr. Emilie said half-jokingly, half-seriously. "Let me start by saying I'm no specialist on anybody's life, but I do know that Kitti's going to be mean to you. Don't sweat it. If you get ticked, punch a pillow or something, but do me a favor and don't beat her up."

Tayoe cracked up, but Jobelle stared ruthlessly.

"Alright, I'll be serious. Any illness is a challenge for everyone in the family, even if it lasts 24 hours. If somebody gets a stomach bug, everything gets thrown off course for a day or two. Kitti will be on medicine for nephrotic syndrome for at least three months. It's not the end of the world, but this *will* affect you, even if it's as simple as not riding with your sister on the school bus. So, here are some 'I Can' Beads for Super Sibs..."

~~~

My renal RN, Nurse Garcia, had hooked my bags to a nifty IV pole on wheels so I could walk around parts of the hospital. On Sunday afternoon, Tay and I explored the colorful hallways of the Penguin and Eagle units.

"What's the freaky yellow stuff in that bag?" Tay asked me.

"It's albumin."

"Cool. What's albumin?"

"It's protein. It's supposed to replace the protein that I'm losing through my urine."

"Does peeing hurt?"

"That's impolite!" I yelled, furious for him for using such terminology. *Wait,* I thought. *Tay's worried about me! That's sweet!* I threw my arms around his neck.

"Okay..." He said. "So does it hurt?"

"No," I answered, suddenly feeling sad again. "Dr. Emilie says that sometimes, if there's protein in your urine, you can see foamy bubbles in the toilet."

"That's cool."

"NO IT'S NOT!" I screamed, my mood jerking back to anger before I jolted to the giddiest I had ever been.

"Hey, watch this!" I put one foot on the base of my IV pole and used the other to push myself along. "It's the best ride ever!"

Finally, the 48-hour steroid pulse ended. Starting on Monday, I was able to take "only" the high dose of 50 mg of prednisone per day.

Jobelle's Point-of-View: Continued from March 3, 2008

"Tay went to school?" Annie asked as she walked into the waiting room and sat exhaustedly next to me.

I nodded. "Yeah, he couldn't wait to play dodge ball," I stated. "I guess I don't blame him, wanting to distract his mind from what's going on. I went on Friday, when she was in PICU, and he didn't, so we're even."

"So, are you okay?" Annie asked me, grasping my hand.

I shrugged and took a sip from my forty-ounce cup filled to the brim with flavored crushed ice.

It was weird. Kitti and I were officially sisters through her adoption, but Annie and I might as well have been. I had probably already spent twice as much time with Annie than I ever will with Kitti. Even so, Kit's diagnosis stung a little worse than Annie's had. My mind raced for reasons. Maybe it was because I knew what nephrotic syndrome was, or because Kitti was younger.

"What are the statistics?" I asked quietly, still staring straight ahead while occasionally blowing bubbles into the ice through my red straw.

"We don't know what she has, but FSGS is the worst-case scenario, so we'll just go by that for now. I'm not sure how accurate this is, but I've heard that with FSGS, about fifty percent of people will need a kidney transplant within five years."

"And the other fifty percent get into remission?"

"No, about twenty percent get into remission. The study didn't say whether or not they stay in remission or relapse occasionally, but that group doesn't need to worry about lifelong health problems. The other thirty percent don't get into remission, but with medicines, their kidneys don't fail."

"Why wouldn't they just let their kidneys fail so they can get kidney transplants and be done with this mess?"

She sighed sadly. "It isn't that easy. Even if it was a cure, organs don't grow on trees."

"It's not a cure?"

"Not at all; it's a *treatment*, just like prednisone or dialysis. It has the potential to be life-saving and life-changing, but it's not without risk or negative side effects. Because you weren't born with it, your body sees a kidney- or heart or lung or any organ, for that matter- as a foreign object. A person's immune system was built to protect against *anything* it doesn't recognize as its own... including transplanted organs. Anti-rejection medications, including prednisone and cyclosporine among others, trick the immune system into keeping the graft... meaning *organ*... safe from attack. The medicines have to be taken every day for the rest of the organ's life, or you run the risk of rejection. Even if you do take your medicine faithfully, there's still the risk of rejection."

I shuddered at that. Basically, if her information was correct, up to seventy percent of FSGS patients would spend at least a good part of their lives on these terrible drugs fighting this awful disease, one way or another. It didn't mean they couldn't live fairly normal lives, but it did mean that everything they did would be more of a struggle than it would have been otherwise.

"How do we know which percentile Kitti is in?" I thought aloud.

"She probably doesn't even have FSGS. Other causes of nephrotic syndrome, like minimal change disease, work differently, and as far as I know, the prognosis is better. This might sound a little harsh, but finding FSGS is like finding out a tumor is an aggressive cancer. Minimal change and other causes aren't good, but it's like receiving word that the tumor's benign."

My worries shifted off Kitti for a half-second. "Wait... how long should it take to go into remission? You said your disease is refractory, meaning it wasn't affected by the main treatment. Does that mean you aren't in that 20% who are completely normal?"

She shrugged. "I don't know. There isn't nearly enough

research, but from what I've read there's slow FSGS- called benign- and fast FSGS, called malignant."

I was so confused. As far as I knew, the words 'malignant,' 'benign'-even 'remission' and 'relapse'- were cancer terms. Nephrotic syndrome and FSGS aren't cancerous, so why use the same terminology? I dropped the fancy jargon.

"How do you tell if you have slow or fast FSGS?" I asked.

"I think it has to do with how long it takes to go into kidney failure, or if you go into kidney failure at all. If a person's native kidneys don't fail, then I guess they have benign FSGS."

I was flabbergasted. "There's no way to know until a person goes into kidney failure? That's insane! Aren't there indicators that give a timeframe of sorts?"

"Blood and urine tests keep track of what's going on. I'm guessing the better your numbers are, the less chance you have of having the malignant variety. Kidney biopsies help as well. Pathologists can tell how many glomeruli are scarred and if there are any specific types of problems, like cellular or tip lesion scarring. The collapsing variant is the worst, I think."

"Which kind do you have?"

She avoided eye contact with me. "I honestly don't know. I've only been told my biopsy results were interesting. When we checked in September, there was already significant scarring and collapsing. There was something else abnormal as well, but your guess is as good as mine."

"I highly doubt that."

You "honestly" don't know, but the "collapsing variant" is the worst, and you have "significant scarring and collapsing?" That's the malignant kind, isn't it, Annie? I asked her silently, this time turning my head to face her and placing my chin lightly on the straw of my huge cup of flavored ice. "Want some?" was the question I actually asked out loud.

"Grape?"

"Blue coconut," I answered. She shook her head and

leaned against my shoulder.

"Why do we both like flavors that match our favorite colors?" She mused. The edges of my lips curled slightly, and I looked down at her.

"We're not the only ones," I stated. "Kit likes bubble gum flavoring."

"Pink," we said simultaneously. We both smiled, but I sobered fairly quickly. "Do you think she can do the diet?"

"If I can do it, anyone can do it," Annie confirmed confidently. "The biggies right now will be sodium and potassium. I'll teach her how to add up sodium the easier way…" she dug through her purse to find her trusty calculator… "And they'll probably just limit her to a couple servings of high potassium foods a day. It'll be easy, and before you know it, she'll be able to eat whatever she wants."

Sure, if she's in that lucky twenty percent…

I could tell she was thinking the same thing.

"You know…" she told me "… it might not be FSGS. There are a lot of things that cause nephrotic syndrome. They aren't even going to biopsy her unless she gets worse."

I nodded, but somehow, I had a nagging feeling Kit had FSGS. *It'd better be benign*, I echoed in my head.

Kitti's Point-of-View: Takes Place March 4, 2008

"Alright, Kit, I've got good news," Nurse Garcia said as she entered my room and squirted hand-sanitizer into her palms. "As soon as Dr. Ballard gets your paperwork processed, you are out of here."

"Really?" I asked, pushing aside my math book.

"Really," she answered. "Say 'so-long' to the IV!"

"It can come out?" I asked in delighted surprise.

"Yep, and hopefully, you'll never have to have another one again. Give me your hand, sweetie."

"Will it hurt?" I asked, timidly holding out my left hand.

"Maybe a little. Usually, the worst part is peeling off this sticky dressing that holds the IV in place. I've discovered a way to make it a little better. This is an alcohol prep." She opened a small paper package and pulled out what looked like a tiny wet wipe, probably an inch wide and an inch long. "Most of the time," Nurse Garcia continued. "We use it to de-germ the skin before we draw blood or give an injection. It's an antiseptic. What I'm going to do is this…"

She carefully rubbed the moistened pad in circles around the edge of the tape for about a minute, purposefully wiping the border of my skin and the tape.

"Okay, Kitti, this part might burn a bit, but the rubbing alcohol will hopefully prevent any pain. Do you want me to pull it off, or would you like to?"

"You?"

"Okay. I'm going to go slowly around the sides. When all of the tape is off, I'm going to slide the tube out of your vein. Sometimes, it doesn't hurt at all. Other times, it will feel like I'm pushing on a bruise for just a moment. When that's over, I'm going to put two pieces of gauze where the itty hole will be. Ready?"

I nodded. She peeled away a little bit of tape. It didn't hurt too badly, but I couldn't help but pull my hand away in surprise.

"Sorry," I said, reluctantly giving my hand back. "It's alright, sweetie. Why don't you close your eyes and take deep breaths?"

"How about singing?" My dad suggested.

Nurse Garcia smiled. "That's a wonderful idea, dad. Do you like to sing, Kitti?"

I nodded.

"Ah, there's my favorite patient's smile. Close your eyes. When you're ready, go ahead and sing. I'll work my magic, and before you know it, you'll be almost ready to go home."

I did as they suggested, and it worked. I could feel

tugging. Occasionally, it would burn for a second or two, but nothing was too terrible. After a minute, there was a mild bruising feeling, quickly replaced by a slight painless pressure.

"Woo-hoo!" Nurse Garcia cheered when I finished the songs. I opened my eyes to see her taping clean gauze over the teeny hole in my skin.

Tuesday, March 4, 2008

Once again, I stepped into the backyard. Brownie was asleep in the laundry room, but Nectar was chasing a squirrel at the far-side of the fence.

The Labrador came running, and I offered her a dog treat. "Hey, you want to see something cool?"

I held out a nearly-empty purple binder for Nectar to sniff. "All the old PFA notebooks are under my bed. This folder will only have the new stories I write. What'd you think?"

Nectar quizzically tilted her head.

"It's crazy, isn't it? I've been writing every moment I can, but I'm also finding myself actually imagining this stuff here and there. I mean, I know it's not real, but pretending it's happening right now... it's helpful."

I tried to sit on the ground but knew I wouldn't have the strength to get up. Even though the cyclosporine was working better than the prednisone alone had, my kidneys were still leaking several grams of protein each day. The water weight was coming back quickly. Eating was becoming increasingly difficult because my stomach and internal organs were also retaining water. I had no appetite but gained as many as seven pounds a night. I supported myself against our house's brick wall.

Nectar looked at me with concerned eyes. "It's okay," I told her. "I'm going to be fine. A lot of things are spinning out of control, but God is in charge. He's given me faith, family, and fantasy." Nectar wagged her tail and licked my hand as if she understood.

FSGS, I thought, patting my sweet dog's head. *Jesus already has the final victory. No matter what happens, you won't win.*

Medical information from the NephCure Foundation and
http://www.unckidneycenter.org/kidneyhealthlibrary/fsgs.pdf

The PFA
Part 3: Seasons

Introduction:

Monday, June 21, 2010

I sat at our room's windowsill, lifeless, holding Pepper and watching my mom drag luggage from our car to the hotel's entrance. It was 1:30 on a swelteringly hot afternoon. Across the street, the metal roof of Hot Springs Christian Medical Center glistened in the sun.

My mom and I had left home early that morning to go to several last-minute appointments with various doctors and hospital staff. My dad and brother would come in a few hours. *Tomorrow morning,* I told myself, *everything is going to change.*

Contrary to popular belief, I wasn't sure if accepting this transplant had been the smartest idea. With all of the possible complications and probable side effects, every logistical, analytical bone in my body was screaming that this surgery might be the absolutely wrong move. I wasn't worried about rejection, but with a sixty-percent chance that my new organ would be attacked by the same disease that had killed my native kidneys...

God, I prayed. *If it's Your will, please make something happen to cancel this transplant. I can't back out now, but I don't want this kidney if it's going to make my quality of life worse than it already is.*

Exhausted, I hobbled over to the nightstand and dislodged a Bible from its sliding drawer. I opened to a random page and read, "Vanity of vanities; all is vanity!"

I smiled. That verse, part of Ecclesiastes 1:2, reminded me of how I felt about "normal" teenage worries. Once, while I cried in the school's bathroom because I was having chest pain, the girl in the next stall was sobbing over her "ugly" prom dress.

I flipped to another page and stopped at Ecclesiastes 3:1-3.

"To every thing there is a season, and a time to every purpose under the heaven. A time to be born, and a time to die; a time to plant, and a time to pluck up that which is planted; A time to kill, and a time to heal..."

Dear God, I prayed as I closed the Bible. *Please let this be a time to heal.*

Wednesday, March 5, 2008

"Hey kids!" I said. "Are you tired of playing with boring toys? Do you ever wonder what this is?" I held up a plastic bag of kid's wax art strings. "Well, wonder no more and buy the amazing Whiskers- the Wonder Cat!" I stuck Pepper's face in front of my purple video recorder. "Whiskers the Wonder Cat is amazing! She can even fly using her invisible super-action string." I managed to twirl Pepper around several times.

"Whiskers the Wonder-Cat is the coolest cat in the world!" I sang before clicking my camera off and petting Pepper between the ears.

"Thirty-three seconds," I told the inanimate stuffed animal. "You think that's close enough to a half-minute? No? Well, I really don't care."

It took a minute, but I managed to stand up. I ejected the disk from my purple web camera, scrawled my name and "English 10 Assignment: Advertisement- February 2008" on the DVD, and stuck it in a CD sleeve.

"Well, that's done," I said out loud. "What else can I do before my blood pressure spikes?"

Most kids create a homework schedule around their daily activities, but I worked whenever my body allowed. It was difficult, because during the rare moments when I wasn't confused or exhausted, I could barely hold a pencil. The cyclosporine gave me tremors that shook my fingers, hands, and sometimes entire arms. There were times when my hand would "lock" around a pen or pencil. I had to pry my fingers off and take a break. I typed when I could, but some assignments had to be handwritten.

Besides homework, I had a variety of ways to entertain myself. I became very familiar with daytime talk and game shows. To keep my mind as sharp as possible, I pulled out our old collection of educational computer disks. It was fun reliving my childhood, and these programs helped me review basic academic skills, which were becoming increasingly difficult because of my medicines.

143

And, of course, I wrote. As my life grew scarier, the Pretend Friend Association's plotlines got darker. Even so, I still found joy etched into these fictional stories.

Darkening Skies- Jobelle's POV
(First-Person "Point of View")
<u>Takes Place: Tuesday, March 4, 2008</u>

I hated running, but I had sprinted for nearly ten minutes. Forget dance lessons- when school got out at 3:00 PM and someone finally decided the coast was clear, I headed straight to the PFA's apartment complex.

It had started at 1:17 in the afternoon. Ironically, I had been in Imaginary-Reality Theory class. The study of the imaginary world included everything from the history of galaxies far away to fictional languages, such as my own world's native tongue. For 70 minutes, Mr. Mode had been droning on about the typical IRT curriculum that every imaginary kindergartener knew. "Our city is unique, built entirely beneath the real ground. It is divided into five levels, like the floors of a tall building. Each level is at least a mile high, connected to the other four by elevators large enough to fit several dozen cars..."

We know, I thought, zoning out.

The past few weeks had been difficult. My best friend had been sick for months, but now that my little sister had been diagnosed with the same illness, life was rough at best.

"Jobelle Newbrey," Mr. Mode called.

Oh, super.

"Miss Newbrey, can you answer the question?"

I shook my head.

"Obviously," Mr. Mode continued. "We must be careful in the real world. You've been told since preschool that real cars cannot see you and that you'll never be able to open a real door, but do you know the dangers of the *imaginary* world? Well, do

144

you?"

Yes, I thought. I was born in a corrupt society, not in the safety of the Underground City. I remembered Mara's many dangers, including the earthquake that had killed my mother.

"Most of you don't," my teacher continued. "This is the Underground City, created by Todd and Anna Grace Shramere, two children with innocent minds. However, what is in *their* minds isn't all that matters... as we know from the third rule of the Pretend Friend Association, which states..."

"Everyone's imaginary worlds combine," I answered, not bothering to raise my hand.

"Precisely," Mr. Mode answered. "The real world is a dangerous, malicious place. I won't go so far as to say that it's outright evil, but there is evil in that world. Whatever is in the real world *will* affect us in the imaginary world. In fact, it already has."

I had never thought of that before... could natural and social disasters enter the Underground City someday and cause terror, just as they had on Mara?

"The Underground City has always appeared safe," Mr. Mode continued. "Thanks to Anna Grace and Todd, we haven't had to worry about catastrophic events. However, many other fantastical civilizations have to deal with extreme conditions every day."

"We have the Fictional Alliance," some random kid said. "They cause all kinds of mischief."

"The Fictional Alliance is good. Despite their odd behavior and the occasional suspicious character, their organization is what has kept danger at bay. You think the fluff balls that throw chips at people are menacing? There are far more dangerous enemies out there. At present, the UC has never been in any real jeopardy, but elsewhere, entire imaginary cultures have been destroyed."

I raised my hand.

"Why aren't we taught about these threats?"

"So far, there haven't been any real threats," Mr. Mode commented. "At this point, it's the city government's job to prevent such problems."

At that moment, a siren alarmed. I had never heard it in the Underground City before, but I had heard something similar- many, many times- back on Mara.

"Everyone! Under your desks! Now!" Mr. Mode shouted, running to lock the door. The lights flickered off and explosions rocked our classrooms. This was not one of the typical, goofy skirmishes with food coloring and tortilla chips.

No one said a word, but it seemed that the Underground City was under attack. It was much too reminiscent of the earthquakes, wars, and tsunamis that had destroyed my home land.

Thankfully, the event had only lasted five minutes and fifty-seven seconds. The school kept us in lockdown until regular dismissal time, when we were allowed to leave. I didn't bother with the school bus and the insanely congested traffic. Running was so much faster.

I flung open the door of the apartment complex, checked in at the front desk, and flew up the stairs. My dad left Ariella and Kitti on the couch and embraced me.

"Where are…?" I began, panicked.

"Lee-Lee and Tay were at Closet School in the Shramere's house when the attack took place," Ariella told me. "The Fictional Alliance isn't letting anyone enter or exit the city yet, so the kids are with Dot."

"What happened?"

"Some sort of attack," dad explained. Since Kitti had gotten out of the hospital the day before, he had taken the day off to care for her. The TV had been on all day, so dad knew more than the rest of us. "It turns out there's a method to the Fictional Alliance's madness," dad explained. "They've been fighting silly cartoonish squabbles over molehills for years. We thought it was crazy, but it was all in preparation for the good versus evil battles they knew were to come. The Fictional Alliance's good soldiers are going to be ready at a moment's notice."

"So we're becoming just like Mara," Ariella worried aloud.

"No," dad answered. "The commanding officer of the Fictional Alliance reported that a roving group of mythical creatures just happened to be in the area and decided to cause havoc before passing through."

"So it won't be a regular ordeal," Ariella asked cautiously.

"No, but it's a reminder that even this 'safe' city isn't as secure as we once believed," dad answered.

Kitti's POV (Takes Place: Wednesday, March 5, 2008)

I drifted in and out of sleep. Daddy carried me from the Underground City's apple tree entrance to the Shramere family's house where Annie was hanging out. When I woke up, I was on the real recliner in the living room. Daddy was hovering over me, brushing loose strands of hair out of my face.

"I don't feel so good," I whispered, feeling gloomy, dizzy, and hungry.

"I know, princess," he answered, holding my hand. "You're going to be okay. I have to go to work, so Annie's here. She'll do her best to take care of you, but you may need to help her as well. I'll be back at 3:30, hopefully before the real people come home. If they get here before I do, hang out on Annie's bed. I love you, my beautiful princess." He kissed my forehead and left.

"Bye," Annie's voice surprised me. I suppose she had been leaning against the recliner since before I woke up, but I had been too dazed to notice.

"You okay?" Annie asked as soon as daddy was gone.

"I don't know," I admitted before spiraling into a major

mood swing. I began crying bitterly, but I didn't know why. There was a dull pain coming from my arm. *Where did that come from?* I wondered. *Daddy carried me. He must have been too rough and bruised me… Dr. Emilie did say I'd bruise easily while on prednisone.*

"My dad shouldn't have carried me!" I screamed in anger. "He bruised my arms!"

"My arms are bruised, too, Kit," Annie said, rolling her sleeves up to reveal numerous gray, purple, and blue dots on her skin.

"WOW!" I shouted happily. "We're like twins, we have matching bruises!"

Annie nodded with a smile. "How much prednisone are you on, Kit?" She asked.

"50 milligrams a day," I answered. Annie slid into the recliner and put her arm around me.

~~~

Nephrotic syndrome wasn't quite as bad as I thought it would be. It wasn't fun, but it wasn't terrible, either. Spring break was coming, so Dr. Emilie excused me from school until after vacation.

I was surprised that Annie had a routine, and to an extent, she made me stick to it. We walked the hallway for a total of thirty minutes (spaced over the entire day), ate lunch at noon, and took our medicines at prescribed times. Homework was more sporadic, but we managed that, too. Annie taught me how to limit sodium and test my urine with litmus-like test strips.

"What does dark green mean?" I asked.

"Plus four," she said. "You're spilling a lot of protein, but don't worry. Prednisone doesn't work overnight… at least, not for nephrotic syndrome."

I showed Annie my blood test result sheet, and she explained the kidney function numbers.

"Creatinine and BUN count the levels of different poisons

in your blood," Annie explained. "If your kidneys aren't working properly, those waste products build up, and your creatinine and BUN rise."

"My BUN was 47,' I remembered.

"As far as I know, that's not really bad. Normal for me is under 25, but everyone's a little different. Yours is probably supposed to be around 25, too, but that's just a guess. I don't really know how it works, but your BUN and creatinine don't always go up at the same time. Last week, my creatinine was 1.1, which is good, but my BUN was 147."

"My creatinine is 0.7," I said. "So if yours is good, mine is too, right?"

"Everyone's normal is different. I think 0.7 would be good for almost anyone. It has something to do with what it makes your GFR."

"What's that?"

"Well, as far as I know, your creatinine is used to find your GFR- your glomerular filtration rate. It's an estimation of how well your kidneys are working, similar to a percentage. Your estimated kidney function is calculated by one of several formulas that add in all kinds of factors, like your age and race. Your creatinine is put in, and when everything comes together, the result is your GFR. You want that number to be high; I think above 60 is good."

Later in the afternoon, we trekked outside to feel the cool winter breeze. Annie sat on a lawn chair, since her legs were very swollen. Thanks to my medicines, I could lie on the grass.

"Do you miss school?" I asked.

"That's a complicated question," she answered. "Sometimes, I miss my friends. I hate how my grades are dropping. B's and C's are good, but I have to work so hard to get them. It's scary that I can't even understand what I'm reading half the time. I can study for a long time and then go blank in the middle of a test."

"Will that happen to me?" I wondered out loud.

"I don't know," Annie answered. "It's possible, but everyone is different. Some people with kidney disease can have difficulty focusing. Steroids, other medicines, and chemical imbalances can cause cognitive problems, too."

I felt a wave of unexplained hopelessness and began to cry.

"This is so stupid!" I exclaimed. "Is there anything good about this?"

Annie looked into the sky. "Yes," she answered.

"What?"

"Look at the sky," she commanded. I did.

"What do you see?"

"Rain clouds?"

"Remarkable, aren't they?" I didn't answer. "A couple weeks ago, they were snow clouds," she continued. "I felt good enough to stand outside for a few minutes. For the first time in my life, I noticed every beautiful snowflake, each with its own unique design. A lot of people would take that for granted, but I didn't. I couldn't overlook anything so spectacular, not after wondering how little time I could have left to enjoy it."

"That's terrible," I whispered. Had she really wondered if she would die? Could she die? Could I die?

"No. It's kind of miraculous. Kitti, we've been given this amazing gift."

"Kidney disease is a gift?"

"Being forced to realize how beautiful life is- that's a gift."

I tried to comprehend what she was saying. "But... couldn't FSGS kill you?" I stammered.

"Anything could kill me. I could die because of a bug bite. Nephrotic syndrome doesn't usually kill people... not to say that it can't, but people have died choking on marshmallows."

"Then why did you think about dying? And when?" I asked.

She touched my shoulder. "There were about two weeks in

December. I felt so sick, and I couldn't imagine ever feeling okay again. Even so, things got better once my doctor changed my meds. I still don't feel great, but it's a huge improvement. I learned that as long as you have faith, there will always be hope."

I wished I had as much faith as the Annie part of me.

Thursday, March 6, 2008

Things were going downhill quickly. Once again, I was inflating like a water balloon and my mental 'fogginess' kept getting worse. I ate so little that my preschool-teacher mother would jokingly use her "one-bite-per-year" system on me, teasingly telling me that I had to eat sixteen bites at each meal.

"I think I'm low on albumin," I told my mom after I urinated for the first time that day. I showed her the tell-tale foamy bubbles in the toilet, indicating protein-packed urine.

"Do you think I need to call?" My mom asked uneasily. I nodded my swollen head. Back in December, my mother's almost-daily phone calls were ignored. This time, a nurse allowed her to talk to an on-call nephrologist immediately. The doctor ordered several blood and urine tests for the next day.

In the morning, my mom and I went down to the lab as instructed. "Hey, Anna Grace," my lab tech, Barb, called. Most phlebotomists couldn't draw my blood easily. My teeny veins rolled. Even if someone did manage to stick me well, it usually left a huge bruise. But Barb was the best! Not only was she incredibly talented and competent, Barb made the lab a fun place to be. Her kind, lighthearted personality was exactly what people facing this harsh disease needed.

"You seem like you feel puny," Barb told me. "Here, have a bunch of pens. Look, this one has multi-colored inks and a highlighter- better than anything anyone else has ever given you, right?"

"For sure," I agreed weakly.

On my first visit to Dr. Jones' office back in August, I had accidentally dropped my purse on the floor. Dozens of gel pens had spilled out.

"Oh!" Nurse Debbie had exclaimed. "You're just like my daughter- she loves pens, too. Here," she reached into her scrubs' front pocket and pulled out several fancy pens. "We have hundreds of special ink pens lying around."

Weekly, they received dozens of pens from various

companies, each featuring the brand name of a prescription drug. I could always expect a treasure or two- or ten- after each lab visit or check-up. There were (mostly!) friendly competitions over "who gave Anna Grace the best pen." I learned the names of dozens of kidney meds through this more-sophisticated-than-a-prize-box reward system that existed solely for me. I suppose it was my own, personalized version of Kitti's I Can Beads.

I got weaker over the weekend. Even though I wasn't eating much of anything, my weight kept climbing. Monday began like a "normal" day. I was on the couch, fighting my geometry homework, when Nurse Debbie called.

"How're you feeling, Anna Grace?" She asked.

"I don't know," I replied. "How do my labs look?"

"Your serum albumin is down to 1.2," she answered. Just as I suspected, my blood levels of protein had been depleted once again. "What's your weight?"

"I'm back up to 132 pounds, and I'm not eating much." I glanced at the chart by the phone, where my mom and I recorded my daily blood pressure, weight, temperature, and pulse rate. Everything was indicating trouble once again.

"Dr. Jones has scheduled you to be admitted to the hospital tomorrow," Debbie told me. "He's prescribing several bags of intravenous albumin and high-dose diuretics. You'll probably be inpatient for a day, maybe two. "

That was fine with me.

Tuesday, March 11, 2008

It was a stormy spring morning. My mom pulled up to the Nectarwood Hospital's patient drop-off area, and I stumbled out of our car, Pepper's paw in hand.

Unlike the time in January, the registration and admission process didn't take very long. A kind volunteer found a wheelchair and took me up to the second floor.

"Such a gloomy day," the elderly man stated to my mom. "At least it's not sunny; I suppose it's a good day to be in the hospital. Well... not that I'd want to see a little girl here anytime, but better during rainy weather than otherwise." He looked down at me as he rolled my chair into the mirrored elevator. "Don't worry, hon'- they do their best to get young people in and out as fast as they can. It's important to get teens out and on with their lives."

My mom and I smiled politely and thanked him as he handed my chair's handles to a nurse.

If Jobelle was real, that man's innocent, intended-to-be-sweet comment would have made her so angry! I thought, knowing that this hospital trip was simply meant to alleviate some of my symptoms. All of my treatments over the next few days would be for supportive, not curative, purposes.

I wished I was in a children's hospital- or at least the pediatric wing downstairs- because hospital life is boring when you're sixteen. My main forms of entertainment were talking to my mom, watching TV with its 68 cable channels, spending way too much time posing Pepper for pictures, and typing on my laptop.

Jobelle's POV- Takes Place: Monday, March 10, 2008

"But I don't feel sick anymore," Kitti was saying to dad as I entered our apartment. "My dipstick tests in the morning still show 4, but I feel a lot better. Really! It's just hard to think, that's all."

"I would let you go to school, but the flu is going around. I'm not even sure I should send Tay the rest of the week; what if he brings whatever it is home to you?"

"Then please let me stay home," she begged. "Annie takes care of herself."

"Annie's sixteen, sweetheart," dad replied. "You've just turned thirteen, and you're still adjusting to your medicines…"

"Why can't you stay with Annie?" I asked.

On high-dose prednisone, Kitti wasn't as intuitive as usual, but I could tell she knew something I didn't.

"Honey," dad said slowly. "Annie's going back to the hospital tomorrow…"

I ran out of the apartment, down the stairs, out of the complex, and into the city. I planned on trekking across the real backyard to ask Annie what was going on, but I didn't get far.

"Belle! Stop!"

I turned to see Graham jogging toward me. Since he lived in an apartment just down the hall from my family's 'house,' he had no doubt heard the commotion.

"The Underground City is going into lockdown," he explained.

"Lockdown?" I exclaimed. "Why?"

"The Fictional Alliance says we're more vulnerable without a real person's protection. Annie's going to the hospital, which means our author is, too. We're more susceptible to an attack from enemies."

"I don't care. I need to know what's going on with Annie…"

Graham touched my shoulder. "I know you're scared. It's going to be okay. Let's go inside and wait this out."

"No!"

At that moment, warning sirens began blaring. Explosions rumbled beneath my feet, indicating an attack on a lower level of the city. I used the distraction as an opportunity to bolt. I figured that I would get out of the city, find Annie, and go to the hospital with her.

From out of nowhere, a creepy-looking creature jumped in front of me. It was something from someone else's imagination... something evil, created to terrorize and destroy everything in its path.

I stopped in my tracks, terrified. The next thing I knew, I was flat on the concrete with something on top of me. No, it wasn't something; it was someone.

Graham.

Around lunchtime, a nurse started my first albumin drip and gave me an IV diuretic push as instructed. I was informed that Dr. Jones was on vacation and that his associate- Dr. Wright- would be my physician while I was inpatient. I secretly called the guy Dr. Freak-Out, because he seemed to do just that. I had difficulty eating; rather than just assume this was a side effect from my many nausea-inducing medicines, he systematically began to rule out other causes. At the time, I thought he was crazy. Looking back, I agree with almost everything he did, even his response to a nurse practitioner who stuck her head into my hospital room, gasped at my very pale complexion, and announced that I would need a blood transfusion "immediately" to survive.

"Her red blood cell counts are low," Dr. Wright agreed, "but she's young. We'll watch it, but I'm sure she'll rebound without any help. We're also watching her caloric intake. She isn't eating much- I can hardly blame her, with all the meds she's on- but it could be that her iron level is low."

The nurse practitioner walked out into the hall, where several nurses and doctors- including Dr. Wright- stood in a circle.

"We don't want to do a blood transfusion if we can possibly help it," I overheard Dr. Wright say to the team. "We need to keep in mind that she's dealing with a very aggressive case of FSGS."

"Her kidney function is good..." someone stated.

"She has an aggressive case of FSGS," Dr. Wright repeated.

"There are several more treatments Mark has in mind if the cyclosporine fails to put her into remission, but we can't ignore the fact that she may need a transplant sometime in the future. Every unit we give her will complicate a transplant; we need to avoid giving her blood products or at least postpone it for as long as possible..."

A nurse walked by my room and closed the door.

The mention of a kidney transplant scared me to death.

"He's overreacting," my mom told me. "At least he didn't agree with that nurse practitioner."

"Do you think my kidneys are going to fail?'

My mom shook her head. "If God wanted you to be on dialysis, you would have already gone into kidney failure."

Even so, this was the first time I had heard a doctor act like my case was more than a "little kidney condition". In my case, it was a disease that could be serious.

It was similar to what had happened it the Underground City. At one time, harmless slobbering fluff balls were the only threat to the imaginary characters. Now, much more dangerous enemies plagued the citizens.

Jobelle's POV Continued

I was sure we were dead. Whatever the creature was, it had huge teeth and seemed hungry.

There was a strange noise, and then I felt it. Heat, as if coming from a fire, seemed to engulf us. I couldn't see much because I was being shielded by Graham, but there was a very bright light, and then silence.

"You okay?" Graham asked as he stood up and helped me to my feet.

"What was that?" I asked, trembling.

"I don't know. It was another attack of some kind."

"No... I mean, what saved us?"

"I don't know," he answered, putting his arm around me. I was shaking more than Annie on cyclosporine, and for just a moment, I could imagine how that felt.

We got inside the complex and ran to my family's apartment. Dad hugged me and thanked Graham.

"What was that noise?" Dad asked, unaware of what had happened outside.

"There must be something going on down the street," Graham lied. He was so convincing that I wondered if I had imagined what had just happened to us. I had almost gotten Graham killed. He had risked his life to protect me, and if it weren't for our mystery hero- most likely someone from Todd's Fictional Alliance…

"Thank you," I whispered into Graham's ear once my family was gathered around the television, watching coverage of whatever was taking place outside.

Wednesday, March 12, 2008

I'd never laughed so hard before, particularly not in a radiology scan room! With fluid building up all over my body, Dr. Wright was concerned about my lungs, so he ordered a chest x-ray to make sure all was well.

I was wheeled to a dimly lit radiology room, where a young woman stood waiting for me. "Is there any way you could be pregnant?" she asked.

You have to understand the situation. An x-ray technician is trained only to use technology, not diagnose. Likely, she didn't know what was wrong with me, just that the doctor needed certain "pictures". Here I was, a nauseous sixteen-year-old girl with a bloated stomach and very swollen feet.

Yep- she was certain I was pregnant! I tried to explain what was going on to no avail. Technicians are knowledgeable and very important in the medical field, but they aren't doctors. A lot of nurses don't know about nephrotic syndrome, so when the tech ran to get a nurse to question me, things got funny.

This senior nurse was very stern and determined to prove I was pregnant. I told them everything I could to convince them otherwise until they asked, "When was your last cycle?"

Oh, this was too great! Prednisone alone is enough to mess with a person's hormones, and with all the other meds I was taking, I had wondered if I was beginning menopause.

"Um... October," I stated with a smile.

You should have seen their faces! They were certainly justified, not knowing me or the situation, but this mix-up was the highlight of my week.

I waited in the room, cyclosporine-shaking and shivering in the cold, while the nurse ran off to grab a form for me to sign, stating I was aware that radiation could harm "my" unborn baby.

After the x-ray, I was taken back to my room.

"Mom, you'll never guess what happened!"

~~~

About an hour later, I began feeling worse than ever. It was as if my energy had been zapped.

At dinner, my nurse brought me medicines. "Don't forget," she told me. "You're NPO after midnight. Don't eat or drink anything."

"Why?" I asked.

"They didn't tell you?"

My mom and I shook our heads. "Well, Dr. Wright has you scheduled for a gastric-emptying test tomorrow morning. He noticed that you're not eating much, and he wants to rule out any other problems. The test isn't really a big deal. They'll give you food with a radioactive material inside. When you're finished eating, they'll put you in a special scanner that will track the radioactive particles as they travel through your digestive system. If we don't find anything during the scan, we'll assume it's the side effects of the medicines."

"Isn't that a little extreme?" My mom asked.

The nurse shrugged, obviously disagreeing with my doctor's knee-jerk reaction but trying to remain professional. "Anna Grace's doctor is Dr. Jones," she said neutrally. "He isn't quite as… cautious…. as Dr. Wright."

In other words, Dr. Freak-Out was a perfect nickname for my temporary nephrologist.

Early the next morning, my mom had to give me a sponge bath before the diagnostic procedure. She was as gentle as could be, but the soft washcloth felt like a thousand knives were piercing into my skin. I usually had a high tolerance for pain, but I was on the verge of tears.

I couldn't imagine what it would be like to be my mom. Even though she was trying to help me, I kept instinctively pulling my arms away from her. What would it be like to see your daughter so sick that physical contact hurt? And worse, how awful would it be to know that *your* soft touch was causing your child pain?

Before long, a cheery woman entered my room. "Hello! You must be Anna Grace. I'm Lisa, and I'll be helping you with your gastric emptying scan today. How are you?"

"Good," I answered.

"Uh-huh," she said with a smile and eye roll as she glanced downwards at my chart. "Well, you must feel absolutely fantastic, the way you're eating an enormous 500 calories per day."

The low calorie number surprised me. Was I really eating that little? But I had felt so full yesterday!

"So, Anna Grace, do you like oatmeal?"

"Not particularly."

Gross, I thought internally.

"We'll make it as easy for you as possible. Now, I'm going to go get the scanner ready. I'll be back in about ten minutes."

The moment she left, I burst into tears. I'd had a kidney biopsy, felt hundreds of needle sticks, taken thousands of milligrams of harsh medicines, undergone numerous diagnostic procedures, and spent seven nights in the hospital over the past six months. Even so, I couldn't stand the thought of eating a bowl of oatmeal. Looking back, I realize that I was simply sick of being sick. Being forced to deal with yet another procedure was "the straw the broke the camel's back."

Lisa returned to my room, and although I had stopped crying, my already-puffy eyelids had nearly swollen shut from the tears. Lisa helped me into a wheelchair and pushed me down the hallway. My mom wisely stayed behind, knowing I would be "braver" without her around.

"Is there any way you could be pregnant?" Lisa asked.

Oh gosh, not this again.

I shook my head. *Nope,* I thought. *Not unless I'm Mary from Nazareth!*

"When was your last...?"

"October; I know that sounds awful, but it's because I'm on prednisone. I'm swollen because I have nephrotic syndrome...."

"A kidney disease," she finished. "Yes, I've heard of it. Impressed?"

I nodded. "It's rare. How'd you know?"

"We have more renal patients than you'd think. How are you doing... honestly? Not just that standard 'good' stuff."

"I'm okay," I answered. "It's a miracle my kidneys are still working." I looked down. "I'm a Christian, but as much as I believe that God can heal me, I can't ignore that the treatment is so hard. The standard steroid thing didn't work, so I'm on medicines that suppress my immune system. They're working, but they make me feel so sick. They make me ugly, too."

"Who?" Lisa asked. "You? Well, you could have fooled me. I think you're pretty."

"But I was *prettier* once!" I told her. "And now I'm just 'cute,' like a little girl. Most sixteen-year-olds can change how they look to an extent, by exercising and eating less cheeseburgers. No matter what I do, even though I'm following all of my doctor's directions, I can't make the swelling go down!"

Lisa pushed me into the elevator. During the short ride to the second floor, she knelt beside my wheelchair.

"As humans, we're control-freaks. We want to control everything, and some of the biggest control freaks on the planets are teenagers." She lowered her voice to a whisper. "From one Christian woman to another, that's the way God designed you guys." The elevator door opened, so she stood and wheeled me through the corridors. "You're growing and changing, and let's face it, it's like your world is spinning out of control. So, as human beings, what do we want more than anything else? It's the thing we can't have, right? So, if we can't have control, we want it. Teenage girls want their clothes neat, their face free of blemishes, and their hair flawless. You kids dream of the perfect prom and graduation. Goodness, girls even dream of a fairytale wedding and adorable children, even if those things are ten or fifteen years down the road."

We reached a door labeled RADIOLOGY- NUCLEAR MEDICINE in bold print. Lisa punched in a set of numbers, opened the door, and pushed me into a cold, darkened room as she continued talking.

"No one knows what's coming a year, a month, a week, even a day ahead of time, but we like to think we do. We like to think we have that control, even though we don't. When someone is diagnosed with a chronic illness, that sense of control is ripped away. Suddenly, everything happens on an hour-to-hour basis. Your physical appearance, diet, weight, routine, and many other things change overnight. The little control you actually had is gone."

She wheeled me to a table, where a bowl of oatmeal sat.

"And now I have to take away the control of what you eat, so I will give you as many choices as I can."

And she did. Even "stupid" choices, like where to sit and the amount of oatmeal I felt I could eat, made things seem easier. Lisa took out as much oatmeal as she could before mixing in the radioactive material, which I couldn't see or taste. After eating, I had to lie very still under a scanner for about an hour as a machine traced the small dose of radiation as it moved through me.

"You did wonderfully," Lisa told me when the test was over. "Now, before I say goodbye, I want you to remember that you can do this. Keep your faith, and never forget that God is in control, no matter what life brings."

She took me back to my room, where my mom waited. I never saw Lisa again, but her words had helped me tremendously.

There was a knock on the door, mimicking the rhythm of a kid's cartoon theme song.

"Hey, kiddo," Dr. Wright said as he made his appearance. "The good news is your emptying scan came back normal- no blockages or anything like that. The bad news is that- like your NP Jeanette said yesterday- you are anemic, and we aren't exactly sure why."

"Anemic?" I asked. *Could that be why I am so sore everywhere?*

"Your red blood cell count is low. We test that by checking your hemoglobin, a special protein particle inside red blood cells. Your hemoglobin is 8.9. Normal for a girl your age is at least 12.0."

"What could it be?" Mom asked.

"People in kidney failure are often anemic." Dr. Wright commented before looking at me. "But don't worry, kiddo- you're not anywhere near kidney failure. Your creatinine is 1.6... that could cause anemia, but it's not very likely. We could assume it's nephrotic syndrome-related, but because your renal function is fairly good, I want to run a few tests..."

Yep. Dr. Freak-Out.

Before he left, Dr. Freak-Out told me the nurse would bring the fecal occult test materials later. On my laptop, I looked up what I assumed was a simple blood test. The search engine took me to a medical website that mentioned using sample cards.

Sample cards for a blood test? I thought. *Maybe it's like the urine dipstick a lot of kidney patients have to use to check for protein.*

I remembered my English teacher's speech about vocabulary skills and root words.

Occult, I typed into the search engine, ignoring all the creepy stuff about spirituality, and found the medical meaning: only seen by microscope or chemical reaction.

Blood they can only see by microscope? That's not a blood draw, so what is it?

Okay, then fecal... and began to type but stopped. *Wait, what?* I thought in disgust. *They want to check <u>what</u>?*

Oh, great.

Jobelle's POV– Takes Place: Tuesday, March 11, 2008

The city's attack had been classified as minor. Several vacant buildings had been damaged, but no one was hurt. For precaution, we remained in lockdown, so school was cancelled for the rest of the week. Other than that, life went on as usual.

Graham and I informed the authorities that we had nearly been eaten, but we didn't tell the rest of the PFA. Nothing terrible had happened, and with everything else going on, it seemed unnecessary to give anyone– especially my dad– another thing to worry about. Graham and I were shaken, and we called each other often.

"I almost got you killed," I whispered to him over the phone.

"You were freaked," he responded. "You wanted to help Annie. I can't blame you."

"You aren't mad?"

"After what I've read about sick kids' siblings? No. Your best friend and sister are both fighting kidney disease."

"Graham," I asked tentatively. "Why'd you do that?"

"What?"

"You know *what*- you could have run from that thing, but you didn't. You protected me. Why?"

There was an awkward pause. "Apparently I have the 'fight' rather than 'flight' trait."

"Are you kidding?" I asked. "That's me, not you, and I was scared stiff. Besides, you didn't fight it. You threw yourself over me, like a human shield. You risked your life for me. Why?"

"I guess it was instinct," he answered. "From a young age, I had to protect my family- my sister and my mom, mainly. With Beth living in another state, I don't know. I guess your family has become my surrogate family."

"So I'm like your sister?"

"Yes…no, not exactly, I mean…"

My phone 'lost connection' somehow. I rolled my eyes.

Speaking of sisters, Kitti was doing very well, all things considered. Her symptoms were less severe than Annie's had been, and while her emotions were everywhere, her body seemed to adjust to the prednisone well enough that her personality was still recognizable most of the time.

By Thursday, people were allowed out of the city for "important" matters, as long as a Fictional Alliance solider accompanied them. Kitti and I asked for an escort out of the city so we could see Annie at the hospital. I was elated when our request was accepted, but then I saw our guard.

"Oh, no," Bubba the Parrot said when I opened our

apartment's door. "Not you."

"You have to be nice today," I commanded. "My sister's sick, and she's coming with us."

For Kitti's sake, Bubba managed to refrain from being obnoxious and we got to the hospital without incident. It was great to see Annie, even though she was hooked up to countless bags of medicines and fluids.

Back in January, Kitti hadn't been brave enough to visit Annie. This time, she seemed more comfortable in the hospital room than I was.

"Don't worry," Kitti told me as we left. "I don't plan on getting any more familiar with hospitals than I already am."

"How did you know what I was thinking?"

Kitti shrugged. "Did you think I've lost my detective skills just because I'm on prednisone? They're still in here," she said, tapping her head. "I just have to work a little bit harder to use them, that's all."

I shook my head. In less than two weeks, my little sister had changed. She was still Kitti, of course, but a much braver version. The little things that had bothered her no longer fazed her at all, except needles.

Thursday, March 13, 2008

At 2:00 PM, my dad dropped by the hospital to stay with me while my mom "went to preschool" for a few hours.

About an hour after she left, a nurse came in to give me a shot that "would give me more blood".

I seemed to "flashback" to the conversation I'd overheard a few days before. Dr. Wright's voice echoed in my head.

"We don't want to do a blood transfusion if we can possibly help it..."

"She has an aggressive case of FSGS..."

"She may need a transplant..."

"We need to avoid giving her blood products, or at least postpone them for as long as possible..."

"Every unit we give her will complicate a transplant..."

Even though the alarming words had come from possibly the most cautious man in the world, I went into "freak mode." Apparently, my internal panic spread to my face, because my nurse melted with compassion.

"Oh, sweetie," she began. "Did you know my daughter is diabetic?"

I shook my head politely but had to bite my lip to keep from sneering.

Both the nurse and my dad thought I was afraid of getting a shot.

After several months of blood draws, a pinprick was the last thing on my mind, but their misunderstanding was logical. Most people aren't huge fans of anything sharp. I'm sure my nurse had seen dozens of people dread injections and figured I was no different. My dad's mistake made even more sense, because once upon a time, I had been a wimp when it came to doctor's offices. Over the previous few months, my mom had seen me transform from a kid who hated getting new glasses to a girl who could laugh during a biopsy. My dad, who had the important job of taking care of Todd, missed most of the action. It wasn't his fault he hadn't seen the warrior I had become, but I was irritated with him.

"My daughter was diagnosed with diabetes when she was six years old. It scared her to death at first, but she learned how to inject herself with insulin. Now she's thirteen and does it several times a day without a second thought!"

As the nurse tried to calm me down through several stories about her daughter, I tried to figure out what was about to be injected into my stomach. Dr. Wright had said nothing about a shot. All I knew was a blood transfusion could make a future transplant more difficult. I wondered if this mysterious blood-giving drug could have the same dangerous effect. The nurse kindly gave me some great advice for people who are afraid of shots but ignored my questions.

"If you pinch your skin really tightly around the spot where the needle is going to slide in, it hurts less," she told me.

"I'm not afraid of the needle. I just want to know what the medicine is because..."

"There's no shame in being afraid, honey."

"I know, but..."

Just as she inserted the needle into my skin and pushed on the plunger, my mom and Todd entered the room.

"See?" The nurse said as she threw the syringe into a sharps container. "It wasn't so bad, was it?"

Now I was even more frantic, knowing there was no turning back from whatever had just been injected into my abdominal tissue.

"What's wrong?" Mom asked, knowing I was no longer afraid of pinpricks.

"She gave me something, but I have no clue what it was. She said it would give me blood somehow."

"Give you blood?" Mom's usually calm voice was shaky.

"I tried to get her to explain it, but she wouldn't!"

My mom ran out of the room and caught the nurse. She was a lot more rational than I would have been if someone had ignored my daughter's questions about a medicine. Even so, I could hear the agitation and alarm in her voice as she spoke.

My poor dad was very confused. "You really weren't afraid

of getting a shot?"

"No," I replied. "I've probably been poked several hundred times in the past few months."

"Then what was the problem?"

I shouldn't have been so angry, but I was. "A doctor said that if I get a blood transfusion, I can't get a kidney transplant if I ever need one. If that medicine really does 'give me blood,' then it could have the same effect. "

It was a cruel exaggeration, but I was ticked at the situation and, unfortunately, took it out on my dad.

I forgot Todd was listening. The young teen spoke from the corner.

"If you can't get a kidney transplant when you need one, does that mean you... die?"

Oops, I thought. For some nasty reason, I wasn't afraid of scaring my dad. Like almost all unkind deeds, it came back to bite me in the foot. Now I had scared my brother as well.

I didn't know much about end stage renal failure, but I did know a few things about dialysis, and I knew that- even without a transplant- a person could live a semi-normal life.

"No," I said, trying to be nice. "There's a thing called dialysis that cleans your blood for you."

My dad sighed in relief. Dad and Todd knew less about dialysis than I did, so my explanation reassured them completely.

Dr. Wright came into my room, followed closely by my mother.

"I'm sorry I didn't explain this to you earlier, kiddo, but I had an emergency in the ER. The medicine in the shot is a hormone called darbepoetin alfa. It doesn't give you blood, and it doesn't hurt your transplant chances. In fact, many renal patients take it regularly," Dr. Wright clarified. "Your stool sample came back negative for occult blood, so we're going to assume you're anemic because of the nephrotic syndrome."

"Is that good?" I asked.

"It's neutral. The good news is that your gastric tests have been normal. The nephrotic syndrome and medicines haven't caused any of the complications that concerned me. The bad news is that, even though your renal function is still fine, the FSGS *has* caused enough damage to your kidneys that your erythropoietin production is being affected."

Mom, dad, Todd, and I learned that kidneys are responsible for releasing a chemical known as erythropoietin. This hormone stimulates blood production by telling the bone marrow to make red blood cells. Kidneys that aren't functioning properly can't release erythropoietin as they should, so red blood cell levels drop. Darbepoetin alfa is a synthetic form of natural erythropoietin. Until my condition improved, I would get occasional shots of this medication to replace the natural erythropoietin my sick kidneys couldn't create.

"No one told me what it was," I said to Dr. Wright.

"I know, and I'm sorry about that. Most sixteen-year-olds don't care," he told me.

"Even if they're sick?" I wondered out loud.

"*Especially* if they're sick."

His explanation was likely true. Whether it was good or bad, I was different.

Of course I'm different, I thought. *Not many teenagers have imaginary friends.*

Friday, March 14, 2008

It was 7:15 in the morning of my last day in the hospital. My mom hurried around my room, getting ready for the day.

"I'd get a substitute if it was any other day, but today is Easter party day…"

"I'll be fine, mom."

"Sweetie, they don't listen to you. Your grandma is good at understanding the hospital system. I told her not to let them give you anything you don't recognize."

"Are you sure dad can't get off work?" I asked.

"I'm positive. Besides, after yesterday…"

"He'll learn," I said, but I knew the truth.

After twenty-five years, my mom and dad were still very much in love. In the past few days, my mom had seen things no parent wants to experience, and she didn't want to expose my dad to the "frontlines" of chronic illness. I wanted to protect my dad, too, but while I preferred my mom to be with me in the hospital for gender issue reasons, I wanted my dad to understand what my mom and I were going through. The only person I wanted to shelter completely was Todd, but that was impossible.

"Hello, Anna Banana Montana!" Grandma cheered as she walked into my hospital room. My mom went to lead her class's spring party, and I was left with my grandmother. I expected to be bored, but something amazing happened. We talked for the entire four hours, and I realized my grandma was one of my closest friends.

"You know," she said. "We may be sixty years apart, Anna Grace, but we're very much alike." She was right. When my mom came back at noon, I wasn't sure I wanted my grandma to leave.

I was discharged within an hour. An orderly pushed me in a wheelchair to the patient pick-up area as my mom went to get the car. While rolling down a long corridor near the admissions department, I heard the sound of an old wheelchair squeaking and creaking down the hall.

I hadn't expected to see a five-year-old girl sitting in the noisy "vehicle." An admissions nurse pushed the child along, closely followed by the girl's mother.

The little one seemed to have no fear of the child-unfriendly environment. In fact, although she looked totally out-of-place, she seemed quite at home. The sparkly plastic tiara resting on top of her red hair clashed with the sterile white walls.

"Oh, it's another princess in her chariot!" My orderly gushed as our two wheelchairs got closer. The precious little girl giggled happily as her rusty, squeaky wheelchair passed mine. I turned around for one last glance of the preschooler.

"Do I have to get another test with the sleepy medicine?" The surprisingly nonchalant voice asked. "I don't like drinking all that yucky juice."

"Not this time," her mother said as they turned the corner and walked out of my sight. "We go to Little Rock for those tests."

Little Rock, where the children's hospital is, I thought. *She must be chronically ill, too.*

Monday, March 17, 2008

Because I had been in the hospital the week before spring break, I didn't have to worry about school for a while. The disease didn't take a spring break, but I was able to finish the few assignments I lacked without worrying about getting farther behind.

On Friday morning, my mom and I headed to the mall's gift shop for its yearly spring event. Unfortunately, the store was in the middle of the complex, far away from every entrance and exit.

What had once been a one-minute walk became a ten-minute trek.

No, FSGS, I told my disease. *No. My mom and I go to this event every year. I don't care that the food has too much sodium or that there's nothing I'm going to buy. I will do this!*

I mentally screamed at my disease. With swollen and achy legs, every step was painful, but I made it to the store! Just as I had expected, the party was lackluster- at least to me. The important thing was that I had gotten there, even if I had to sit on the floor the entire time!

Except for my mom, no one noticed I was camped out next to the winter clearance rack. I imagined that Pepper's invisible form was scampering around the store, dodging feet and snatching dozens of cookies.

People watching always gave me inspiration for the PFA. From my spot on the ground, I could clearly see out the doorway and into the mall. There was a toddler smearing ice cream all over his face. A middle-aged man was fast asleep on a couch. An elderly woman went by in a wheelchair.

Another princess in her chariot.

I began to think about that preschooler. What had happened to her? What illness did she have? Was she still at Nectarwood General, or had she been transferred to Little Rock? Why did she need to have a scan with the "yucky juice"? How did she cope with being sick? Had her nickname become "princess," just as mine had become "penguin"?

Just then, something on the bottom shelf of the winter clearance rack caught my eye. There, by itself, sat a stuffed animal penguin. That alone would have been a miracle, but this particular plush toy had puffy cheeks and overstuffed webbed feet.

It looked like it was on prednisone.

I picked up the plump plush, holding it casually as if I wasn't acting insane.

Hello, I told it silently. *What's your name?*

I wish I'd known that sick child's name, but I didn't. All I could remember were the squeaky wheels of her wheelchair.

"Squeaky," I imagined myself hearing. *That's a nice name. I'm going to take you home with me. The Underground City has a lot of doctors; they can help you feel better. We'll make a string of I Can Beads for you.*

At that moment, Pepper got a new friend- Squeaky, the penguin who had nephrotic syndrome.

~~~

I went back to school the day spring break ended. It was tiring and painful, but I was determined to make it through the day. Miraculously, I did.

I was thankful for my lenient school schedule. FSGS sucked all the fun out of tenth grade. A weird instinct told me to protect my more sensitive friends, so I did, even if it meant acting like I was fine when I wasn't. Rather than socializing at lunch, I had to focus on eating without vomiting, and during the minutes before seventh period started, I would usually fall asleep on Kris' shoulder. When I walked down the hallway, everything was a blur. I had to hold on to Kris' arm to keep from falling over or bumping into someone. I often had to ask her which class I was heading to, because I couldn't remember my schedule.

Going to school wasn't a distraction from my disease; it felt like pure work and quickly became misery, no matter how nice everyone tried to be. Through the end of the year, I was able to make it to school twice a week. It was a struggle. I had virtually no free time after I got home, because I was done for the day. Once I went to a band concert and played amongst the other clarinets. It took me three days to get back to my "normal" level of sick again.

Going Back- Kitti's POV
Takes Place: March 24, 2008

I was excited to go back to school. I felt heavy with water weight and a little bit "foggy," but nothing too out-of-the-ordinary. The one-room school had a "welcome back" party for me, which was nice.

Even though I was at school, my disease was active. I wasn't 'all-better' as the kindergarteners kept saying, but I was okay. I didn't miss as much school as expected. In fact, I felt a lot better than I thought I would.

Unlike Annie, who hadn't been hungry at all during prednisone treatment, I was starving! Going to school was good, because I couldn't eat all day like I could at home. (My weight stayed the same- because I had lost about fifteen pounds of water, the ten I gained in what Dr. Emilie called "real weight" seemed like nothing.)

Socially, nothing changed. Pepper was still a math genius, even though she couldn't say the alphabet. Tayoe was still my brother, although he did seem to watch out for me more. As a seventh grader, I still tutored the little kids, including Squeaky the Penguin. Squeaky and I became close friends, despite our age differences. We bonded because we understood each other's struggles with nephrotic syndrome. We strung our I Can Beads into necklaces and bracelets and wore them all the time.

While the Underground City didn't get attacked by anything evil again, our imaginary world did seem to be going through difficulties. Just like in the real world, there were imaginary funding cuts. Because Anna Grace and Todd were growing up in real life, Closet Elementary and Middle School would close after school let out for the summer, meaning we'd all be dumped into the Underground City's public school system come August. I'd miss being with younger kids all day, especially

Squeaky.

One day during reading groups, our teachers paired the elementary kids with junior high students. I wasn't feeling good and was allowed to rest at my desk. Bored and dizzy, I watched Tayoe's best friend Tomes read out loud to several kindergarteners, including my niece Leah.

Tay and Tomes had been best friends from the moment we arrived in the PFA. (Quite literally- we met him at the Halloween event the night we came to the Underground City.) Tomes had been to our apartment often, but I had always stayed out of the way. I thought Tomes was annoying; as much as I loved my brother, Tomes seemed to bring out the 'wild side' in him. When those two were together, everything got rowdy, and our house would change from calm to crazy. I always wanted Tomes to go home.

On this particular day, Tomes was different. He was the same person, obviously, but this time, I didn't want him to go away. He read well to the little ones, using a variety of voices to distinguish the characters. It was a cute sight, but not the same cute as a baby or something like that. Tomes was a new kind of cute, the kind I never understood before.

When the story was over, the little kids ran to the book nook center of our classroom, leaving Tomes sitting across from me. Our eyes met, and my heart fluttered a little. I knew Annie had heart palpitations because of her medications, but I had also heard of the term "heartthrob."

"How much of that did you see?" Tomes asked.

"Since the 'once upon a time' part," I admitted. "You're Tomes, right?"

"Yeah. You're Kittina, right?" He held out his hand, and I remembered Dr. Emilie's mini speech on avoiding germs while on prednisone.

"Kitti," I corrected. "Sorry- I can't shake hands. I'm on this medicine…"

"I know. Tay's been all freaked out about you."

"He has?" I asked, worried about my brother. I knew Jobelle struggled with my condition, but Tay... had he been more concerned than I thought?

"Yes. He says you're on a steroid, and that the side effects are really bad. I'm sorry you have to deal with all that. It must be really hard."

"Thanks," I gushed genuinely. "I'm fine."

"Are you? 'Cause every time I come over, your bedroom door is closed, and Tay says you're asleep. You never used to do that."

"Maybe 'okay' is a better word than 'fine,' but it's not too bad."

"Do you mind talking about it?"

"No. I just don't because no one cares."

"You're my best friend's sister. Tay and I are like brothers. We made up a secret language and had a handshake when we were little. He really loves you, and if anything bad happened to you... it wouldn't be cool for him. So, yeah, of course I care."

I began going through the story of my diagnosis and current treatment. I took off my I Can Beads necklace and showed him what each bead represented, pretending to forget what the orange "catheter and bedpan" beads had represented.

When school was out, Tay and I walked from school to the city's apple tree entrance. Before I got sick, we'd always walked home from there. Now, we decided each day whether or not I felt good enough to make the long hike. My joints hurt- a side effect from a blood pressure medicine called a beta blocker- but I told Tay I was symptom-free.

"So how old is Tomes?" I asked.

"Ten months older than we are, so fourteen and in eighth grade," he answered immediately, and I was glad he hadn't asked why.

"Why?" He asked, suddenly stopping in his tracks.

"Just curious," I replied innocently.

~~~

"You still feeling alright?" Dr. Emilie asked at a routine check-up the next day. "Are you having any prednisone side effects?"

"Everybody says my emotions are crazy," I answered, "and sometimes I get really confused."

"How about swelling?" She felt my ankles. "Good, it's down. Can you feel it- the heaviness?"

"Not as badly as in the past." I thought for a moment." Heaviness- that's a perfect description! How did you know that?"

"Kidney disease seems to run in my family. My mom had lupus nephritis." Dr. Emilie switched subjects. "So, the good news is that there's already a significant decrease in your protein loss. The bad news is your blood pressure and cholesterol are still through the roof, but once you get into remission, everything should stabilize. Now, on to the fun stuff…"

Dr. Emilie reached into the bag she had brought into the room. She pulled out three plastic organizers filled with beads.

"I actually had a few spare hours last night, so I went to the crafts store downtown and made this."

She opened a lid on one of the boxes to reveal a key to the dozens of colorful beads. Rather than reading "radiation" and "spinal tap", all of these plastic beads stood for kidney-related things, including dialysis and prednisone.

"I tried to keep everything you already have the same- white is prednisone, cranberry is lab, blue is clinic, hearts for inpatient nights, and so on- but I added a bunch more. I've already shown the dialysis/transplant child life team, and they love it."

I opened the plastic box, which stored dozens of fancy glass beads labeled "special choice for special stuff" in my doctor's handwriting. There were shapes of every color and size. "You bought all these last night?" I asked in awe.

"Nah- just the plastic ones; I stole the fancy glass beads from oncology's child life storage room."

"They told me the storage room was downstairs, by the adult wings," dad commented, finally speaking from his corner of the room.

"You're right," Dr. Emilie agreed. "Pediatric oncology has their own, as they should."

"So should nephrology," he added.

"And hepatology, cardiology, neurology, pulmonary, hematology, and everybody else," Dr. Emilie continued. "You can thank a fellow NS kid for the playroom over on the transplant floor. She was so hyper on the pred that they practically built the thing for her."

My heart dropped. "So she needed a transplant?"

"Oh, gosh, no- she was in and out of remission for ten years before the minimal change finally decided to get lost. She's almost completely normal today. They put the playroom by the transplant ward because those kids are considered 'sicker' than 'regular' kidney kids."

"Aren't they?"

She shrugged. "It depends on the patient. Anyway, you're leaving a legacy in this hospital as well- the other kidney kids can thank you for the I Can Beads Nephrology Program."

She let me pick a glass bead for helping spread awareness of kidney disease by participating in the new program. I chose an orange bead with a smiley face because it was cute.

The regular cute, not the Tomes kind of cute.

Wednesday, April 2, 2008

Before I'd gotten sick, I learned academic stuff at school. After my first hospitalization, I taught myself "survival skills."

"When you say you couldn't 'make it', what did you mean," my friend Amanda asked kindly. I looked up from my Spanish notebook, pleasantly surprised that someone was talking to me about my illness. People very rarely asked me questions, and when they did, it was often sarcastic things like, "have you ever tried to steal drugs from the cabinets when you're in the hospital?" I was willing, even eager, to talk about my experiences, so any serious question was more than welcome, no matter how stupid it may have seemed. I must have looked shocked, as if I didn't understand her, because she clarified. "I mean, at the beginning of biology I heard you tell Kris you couldn't make it all the way through the mall in Little Rock. Does that mean you threw up, or passed out, or something else?"

I smiled, my uncomfortably swollen cheeks rising and, therefore, cutting off more than half of my vision.

"I usually feel like I'm going to throw up," I explained. "I always have this pain in my feet and legs when I walk, but I can push myself pretty far. Sometimes it's hard to breathe, but I ignore that. When I 'don't make it', it means I literally cannot take another step or another deep breath, depending on the situation."

"What do you do?" She asked.

"Sit immediately, even if it's on the floor," I said. "After a couple minutes, I get up."

I didn't mention getting up was an incredible struggle. Once I'd "crashed," it was only a matter of time before it happened again. To compensate, I had memorized every possible place to sit down in every store I visited, just in case.

On one boring stay-home day, I decided to call my grandma, just to talk. At first, she thought that something was wrong, but when she learned I just wanted to say hi, she became very happy. Anytime I didn't go to school, I called her, and we would talk for about an hour or two. She was one of the many gifts God gave me to combat what I finally understood was a potentially life-threatening illness.

Sleepy Friend- Squeaky's POV
Takes Place: April 2008

My name is Squeaky. I'm in third grade. I like soccer and singing, but my favorite thing in the world is swimming. Fishing is fun, too. My favorite color is blue-green, and if I could have a super power, I'd fly. If I could do anything in the world, I'd be an Olympic swimmer, but unfortunately, imaginaries and penguins aren't allowed, and I'm both. So I'd settle for swimming in the ocean.

I'm a penguin chick, but I look like an Emperor adult. That's because I have nephrotic syndrome. That means my kidneys are sick. My medicines made my swim feathers grow in early.

I live with a group of penguins in an igloo, but sometimes, I go to the Newbrey's apartment. One day, I came over after school. I wanted to say hi to Kitti because she had missed school for several days. It didn't go too well. Kitti's nose was bleeding, so I ended upstairs. Tayoe was supposed to be playing video games with me, but he just sat on the stairs listening to what was going on.

My friend, Kitti, has nephrotic syndrome... just like me! I'm in remission and almost totally normal, but her nephrotic syndrome is "awake". She's sort of normal right now, but sometimes, her diseased kidneys make her awfully sick.

"Squeaky!" I heard our friend Annie call my name. (She has nephrotic syndrome, too! Her kind is called FSGS. My kind is called minimal change.)

"Squeaky!" I tobogganed down the hallway as quickly as I could.

My friend Kitti was on the comfy chair. She didn't feel good. I heard the blood pressure machine hug her wing- I mean, arm. I hopped onto the soft recliner to get a look. Her blood

181

pressure numbers read 189/111.

That's really high.

"Well, that's better, but it's still above the safety level," Mr. Newbrey said. He held out a little white pill to Kitti. "You need to swallow this, princess."

Kitti shook her head.

I knew that little white pill!

"That's my sleepy friend!" I shouted, happy that I could recognize a pill.

Annie picked me up. "See? Squeaky has taken clonidine, haven't you, Squeaky?"

I nodded my head many little times, up and down.

"Well," Annie said, "sometimes when I take clonidine, it makes me feel confused. Kitti's worried about what that feels like. Do you think you could tell her?"

"I call it my sleepy friend," I said. "It can make you feel like you're moving your wings when you aren't. It makes you feel tired, and once, I hallucinated and saw lots of bubbles. But that's it! You just take it- it doesn't taste icky like prednisone- and then you just close your eyes and take a nap. And that's why I call it my sleepy friend."

Squeaky- Jobelle's POV
Takes Place: April 2008

"... And that's why I call it my sleepy friend," Squeaky answered. Kitti turned the pill in her fingers one more time before she put it in her mouth and swallowed. Annie and dad praised Kitti, for her bravery, and Squeaky, for her help. Dad, Annie, and Kitti decided it would be best for Kitti to sleep through the medicine's effects in her own bed. When they began to walk past the kitchenette and up the stairs, Tayoe and I shut the door and dodged backward, pretending we hadn't been eavesdropping.

"When is it going to be over?" Tayoe asked.

"It takes time," a high-pitched voice chimed. I looked down to see Squeaky at my feet, looking up at me with her beady penguin eyes. "Nephrotic syndrome doesn't go away fast. A lot of sicknesses last a while- like cancer and rheumatoid arthritis and Crohns and heart disease and so many more. Some never totally go away, but things can get better with time and treatments and stuff." She shuffled her little feet. "I've been in and out of remission lots of times. When I'm in remission or partial remission, I'm almost totally normal, just with a few pills to take in the morning and a couple of foods I can't eat. Sometimes I am totally normal, with no medicines or side effects or anything! There are times things are different, like when I have to go to the hospital, but even then, I'm still me. Anyway, I'm gonna go swimming now. Wanna come?"

Tayoe wanted to play a videogame in his room, but I agreed to go with Squeaky.

"Let me ask my dad if I can…" I began, wondering where in the Underground City I was going to take this sweet kid- or, penguin.

"Oh, I already did!" Squeaky announced happily. I was surprised when she led me to our family's bathtub.

"It needs to be eighteen inches deep," she instructed. "Cold water please."

I turned on the faucet and waited for the "pool" to fill. Squeaky stood in the bottom of the tub, smiling gleefully as the water rose around her.

"What was your longest time without taking medicines?" I asked the flightless bird.

"From the day before Valentine's Day to the day the leaves turned yellow and red. It was winter, spring, summer, and a little bit of fall, too! That was the best year ever!"

"That's probably February to October, not a whole year," I commented.

She shook her head. "I meant a whole year in seasons... that's Valentine's Day and Easter and spring break and ALL of summer break and the first day of school and the fair! See, I've had nephrotic syndrome since I was a baby chick. Before I knew how to say the days of the week and the months of the year, I knew the order of seasons and holidays. That's how I told time back then. I knew that my illness would usually only wake up for a season or two at the most. I learned how to love every day, even the bad days."

"What was the longest time the disease was...?" I started to ask.

"Awake?" Squeaky finished. "Right after its longest time asleep- from the fall equinox to Halloween... and I mean the next Halloween, not the one that happened a few weeks later. I went trick-or-treating in the hospital those years. But I'm in remission now. Maybe it won't come back this time! It can't keep relapsing and remission-ing forever, right?"

"I hope not," I answered. "Are you on any medicines now?"

"Prednisone," Squeaky said sadly. "I'm steroid dependant. That means I can't stop taking the prednisone because the disease could come back. But my new nephrologist and pediatrician and veterinarian want to find another medicine- a steroid sparing agent- I could try instead of the prednisone. Prednisone makes my blood sugary and my bones weak."

The water was up to her waist, and she began splashing her wings. "What I'd like more than anything is to swim in the ocean," Squeaky said. "Or be an Olympic swimmer or diver, or maybe fly. I'm not sure what I want my dream to be."

"Your dream?"

She nodded her head several times. "You know the dream people? They make one of your dreams come true. I've applied a couple times, but I've always been told no. My kidneys work well because of the medicines, so I always get denied. Hey, wanna see me go slow?" The water level was at her neck, so she was able to duck underwater and swim at an incredibly fast speed.

"You're fast."

She giggled, making a unique penguin sound. "You think that was fast? That was nothing! Just wait!"

Squeaky was right. She was fast, even for a penguin. When the water was deep enough, she flew around like an underwater jet. You never would have guessed she had been battling nephrotic syndrome on and off throughout her life.

I hoped Kitti and Annie would be the same way. Maybe someday, we would never guess that they had once faced such difficult physical challenges.

Friday, May 9, 2008

Time is a strange thing, especially when you're sick. It either flies or creeps by slower than a snail.

I anxiously awaited the end of the school year. Thanks to prednisone and anemia, concentrating was nearly impossible when I took the lengthy state standardized English tests. The only writing that seemed easy was the PFA.

Best Summer Ever! – Kitti's POV
Takes Place: May and June 2008

"Hey, Kitti," Dr. Emilie said with a gigantic smile on her face as she entered the exam room. She handed me a thick folder with the words COMPLETE REMISSION carefully written on it. There was a purple, heart-shaped bead taped to the front.

"Let's start tapering you off those steroids, shall we?"

"All the way off?" I asked. I had only seen Annie's case of nephrotic syndrome, so I didn't know what a "good" case looked like.

"Within a few months, yes."

I squealed and hugged daddy, but then a very scary thought hit me.

"Dr. Emilie?" I asked. "What if it comes back?"

She shook her head. "We'll cross that bridge if we come to it. For now..."

"No," I said quietly. "I promise I won't worry about it, but I need to know. If you don't tell me, I'll probably imagine something so much worse."

Dr. Emilie raised her eyebrows and smiled. "Good for you," she commented. "If you were to relapse, I'd schedule a biopsy. You'd be sedated, so you wouldn't feel a thing. My guess is you have minimal change disease. Since you respond well to corticosteroids, I think we'd redo a prednisone course."

"If it doesn't work…"

"We'd go from there, depending on the diagnosis. But for now, I want you to go home. Have the best summer ever. Eat whatever you want, within reason. Go on vacation, spend time with friends, and enjoy life. Celebrate!" She patted my back. "You did it, and I'm so proud of you."

She gave me a glass smiley face bead and a t-shirt. I unfolded it.

"Remission accomplished," I read out loud.

"Let me guess- pediatric oncology storage room?" Dad wondered.

Dr. Emilie nodded.

June and July 2008

The school year ended, lifting one of my biggest burdens. As more and more protein was lost through my urine, the water weight was slowly coming back. My kidney function was okay, so although the side effects of cyclosporine were awful, I had to remain on the drug.

Before kidney disease, I had been pretty. I didn't outwardly brag, but I was conceited enough to think I was good-looking. Between the medicines and the disease, my appearance changed drastically. I hated my prednisone-induced "moon face", especially when referred to as "chipmunk cheeks." The loose-fitting glasses I had gotten in June 2007 dug into the sides of my head by July 2008.

Cyclosporine caused an overgrowth of hair everywhere! It grew so quickly that my mom frequently used an electric razor to shave my legs, arms, and face. In contrast, the hair on my head fell out in clumps. Sometimes, I could pull it out by the handful.

"You're not going bald," my mom assured me. "It's just thinning."

She was right. I didn't mind losing half the volume of my very thick hair. I had planned on eventually getting it thinned anyway. Depending on my dosage of steroids, it grew differently. It could be straight, wavy, or curly at any given time. It grew in blonde for a month or so, giving me highlights that eventually disappeared.

It's difficult to describe how my swollen body felt. For a lack of a better illustration, it was like there were a million fists under my skin trying to punch their way out. I was afraid to bend my elbows and knees, because I had an irrational fear that my skin would burst like a balloon, causing my bones to break through. This fear combined with my extreme fatigue made it almost impossible to sit on the floor. If I did manage it, it was equally impossible to stand up.

Even so, I volunteered to teach children's church for about eight weeks. I loved working with those kids so much that there were times when I forgot I had kidney disease. Believe it or not, I'd actually wonder why I felt like I was dying. Several times, I dropped to my knees to talk to a child or lead an activity. After I struggled to get up, I would be out of breath for at least an hour. No matter how much I loved my 'job', my symptoms never went away.

I did think about my faith during those times. I often wondered why I had FSGS- why not some other disease, one that had a cure or at least a standard treatment. I never questioned "why me". My reasoning was simple... why not me? In fact, I was glad it was me instead of anyone else in my family.

My family was amazing. There are tons of awful stories of how families with a "sick kid" spiral out of control. Divorces are common. Parents do things they never would have considered before their child became ill. "Good kid" siblings become drug addicts. "Bad kid" siblings end up in jail. Thankfully, none of those things happened to us. Even so, I learned that a family with a seriously ill member cannot completely escape unscathed. There were conflicts that arose, as small as they were. Dynamics changed, even though they were hardly noticeable to an outside observer. We went from no quarrels ever to an occasional squabble. We never broke, but we acquired a hairline fracture or two.

My life was very hard, but it wasn't agony. In fact, having kidney disease made me appreciate each joyful moment that much more.

I had gotten a video camera for my sixteenth birthday, so I videotaped everything... and I mean everything! From Todd racing the clock to see how many French fries he could shove into his mouth to the Fourth of July fireworks, everything was captured on film.

Besides the nephrology clinic and local super-center store, I went to the local amusement park. Visiting my childhood "summer escape" made me feel normal, even if I couldn't stay at the park for longer than ninety minutes. We stayed mostly in the water park areas, and I challenged myself to make it to the top of the waterslide tower once or twice at each visit. The downside was the pool's chlorine that turned my skin orange. We never exactly figured out why, but we assumed it had to do with the medications in my body mixed with the chemicals in the chorine and sunscreen. Changing to an all-natural infant sunscreen seemed to help.

People-watching during these excursions expanded my ideas for PFA adventures.

Jobelle's POV– Takes Place: July 2008

A busload of PFA citizens and I went to Awesome Happy Fun World's new water park every Thursday. I loved water almost as much, if not more, than dancing. It was my job to watch out for Tayoe, Tomas, Kitti, and Tomas' eleven-year-old sister Tori as we tackled the various water slides. I would have ridden the slides anyway, so I didn't mind keeping an eye out for my siblings and their friends. The dynamics of the quartet were rather cute, especially when Kitti and Tomes began to flirt.

When we were finished with the water slides, which usually occurred about halfway through each trip, dad accompanied the preteens to the pools. I was free to go wherever I wanted within the gates. Usually, I followed other PFA members from a distance, just to see what everyone else did. Squeaky loved the wave pool ("because it's like the ocean") and open-air tower slides ("because it's like flying with water"). Pepper tagged along, even though she hated water. Each time, without fail, she'd start off on the sandy beach play area. Within an hour, she'd end up shouting "DIE OF HEAT," jump into the nearest pool's deep end, and need to be rescued by a lifeguard.

"We're technically inside," I told Pepper one day. "It's not too hot here."

"DIE OF BOREDOM, THEN," Pepper answered. Reasoning with Pepper is like reasoning with Kitti on high-dose prednisone; it's not worth it.

Friday, August 8, 2008

I zoned out a lot that summer. Your average person thinks of *something* while in la-la land, but I would stare into space with my mind totally blank. Even when I was completely engaged in something, I would space out. This was one of the reasons I avoided learning how to drive. Just in case my medicated brain suddenly wanted me to stare at the sun for a while, I didn't want to risk that I'd be behind the wheel.

Light was so pretty during that time. It made me feel happy. I was especially captivated by the tiny floor lights in movie theater aisles that stay lit while the film is rolling. I went to see a kid's movie with some friends in late July. One of the girls had to keep telling me to look at the really big light with the moving picture on it. I actually told her the little lights were more entertaining. I would always joke around before I got sick, so whether she believed me is a mystery. For the record, I was dead serious.

"When You Hate Your Job"- Kitti's POV
Takes Place: Friday, August 15, 2008

I was on 12.5 mg of prednisone and feeling great. I had monthly labs and visits to the clinic, but everything seemed fine. School was going to begin on Monday, and although I would miss Closet Elementary and Middle School, I was excited about starting at a large junior high.

I had a doctor's appointment before lunch, so we assumed it would only take a few minutes. When my doctor knocked and opened the door, I knew something was wrong.

"How're you doing, Kitti?" Dr. Emilie asked.

"Fine," I answered slowly. "Why?"

"Really fine? No swelling, foamy urine…"

"No," I whined.

"Okay," she said slowly, taking my hands. "There is protein in your urine again. You're losing about the same amount that you were at your diagnosis in March. Your creatinine and BUN are a little elevated- 1.4 and 38 respectively- and everything else is indicative of nephrotic syndrome."

"No," I repeated. My eyes blurred with tears. I reached for daddy, who held me tightly.

Dr. Emilie looked back and forth, from my dad to me. "I want to redo the tests before you go home, but most likely, this is a relapse. I am so, so, sorry."

"I don't want to do it again! I don't want to do it again!" I cried.

"I know," Dr. Emilie said quietly.

"No, you don't!" I screamed.

"Kitti…" Daddy spoke gently.

"It's okay," Dr. Emilie answered. "You're so brave, Kitti," she said sincerely. "You've probably kicked this thing close to a dozen times before. You can do it again."

"Is this when you hate your job?" I asked, trying to take the focus off of my teary eyes.

"I love my job," she stated. "I hate relapses."

I wiped away my tears with the back of my hand. Dr. Emilie handed me a soft tissue for my nose and pulled a huge plastic box out from behind her back.

"Pick a relapse bead, Kit," she said sweetly. I found a bead with purple and white bumps.

"So what's the plan?" I asked, trying to calm down. "Is it like you said? More prednisone?"

"For now, yes," Dr. Emilie assured me. "I want to get a biopsy as soon as possible, but it will probably take a few weeks because you aren't an emergency case. When we get the results, we might change your treatment, but my guess is still minimal change disease"

"Should we be able to get her back into remission?" Daddy asked.

"I can't promise you anything, but because she's

responded so well to prednisone, it's hopeful she will again."

I had to go back to the lab to redo my blood work. They also scheduled me for a biopsy in the first week of September.

I didn't want to tell Belle and Tay, but I didn't want to dump that responsibility on dad, either. It wasn't easy, but I managed to give them the news.

"I'll tell Tomes," Tay said while excusing himself. I think he probably cried before he made that phone call. Belle pretended to be brave, but she locked herself in her room and must have texted Graham and Annie for hours.

On Saturday morning, I started 50 milligrams of prednisone once again.

"Round two has begun," I joked with Annie and Squeaky.

Monday, August 18, 2008

On the first day of school, I literally bounded into the car with high hopes for my junior year. My goal was to go to school four days a week, skipping Wednesdays, with the principal's approval, and doing as much in band as possible.

Unfortunately, the four-day plan only lasted one week. Between the swelling, exhaustion, dizziness, and lack of concentration, I was doing great to get in two days per week.

My biggest motivation was band. Playing clarinet was difficult for someone who was swollen, but it was one area in which I still excelled. I had been very familiar with the instrument before becoming sick. As long as we were playing the old band stand tunes that didn't change much from year to year, I could be a pro. I didn't march much, but I did show up for two of the football season's home games and even one of our away games. It was painful and exhausting, but it was worth it. My band director understood and treated me as if I had never missed a day.

I quickly learned who my real friends were. I was a part several groups of "band buddies"- kids who had their own 'circle of friends' but became inseparable while at band practices and events. These guys, especially the two clarinetists who usually ended up beside me from chair tryouts, included me whenever they could. It was as if I wasn't sick, although we all knew differently.

There were several cliques who seemed to ignore me, but that was okay. I later found out many of those kids had been talking about me, and everything said was kind and caring. They simply didn't know what to say. There was a freshman who made fun of me, but he annoyed everyone anyway. One of my fellow clarinetists verbally pummeled him.

I actually became closer to friends I hadn't talked with since elementary school. An old pal from sixth grade was the first to show concern if we happened to bump into each other in the hall. He and his brother prayed for me every night, and that meant the world to me.

And just as I'd expected, Kris never left my side anytime I showed up, although I had this weird instinct to protect her from what was really happening.

One afternoon, I decided to keep track of the days I was able to attend school. I printed a school year calendar and marked each date with one of three crayon colors- green if I made it through an entire day, yellow if I made it to school at all, and red if I didn't attend.

There were a lot of reds on that chart, but I somehow managed to stay caught up with my schoolwork.

Kitti's POV- Takes Place August 2008

By the first day of school, my nephrotic syndrome symptoms had returned, and sure enough, my daily albumin dipstick tests showed plus 4. I gained weight quickly, but this time, I wasn't hungry at all.

Regardless of how I felt, I went to school. The junior high included seventh through ninth grades, so Tomes, Tay, and I were in the same building. They looked out for me, and with their help, I was able to be pretty normal until Friday, August 29.

When I woke up on that particular day, I was so swollen that it hurt to move. I "rushed" to check my urine, and not only did it read plus 4, but it was tinged pink.

"Blood," I whispered to dad, terrified.

"Okay," daddy told me. "Go to your room and shut the door until I get Tay and Belle to school. The minute they're gone, we're going to the hospital."

I did as I was told, listening carefully to the routine sounds of breakfast. Daddy acted amazingly calm, but I knew he was internally panicking. He told my siblings that I wasn't feeling well and that he wanted to take me to the doctor, but he made no mention of the hospital.

My nose began bleeding when I heard the school bus pull up to the apartment complex. I grabbed a tissue and leaned forward, doing my best to stay composed.

"It's okay," I whispered to myself.

"Daddy!" I called as the bus rolled away. "My nose is kind of bleeding a lot."

We didn't call an ambulance, but dad drove at lightning speed to the emergency room. We didn't wait for long. Actually, we didn't wait at all, which surprised and frightened me.

"Hey," the man at the sign-in desk spoke into a walky-talky, "we have a little girl with kidney disease having a nosebleed out here. Her dad says there was visible blood in her urine this morning. You want to come out here and get her?"

In a less than a minute, a nurse showed up with a wheelchair. When the nurse took my blood pressure, she gasped and refused to let me see what it was, although the rest of the emergency department seemed very interested.

"She takes clonidine?" Someone shouted at daddy.

"For blood pressure over 180/110," Daddy answered.

"So should we give her, like, two?" An obviously-inexperienced intern asked. I told him 'no' before anyone even responded. Someone started an IV in my hand and gave me an IV push. I searched the crowd for Rachel, the ER nurse who had seen me at diagnosis, but she was nowhere to be found.

A phlebotomist drew my blood and did a strange test that involved using a device to make a tiny cut in my upper arm.

"We're checking how well your blood clots," the lady told me.

Within thirty minutes, Dr. Emilie rushed into the emergency room.

"Thanks for the wake-up call, Kit," Dr. Emilie joked. "Looks like you freaked some people out this morning. BP 201/138? My gosh! What are you trying to do? Give me a heart attack?"

She examined my heart, lungs, abdomen, and ankles.

"I'm a water balloon," I said, looking at my swollen legs.

"Well, you're a very pretty water balloon. Let's take your BP again."

As the machine was pumping, she silently handed me several beads, each representing emergency room visits and blood draws. The machine beeped. The results showed that my blood pressure had "plummeted" to 137/92.

Dr. Emilie breathed in relief. "So, it seems the prednisone isn't working. The protein in your urine has increased significantly, so the albumin in your blood is alarmingly low. It's expected that you'd have a few red blood cells in your urine with nephrotic syndrome. There were more than typical, but with all the protein you're losing, I'm not surprised. The good news is you aren't in acute kidney failure; that was my worry when they paged me. Your creatinine is very good... normal, surprisingly. Your BUN isn't great, but it isn't bad considering you had a malignant hypertension episode a few minutes ago. I'm pretty sure that's why your nose was bleeding."

"What's the bad news?" I asked. "There's always bad news."

Dr. Emilie sighed. "Kitti," she asked slowly, "can I speak to your dad for a second?"

"Why?" I asked.

"Kit, you have to trust me," she said. "Listen, I promise you aren't dying. Death isn't even remotely likely, and we won't even bring it up, but there are some things I need to discuss with your father before I tell you, alright?"

"Okay," I reluctantly agreed. They were only gone for a few minutes when they returned. Neither looked sad or afraid, but even so, there was something scary about the mood in the room.

"Here's the deal," Dr. Emilie said. "I need to run a biopsy to see exactly what's going on in your kidneys. It's not the most fun thing in the world, but they'll give you medicine so you won't feel a thing. The sedation will make you drowsy; you'll probably fall asleep, but even if you don't, you won't have a clue what's going on. If you do, you won't care."

"So what's the problem?" I asked.

"It seems that whatever underlying disease you have has worsened. Whatever it is, we need to treat it quickly, but we can't until we know what it is," Dr. Emilie explained slowly. "The problem is that I'm not sure what happened this morning. Everything indicates that your blood clots great, and it seems that your kidneys aren't further damaged beyond what the NS has done. We can assume that your blood pressure sky-rocketed because you have such a low serum albumin level, and we can assume that's why your nose bled, but I don't like assuming things... at least, not right before a renal biopsy."

"Why not?"

"All kidney biopsies have risks," Dr. Emilie explained. "Some people bleed a little. Some people bleed a lot. In less than one percent of patients, the biopsied kidney shuts down. When there's a possibility that the patient has a bleeding issue or injured kidney, the risks increase."

"So we have to biopsy my kidneys, but it's not safe?" I asked.

"It's safe," Dr. Emilie assured me, "but your risk of complications is higher. It's a catch 22. Your dad and I have decided to admit you to Penguin Unit. We're going to monitor you for the next 24 hours. During that time, we'll run a non-invasive kidney scan called a DMSA, give you lots of IV albumin, and see what happens. If all goes well, we'll do a biopsy tomorrow and go from there."

"Do you still think it's minimal change?"

"I don't know," Dr. Emilie replied. "We'll find out soon enough."

Jobelle's POV- Takes Place Friday, August 29, 2008

I walked out of the high school and headed to where the school buses were lined up. I'd be the lone PFA kid onboard until we stopped by the junior high and elementary schools, where more familiar faces would join me.

It had been another dull, terrible day at school. So far, I absolutely hated my senior year. It was as if everything was falling apart. Academically, I was already behind. I was about to head to dance class, which unfortunately, was no longer the escape it had once been. As high school seniors, the competition was ramping up.

I realized I wasn't excelling anymore... but it wasn't because I wasn't good. I had become too good. I was missing too many rehearsals. My instructors were ticked at me, and I could hardly blame them. At the same time, I knew what I was doing... keeping Annie company from three to five... was the right thing to do. It was the only thing I could do that, indirectly, helped my sister.

I also knew my natural talent was the only thing keeping me from being kicked out of the dance program.

My cell phone vibrated.

"Hello?"

"Hi, Belle," my dad said. I could hear beeping in the background and recognized the sound of a heart monitor, which was becoming all-too familiar between Annie and Kitti's recent "adventures."

"What's going on?"

"Kit's okay, but we're at UCMC again. She swelled up last night, so they're giving her albumin."

I felt like someone had punched me in the stomach. "It's worse, isn't it?"

"Honey, she's in good hands. Listen, I'm going to have

someone come get you after dance. Don't worry about Kitti; I wouldn't have even told you, but I wanted you to know not to expect me."

"Who's coming?"

"I haven't had time to figure that out yet, but I promise, I'll think of someone."

Once upon a time, walking home would have been fine, but with the recent threats and heightened security of the city, even I knew walking home was foolish, especially after my misadventure with Graham.

So suddenly Princess Kitti runs the show, and I'm an afterthought, I almost said. Thankfully, I caught myself before a word slipped from my tongue. That accusation wasn't fair. Kitti was sick; Tay and I were suffering as her siblings, but as her father, how much more must he be hurting?

"Okay," I said quietly. "Thank you."

"You're welcome." His unsteady voice hitched. "I love you so much, Belle."

"Love you, too. Bye."

I clicked the phone shut.

It's worse, I thought. It must be worse.

I stood like a statue at my bus door while dozens of kids got in before me. Opening my cell again, I scrolled through my contact list and selected Graham's name.

"Hey, Belle…"

"Shut up," I told him harshly. "What do you know?"

"About what?"

I rolled my eyes. "About Kittina! Hasn't my dad talked to someone? You know how gossipy people are!"

"Belle, go to dance…"

"No," I said firmly. "Listen, the school bus heading toward the studio is leaving soon. You tell me what I want to know, or I'll let it leave…"

"She swelled out this morning. I don't know exactly what's

going on, but she has a biopsy scheduled for tomorrow."

My heart fell. She wasn't supposed to have a biopsy until next week. Why had it gotten pushed to tomorrow?

"You alright?" Graham asked after I was silent for a few seconds.

"No," I answered. "But thank you."

"Hey, are you coming?" The bus driver shouted to me.

I shook my head, and the bus left.

"Graham, can you come get me?" I asked, fighting to keep a steady voice.

"No, Belle. Your dance teachers…"

"…don't understand me!" I finished. "They don't understand me. They don't care. Nobody cares! My sister is sick and nobody cares! They can kick me out of the studio, I don't care!" I stopped screaming and listened for Graham's reaction.

Silence.

"But you do," I spoke into the phone, not sure if Graham was still listening. "You might not fully understand, but you care, and that's why I need you."

I clicked the phone shut and was surprised when Graham texted me immediately.

Be there in 5 minutes. G

Fifteen minutes later, I leaned my head against the window, watching the vast metropolis roll by. I wasn't in any mood to talk, and Graham knew me well enough to keep quiet.

Once at the hospital, Graham came with me to Kitti's room. We were surprised to find her bed empty.

"She's down in radiology," dad explained before I could panic. "They're doing a scan on her kidneys. It's similar to an x-ray. Why in the world are you here? Your dance teachers…"

"I'm done," I announced suddenly. "I can't do that anymore."

My dad was stunned. "Belle, don't do this. I know this is hard, but Kitti is going to be okay."

"It's not about Kitti," I replied, mostly truthfully.

~~~

Graham and I picked up Tay and brought him to the hospital. On the way, I tried to explain everything I knew about Kitti, but I didn't know much. Graham, Tay, and I ate dinner at the hospital's cafeteria. Tay seemed much more resilient than I felt. Perhaps it was because he was younger or easier-going. Obviously, he was shaken, but compared to me, he took everything in stride.

"I need to go home," Graham told me at about six. "Are you going to be okay?"

"I'm fine," I assured him. "Tomorrow is homecoming. Half the kids are going to be absent, so dad is letting Tay and me stay here. What are your plans?"

"I've gotta get ready for Sunday," he reminded me. Graham had recently become one of the children's ministry leaders at the Annie Room Church. "I'll call you sometime tomorrow afternoon."

Kit was on strict bed rest because of her blood pressure issues, but a child life expert still came to talk about tomorrow's procedure with us. Kitti was amazing; it was as if she had suddenly become braver than me, dad, and Tay combined.

Dad and Tay left at about 8:00 and headed to the hospital hotel. I elected to stay with Kitti for the night.

"You don't have to act brave for me," Kit told me as soon as our guys were gone. "Seeing me hooked up to oxygen, an IV, and a Foley have got to be freaky."

"No," I lied, carefully sitting on the edge of her bed.

A Foley? I thought. *What's a Foley?*

Kitti smiled. "Oxygen," she said, touching the tiny tubes she wore in her nose. "IV." She raised her hand that had a tube attached. "Foley." She pointed off the side of the bed. I looked down to see a jug of urine attached to the frame of the hospital bed. "It's a catheter."

"You're getting too good at this," I said sadly. Kitti only shrugged.

"I'm getting used to it. I'm not afraid of needles anymore, either."

"No?" I asked in surprise.

"They drew my blood and started my IV before we could apply numbing cream to my skin. I was too worried about what was happening to cry over the needle."

"What was happening?"

"My BP- sorry, blood pressure- spiked. It made my nose bleed."

"You're a warrior," I told her, brushing wisps of beautiful blond hair from her puffy face.

"I'm just doing what I have to do," she replied, smiling as if nothing was wrong. "Dad told me you're quitting ballet."

"So?"

"Don't, Belle. Don't do that for me. I don't want you to stop doing anything because I have nephrotic syndrome."

"This isn't about you. The last thing I need right now is to be around people who only care about my stupid skills. Life is too short."

Kitti studied my face, trying to process every word and decode the thoughts running through my mind. "You're right," she said finally. "Life is short. But if you quit, do it for you, not for me. I don't mind adapting my life around my disease, but I don't want nephrotic syndrome to take something away from you, too."

Kitti's POV- Takes Place Tuesday, September 2, 2008

My biopsy on Friday went well, although I couldn't get out of bed for a few days afterwards. Usually, they only make renal biopsy patients stay still for four hours or overnight at most. With my risk, I was stuck until late Sunday afternoon.

Monday was Labor Day, so child life had a big party in a general playroom downstairs. On Penguin Unit, they gave us hamburgers with salt-less seasoning and low-sodium hot dogs.

"How's my favorite patient?" Dr. Emilie asked as she entered my room on Tuesday. She held a thick folder with my records.

"Awful," I said quietly.

Dr. Emilie looked genuinely sad. "I know, Kit."

She did it again! I never liked it when people said they knew what it was like to be chronically ill when there was no way they did, but Dr. Emilie was different. I didn't know why, but it was as if she really did understand. She sat on a rolling chair, pulled herself up to my bed, and handed me another bead. It was a single playing die.

"It's unlucky to get sick," Dr. Emilie told me, reminding me what the bead stood for- a diagnosis. The results of the biopsy were in.

"It's FSGS, isn't it?" I asked.

"Yes." She spun around to look at my dad. "I'm so sorry."

"Is it bad?"

"The sample showed a lot of damage, but it isn't the collapsing variant. I think there's a chance that she could still beat this without needing dialysis or a transplant, but it's going to take some very powerful medications."

"Like what?" I asked. "Cyclosporine or MMF...?"

"How do you feel about trying cyclosporine?"

"A lot better than I do about taking chemo," I answered.

My dad agreed, and I took my first palm-full of pink and red capsules that night.

I stayed in the hospital for eight more days, just because my blood pressure kept acting strange. Dad went back to work during the days, but Annie usually stayed with me. One day, I woke up at noon with hair all over my pillow. Annie tried to casually collect it without me seeing, but I couldn't help but notice.

"It's just thinning," she told me. After several months on cyclosporine, prednisone, and many other medications, Annie had lost at least two thirds of what she had once had, but she could afford to. Goodness, she probably needed to! I know hair, and Annie's hair was probably the thickest I'd ever seen. My hair, on the other hand, was fairly thin. If I was going to lose as much as Annie had, I would likely have bald spots. Tentatively, I ran a hand through my hair, came back with a fistful, and looked at it in horror.

Even with hair loss, I preferred high-dose cyclosporine combined with moderate dose prednisone over the high-dose steroids. I didn't like cyclosporine, but I didn't hate it, either. When I was finally discharged several days later, the protein in my urine had dropped. I wasn't in remission or even partial remission, but I was ready to keep fighting at home.

Thursday, September 4, 2008

When I wasn't doing homework, talking to grandma, or writing, I enjoyed watching the 2008 Presidential race. I cared about politics to an extent, but since I was too young to vote, I watched the current events to understand the endless parodies on the Internet. I actually learned a satirical rap and "performed" it for Barb at Dr. Jones' office.

Autumn took a destructive turn when several hurricanes pounded the Gulf. Nectarwood is too far inland even to get a tropical storm, but the remnants of Hurricanes Gustav and Ike managed to flood roads, down trees, and leave us without electricity for several days. This was not a good thing since living on non-perishable foods is almost impossible on a strict low-sodium, low-potassium diet. There was also something disgusting about taking prednisone by candlelight, although I'm not sure what.

Saturday, October 16, 2008

I'm alive, I thought as I sat up in bed. *I made it through the week! I made it through a severe case of hyperkalemia! Nurse Karen said my potassium was higher than what was compatible for life, and I'm still here! Thank you, God!*

Potassium is an important element. In fact, without potassium, the human body can't function. This electrolyte is vital to many organs, including the heart and muscles. It can be found in many foods with especially high amounts in oranges, potatoes, tomatoes, and bananas.

However, too much potassium can be fatal. Because excess potassium is removed by the kidneys, people with kidney disease are at risk of having too much potassium in their blood.

Since September 2007, I had been instructed to limit potassium-rich foods. I tried to have less than three small servings of potassium-rich foods per day, if my frequent potassium blood tests were good. If my potassium levels were border-line, I would eliminate all potassium "mines" until my results improved, which usually took a day or two.

It was a difficult balance. Low potassium is just as dangerous as high potassium. Diuretics have a bad habit of depleting a patient of potassium. There were a couple of times I had to take supplements because my potassium had gotten too low.

On Tuesday, October 14, I had gone to a field competition with the band. I didn't feel halfway good enough to march, but with my mom's help, I was able to watch the performances. As we climbed the stairs of the bleachers, I noticed a strange pain in the back of my legs. It seemed twice as hard to for my brain to tell my feet to move, as if my knees were rusty door hinges. We left the competition early, and on the way home, I had a strange craving for potato wedges. With all the medicines I was taking, it was rare that I wanted to eat anything, so my mom was determined to feed me. We made a stop at one, then another fast food place. Unbelievably, both were out of virtually all potato products.

Disappointed, I settled for chicken strips.

The next morning, my legs felt even stiffer, but I went to school to take a college entrance exam.

"No one is leaving this room for any reason," the counselor commanded as she handed out the booklets and answer forms.

A girl raised her hand and asked sarcastically.

"Well, what if someone drops dead?"

Everyone laughed, but I felt my heart palpitate. *That's actually not a bad question,* I thought jokingly. After the exam, I forced myself to finish the day. When school was out, we went to the nephrology clinic for my biweekly blood draw.

When I woke up on Thursday, I could hardly move. Without question, I stayed home from school. At noon, the phone rang, and as always, I let it go to voicemail.

"Anna Grace?" My nurse Karen said in the message. "Pick up the phone, sweetheart, I know you're there, there's no way you could have made it to school."

"Hello?" I asked when I reached the phone.

"Anna Grace? Oh, I'm so glad you're responsive!"

Way to be assuring, Karen.

"Your potassium level was 6.9 yesterday."

6.9? Whoa, that was high! Normal was somewhere between 3.5 and 5.2 at our lab, and I remembered how I had once panicked Dr. Jones at 5.9.

"Listen, sweetie. You need to get your parents to pick up the prescription Dr. Jones called into the pharmacy. It should be ready in five minutes or so since he had it on STAT. You need it as soon as possible, because we need to zap that stuff out of your system. This is very, very important."

I thanked her, hung up, and immediately called my mom. My dad brought the prescription home within thirty minutes. Dr. Jones wanted me to drink the entire bottle of syrup as a one-time dose to flush my system, which I did quickly.

God, I prayed as I chugged, *I know hyperkalemia this severe could kill me. Please save me.*

My mom came home with Todd at the usual time. "The

potato wedges," she told me as she entered the door. "Oh, Anna Grace, the potato wedges..."

I gasped as realization dawned on me. With insanely high potassium levels, a few French fries possibly meant the difference between life and death.

In other words, if both of those drive-through restaurants hadn't been out of their signature side item, I probably would have died.

"Thank you, God," I had prayed out loud.

It was the strangest miracle I had ever heard of, but I was glad to have been a part of it.

Rachel- Kitti's POV
Takes Place: Sunday, October 5, 2008

There were a lot of bad things happening. The previous week, little Squeaky had relapsed, even though her prednisone dose hadn't changed. She began taking cyclosporine, and fortunately, it made her feel a lot better. It also suppressed her immune system, making it unsafe for her to continue living with the large penguin colony. She lived with us for a while, but with daddy working during the day, her doctors wanted to find a nurse who would be willing to be a short-term foster parent.

"Nobody wants me!" Squeaky had cried at a clinic appointment.

"It isn't that no one wants you," Dr. Emilie told her. "It's just that we need to find a safe place for you to live until you get better. The Annie Room Church is hiring a campus nurse to be around for their worship services and special events. The church will pay her to take care of you, too. Mr. Newbrey wants you close by, so the PFA has offered her a free apartment. You and Kitti will be neighbors."

Squeaky was unlucky to have to move, but she was more fortunate than me when it came to cyclosporine results. Her swelling decreased significantly while my weight continued to climb.

"Do you think you could wait this out for about four more weeks?" Dr. Emilie asked. "I don't want you to be completely miserable, but this could work if we give it enough time. It usually takes a few weeks for cyclosporine to help."

I agreed, partly because I was afraid that the next step could be chemotherapy. My hair was falling out enough on an immunosuppressant. The last thing my scalp needed was actual chemo.

"It's not so bad," Tomes' sister Tori told me at church after Sunday school. "I don't think it's thinning."

I gently tugged on a handful of hair and lost half of what I had touched.

Tori smiled too brightly. "You can always braid my hair, you know. You're so good at hairstyles."

"Kitti?" A vaguely familiar voice called.

I turned to see my dad standing next to a red-headed woman.

"Rachel!" I exclaimed, remembering the emergency room nurse who had been with me the night I was diagnosed. "Remember me?"

"Of course!" Rachel said, spreading her arms for a hug. "How could I forget my favorite patient?"

"I got into remission last summer, but I relapsed."

"Your dad told me," she said sympathetically. "I'm so sorry about that. How are you feeling?"

"I'm fine. What are you doing here?"

"This is my job," she told me. "The Annie Room Church needed a nurse on staff, so here I am."

"You're going to be Squeaky's guardian?" I questioned.

"Yes, for as long as she needs me. I hear we're going to be neighbors! You know, if you ever stay home when Annie is in school, be sure to visit me. I'm getting paid a lot to take care of Squeaky and show up here on Sundays. Between that and the free lodging, I figured I'd buy a few cool things for our new place. Come upstairs and check out the technology sometime."

"Okay," I said with dad's approval.

"Great!" Rachel gleamed.

Squeaky went home with Rachel that afternoon. The penguin called me around dinnertime. I was afraid she'd be upset, that maybe she didn't like Rachel or something had gone wrong. Of course, that wasn't the case.

"Rachel is the best human in the world!" Squeaky exclaimed. "I was scared that she wouldn't know what it's like to feel sick. I know she's a nurse, but sometimes, people don't really understand. Well, Rachel knows 'cause her husband died from liver disease a few years ago. Anyway, she wants to know if you guys want to come over for dinner- we're having fried cod and onion rings. It's kidney-friendly, 'cause we're not putting any salt in the fish fry batter! It's just flour and red pepper! You can eat it, too!"

Our family made a great friend that evening. Rachel became an "official" part of the PFA in no time. After that, anytime Annie went to school, I spent the day at Rachel's "house."

Trying Times- Kitti's POV
Takes Place: Friday, October 17, 2008

I sat in Rachel's living room, staring out the window that overlooked the sidewalk and street. Graham entered the apartment and grabbed one of the wrapped candies that sat beside me on the couch.

"Hey!" I exclaimed, grabbing the rest of my mints with both hands and guarding them protectively. "That chocolate-covered mint patty happens to have albumin in it. Amazing things happen when you read the ingredients. No sodium, either." I tossed another candy at him and giggled when it bounced off his face. He picked it up, tossed it back, and stared out the window. *Aw,* I thought.

"Four minutes," I said innocently. Graham turned to look at me. I stood up weakly "Oh, don't give me that face," I said. "The school bus comes in four- now three- minutes. Belle will be here in three minutes."

"Why would I care?" He asked. I shook my head and leaned against his arm. When Tayoe was at school, Graham was one of the people who took care of me. He was practically my big brother... and I hoped someday in the far future he would be.

"You care about Belle because you like her."

"We're best friends..."

"Yeah, and that's great, but honestly, Graham. You told me that kid at school thought I was psychic because I noticed so many things. I don't need a lie detector."

"I know," he agreed. "So, what do you think? Is it that obvious?"

"I'm gonna say yes."

"Do you think Belle knows?"

Before I could say anything, we heard the bus pull up to the apartment complex, and I knew something was wrong.

The entire group of PFA kids rushed off the bus, except for Tayoe, Tomes, Jobelle, and Squeaky.

Graham picked me up and carried me outside.

Poor Squeaky's little face was unrecognizably swollen. Tears seeped out two little slits where her eyes were supposed to be.

"Jo-Jo," the little chick cried to my sister, who cradled the inflated bird lovingly.

"Squeaky, what happened?" I asked, carefully taking her from Belle's arms and into my own.

"They were calling her names," Belle explained angrily. Tayoe had a hand on her shoulder. It was probably the only thing that kept her fiery temper under control.

"Like 'fat face' and 'chipmunk cheeks,'" the little one blubbered.

"Oh, but you're beautiful," I told her.

"BYE, UGLIST PENGUIN IN THE WORLD!" A scrawny-looking raccoon screamed through an opened window on the moving school bus.

My sister always has the best intentions, but she doesn't always think before she acts. Okay, so she rarely thinks before she acts. I'm glad I had the foresight to cover Squeaky's unseen ear canals, because as I had anticipated, Jobelle exploded. As the bus rolled away, she colorfully told the raccoon to never say such things again.

Tomes laughed in shock.

"It's not funny!" I scolded, pushing Squeaky into my brother's arms. "Take her to Rachel! I'll be there in a few minutes."

The bus stopped. It burned my lungs and legs, but I forced myself to run a couple paces to where Jobelle stood.

"You can't do that!" I told her. "When you say stuff like that, how are you any better than the bully himself?"

Guilt hit her, as it always does, as the livid driver got off the bus. Dad came running out of the apartment complex.

"You and your father need to report to the principal's office at 4:30 this afternoon," she said before getting back on the bus and driving away.

"Hey, daddy," I said after glancing at my watch. It was 3:37.

"Hello, princess. How are you feeling?"

"I'm okay," I said, hugging him. We walked into the building, arm in arm, with Jobelle following slowly behind us. I wished I could hold her close and thank her for standing up for Squeaky, but I knew now was not the time.

I Can't Do This Anymore- Jobelle's POV
Takes Place: Friday, October 17, 2008

Don't cry, I told myself, although the tears threatened to spill. *Don't cry. What's done is done.*

"Get in my car, Jobelle," dad ordered in an eerily neutral tone. I did as I was told, desperately trying to hold back the tears.

Dad stayed inside the apartment complex for at least fifteen minutes. When he finally got into the driver's seat, he didn't put his keys in the ignition or even buckle up. Instead, he turned to me. His face looked like he had been crying.

"I'm sorry," I apologized in a whisper.

"I know, honey," he said with a gentle nod. "The last few months have been very hard for all of us. I'm proud of you for sticking up for Squeaky. I'm upset with myself for not helping you better navigate these difficult times."

"You're the best dad in the world," I told him. "I'm the one who screw…"

His facial expression didn't change, but it was as if the light in his eyes faded in sorrow. "…messed up," I corrected myself. "How is that your fault?"

He smiled sadly and pushed a loose wisp of my hair behind my ear. "Out of the overflow of the heart, the mouth speaks," he quoted. "Honey, if you feel the need to say such vile things, you're obviously feeling very angry inside. Am I right?"

I bobbed my head hesitantly. "I was mad at that little kid who was saying awful things to Squeaky…"

"… and you set such a good example by saying such wonderfully affirming things back," he quipped sarcastically. He drew in a deep breath and closed his eyes, as if he had regretted what he had said, and turned back to his gentle tone. "Belle, do you think your words will stop the teasing?"

"No, sir," I whispered.

"I'm sorry, Belle," dad said suddenly, which shocked me

beyond belief. I expected to be in the biggest trouble of my life, but here was my father, apologizing to me.

"Dad…"

"Belle, this isn't fair to any of us. I know a lot of people think that only Kitti is affected. It's true she's taken the brunt of her disease, but it's hurt you, too. Your kidneys may be fine, but I know your life has changed drastically. I've tried to keep things normal for you and your brother, but…"

For the second time in my life, I witnessed a tear trickle down my dad's cheek. The strongest man I knew was crying, and it was entirely my fault.

"Dad, I'm so sorry," I said through tears. He held me tightly.

"Jobelle," he told me. "It's not your fault, baby. FSGS is not your fault."

~~~

The conference with the principal and a guidance counselor was less-than-pleasant, although I was amazed by how my dad stuck up for me.

"I'm not saying she has an excuse for her behavior," my dad stated honestly. "She made a mistake, but I wish you'd realize that I know the reason this happened."

Neither school official did. They nailed me for dropping grades, daydreaming in class, and… of course… the school bus incident.

"Jobelle, you used to be such a sweet girl," the principal said. "I can see something is going on."

It took all my might not to yell "NO DUH" to her face, but I didn't. She implied I was doing drugs or drinking, or maybe I was hanging with the wrong crowd. She listed every reason except a sick sibling.

When the principal proposed that my dad was in denial about my problems, he turned bright red with frustration. I was shocked at how calm he remained, once again trying to explain our insane home life that involved a thirteen-year-old struggling on steroids and "chemotherapy-like medications."

"Why didn't you say her sister has cancer?" the principal asked, as if that would have been enough to automatically forgive me.

"She doesn't," dad said slowly, and we were back at square one.

~~~

I shook my numb hand and glanced up at the clock. It was 5:27 on a beautiful Saturday afternoon, and I was in Saturday detention for protecting a child with nephrotic syndrome.

Alright, so technically, it was for cussing out an eight-year-old.

The principal had wanted to suspend me for a week, but dad wouldn't allow it. "This is not entirely her fault," he had defended. I was hoping dad would get me out of Saturday school, but he didn't even try. Getting up at 7:00 on the weekend in order to get to school by 7:30 was awful, but dad wasn't as grumpy as I thought he'd be. In fact, he was remarkably nice about the whole thing.

"You absolutely deserve this," dad had finally said as he drove. He went on about it, but not in a scolding manner. It was more explanatory. After all, my dad had a habit of repeating something he was unsure of time and time again. It was his way of hoping to convince himself.

"I accept the fact that I did something wrong and am being punished for it," I mumbled groggily. I glanced toward him. "Why are you having a hard time with this?"

"It's not fair," he said as we parked at the high school campus. "The reason this happened was because a child was bullying another child."

"Dad, it…"

"Get out, sweetheart. You're almost late. I'll be here at 5:30." His cell phone buzzed to alert a text message. He read quickly and snapped the phone shut. "Kit's vomiting again. If I can't pick you up, I'll find someone who can."

It was finally 5:28, and I wondered who that someone would be.

Please be Graham, please be Graham, please be Graham...

They let us out, and I was almost trampled by the stampede. I exited the school and immediately saw Graham's green truck.

"You are such a troublemaker," he teased with a sweet smile.

"Don't be mean. My hand hurts; I've been writing all day."

"Writing what?"

"You name it- apology letters, 'bad word alternatives,' sentences..."

"I sort of feel sorry for you, and then again I sort of don't."

Once in the truck, we drove toward a fast food place.

It was where they made my favorite cheese fries, but Kitti loved them, too.

"Stop," I said quietly. "I don't want to eat here."

"Why not?" Graham asked, concerned.

"Cheese fries," I replied in a whisper. "Squeaky and Kitti can't have them. They're packed with sodium, from the salt, cheese, ranch dressing, bacon bits... and if Annie were to eat a few potassium-rich fries right now, her heart..."

Graham knew the answer and held his index finger to my lips.

"Don't finish that," he whispered.

"Just because it goes unsaid doesn't make it untrue," I countered. "Their diets are so important to their health. I suppose that's true with everyone, but Annie's potassium is so high that with one false bite... Graham, I can't do this anymore. I can't pretend nothing's wrong. She could've died from eating a potato yesterday. A potato! Something as harmless as a French fry could

217

have killed her! And Kitti's blood pressure was so high her nose started gushing blood; I saw the pictures. That could have given her brain damage! If they can't eat pizza and fries, then neither can I!"

Graham pulled over and listened to me rant for a while. When I finished, I leaned against the window, exhausted.

"I'm sorry you had to listen to that," I said after a few deep breaths.

"No, Belle," Graham responded. "I'm sorry you have to deal with this. You're so strong, and you're so brave."

"Me?" I asked. "I think you mean Annie, or Kitti, or maybe Squeaky…"

"No," he replied. "I know what it's like to watch someone you love struggle," he reminded me. "My mom had cancer. It was one of the scariest things I've ever been through, even though I wasn't the one with leukemia."

His eyes got misty, and I took his hand, just like in the "old days…" before chronic illness had impacted my life.

Suddenly, I realized something- back then, my world hadn't changed yet, but Graham's already had. I looked at him in admiration.

"Thanks," I said quietly.

"For what?"

"I don't know. For always being here, I guess."

Thursday, October 30, 2008

As warm temperatures dipped into the fall's crisp coolness, it became clear that cyclosporine wasn't working anymore. Even so, Dr. Jones had me continue it as my creatinine began to climb. When a lab revealed it to be 2.5, I suddenly started wishing it would "plunge" back to the once-considered-terrible 2.0.

On my seventeenth birthday, I reminisced about the past year. It was remarkable how much I had endured, and as terrible as it was, I couldn't help but be in awe of everything God had carried me through. Even so, I prayed earnestly for a "sweeter seventeenth".

I went to have a routine lab draw done on Halloween, but I dreaded my appointment with Dr. Jones. I had gained several pounds overnight and could practically feel the albumin leaving my body every time I urinated. I had no doubt that the disease was getting worse. My kidneys were weakening, and I was getting sicker. Chances were that I'd be pulled off the cyclosporine and placed onto another experimental treatment in the near future. That scared me to death, because I had no idea what medication Dr. Jones would suggest.

I was no longer strong enough to go to church weekly. The service started too early and interfered with my prednisone routine. The drive made me nauseous and I had a hard time sitting in a pew for two hours. I missed going, but staying home never kept me from praying.

November 2 was just like every other Sunday, except it was colder than a typical autumn day in Arkansas. While my family was gone, I sat on our front porch with Pepper, staring at the dismal sky.

God, I prayed. *I don't understand. I know you have a plan for me, but I don't get it. Please show me, because I don't know how much longer I can do this.*

Seconds later, flurries began to pour from the sky. After enjoying the beauty of God's creativity, I went inside and typed about what had just happened to me.

My Life Is Like Today- Kitti's POV
Takes Place: Sunday, November 2, 2008

I sat on the floor by the church's youth wing's glass doors. It was a cold and dreary November day with below-normal temperatures. Even though our imaginary city was underground, the images projected onto the giant ceiling came from a live-feed video of the real sky. We saw billowing gray clouds above us.

It was 11:45 on Sunday morning. Most of the congregation was in the sanctuary; everyone else was in the nursery building or children's complex.

My weekly escape worked well. The adults thought I was helping in children's church. The young children never tattled; they assumed I was in the adult service. I didn't worry about the high school and college students; for some reason, they understood.

Most people would think that I was skipping church because I was bitter and angry with God. I wasn't. The previous six months had drawn me closer to God than ever before. After all, faith was literally keeping me alive. Besides, it wasn't like I skipped church completely. I was as active as possible in the youth group and attended Sunday school. The 10:45 service was the only thing I secretly avoided because I found it easier to pray alone than with the pastor.

I existed on a day-to-day basis. It was hard to plan anything in advance, because no one knew what was going to happen. This cloudy Sunday was a particularly bad day. I had gained three pounds overnight and felt worn out when I woke up.

Nephrotic syndrome and FSGS aren't terminal illnesses, but even so, sometimes I feared I would die. Kidney failure, heart disease, dangerous side effects from the medicines... there were lots of life-threatening complications that could happen. I stared at the artificial sky, imagining what heaven was like. Where was heaven- the real heaven, I mean? Was it in another dimension in the clouds, or was it in outer space on another planet?

I had been completely still for an hour now, and Dr. Emilie's words echoed in my head: "You've got to keep moving, especially now that I have to take you off the aspirin." I stood up and stretched, but doing so felt as strenuous as running a marathon.

It's worse, I thought glumly. *It's worse, and every time it gets worse, my kidneys have less of a chance. Those things have survived two bouts of nephrotic syndrome in the past six months, and I probably had dozens of episodes as a kid. Why do I have to keep getting sicker? Can't I just get back into remission and stay there forever? And if I am going to go into kidney failure, why can't it just happen fast so I don't have to keep fighting?*

God, help me understand, I prayed. At that moment, something peculiar happened in the mock sky. On the giant screen, a few snowflakes silently drifted downward. It seemed to be a gift from God; a comforting promise that everything was going to be okay.

Elated, I forced myself to speed walk to the children's ministry area.

There were a couple ways to get into the oversized children's church room. Because it was in the basement, I could either walk down several flights of stairs or zip down the twisting ocean-themed slide. I missed the slide so much, but even though it was hard for me to navigate stairs, going down the slide wasn't very safe. The plastic tubing had little kids' germs all over it. Besides, my blood pressure had been too high that morning. There was no way I wouldn't bruise when I reached the bottom.

So I "submerged underwater" the boring way.

In the oversized space, elementary-aged kids were in the middle of their favorite worship song. It was a rather spirited rock and roll rendition of "Jesus Loves Me." The room was bursting with energy. Graham had hooked up his bass guitar to a loudspeaker, which he played wildly along with the CD. Besides singing, there was excited shouting, hyper leaping, and plenty of "air-guitar" playing.

Tayoe and Tomes stood at the back of the room, a yard or two in front of the stairs. I tapped Tayoe on his shoulder. He freaked out, likely assuming I had come downstairs for help. I told him I was fine. I was, even if I was exhausted and almost completely out of breath. Tomes hugged me, and I leaned against him.

Tayoe stuck his tongue out at us. Tayoe hadn't been a big fan of romance as a younger kid. He didn't mind it as much anymore- unless I was the girl who had stolen a boy's heart.

"So…" Tayoe said, pulling me out of the hug. "What are you doing running down those stairs, Kit? If this was a game to see who could be less tired, I think the stairs won."

"You have to come with me," I said, taking Tayoe's hand. Tayoe was going through a stage in which he hated any signs of affection, like hand-holding or hugging. He drew his hand away and lightly slapped my arm.

"You're going to hurt her!" Tomes scolded, playfully pushing my brother away. He took my hand and kissed it.

My heart started pounding.

"Oh, for crying out loud, you've probably given her tachycardia!" Tayoe said over the music, although his smile showed that he was amused.

I dragged both boys to the basement-level window and let them peer outside. I think they were as excited as I was, because they turned toward Belle, who was leading a game that was meant to transition the kids from music time to an object lesson.

"It's snowing," Tomes and Tayoe mouthed silently. They flittered their fingers downward like snowflakes. I nodded in excitement.

"Really?" Jobelle exclaimed, forgetting everything she was saying. She dashed out of the room and ran up the stairs.

The children were a little confused.

"Okay, change of plans," Graham stated as he grabbed the microphone. "You know, just a minute ago, we were worshipping God through singing and dancing, but there are hundreds of ways to worship God. One way to worship God is to praise Him for some of the wonderful things He created. So, we're going to go on a little nature walk."

"But there not no nature in the city," Pepper called out. "It's all for fake here."

"We're not far from the western gate," Graham answered. "We're going to go just outside the city's gate."

It was a five minute walk from the church's front door to the real world's entrance, so Graham carried me. When the kids saw the snow, they screamed with joy. Their straight line was destroyed as children ran all over the grass, catching flakes on their tongues and laughing. The flurries poured from the sky, creating ultimate excitement for the kids.

When Graham put me down, I slowly walked around in wonder, gazing at the sky and thoroughly loving every moment. Nothing else mattered. Even though my symptoms didn't go away, it was as if I wasn't sick.

As Tayoe and Tomes ran around like monkeys, I walked back towards Graham, who was now standing with Belle. I leaned against Belle, and she held me tightly.

"I don't know what it means," I said quietly, "but this snowfall was an answer to a prayer for hope."

"Hmm…" Graham said thoughtfully. He moved between me and Belle, holding us both closely.

"I think I know, Kit," he finally guessed. "It's an ugly day, isn't it? I'd say it's cloudy and dreary, cold and bitter, upsetting and depressing. But on such a miserable day came a wonderful thing."

"And my life is like today," I concluded. "And, no matter what happens, I'm going to be okay."

And no matter how many gloomy seasons I have to endure, I thought as I closed my laptop. *God will make it okay.*

The PFA
Part 4: Decisions

Introduction:

Tuesday, June 22, 2010

6 AM. Transplant Day. My body was shaking with fatigue, and I hadn't even gotten out of bed. I wasn't nervous, although I'm sure some would think otherwise. I began praying.

Dear God, please let something cancel these surgeries. I don't want a transplant, and I don't want my cousin to have to endure pain for me. I don't want to be on steroids forever, and that's assuming this transplant works. If You don't interfere, then I'll know it's what You want. I know You're greater than statistics, but the odds are against me.

Please, God, give me peace. I'm doing this because physically I don't have a choice. I don't even know what to pray. I guess just use me for Your glory. Even if I stay on dialysis the rest of my life, please use me. Show that You win over the powers of this world, including kidney disease. No matter what happens, I know that nothing can separate me from Your love. Please keep my cousin safe during surgery and be with my family. Amen.

"Alright, Pepper," I said silently as I picked up my stuffed animal cat. "Wake up. It's time."

Tuesday, November 4, 2008

"Alright, Pepper," I said out loud. "Let's get you dressed. Would you like a patriotic red or blue bow? No, you cannot wear a green bow. It's Election Day. Okay, I guess you can wear white instead. Would you like it around your neck or your tail? No, Pepper, you cannot wear it over your eye. I know you like to play dress up, but you are not a pirate."

Speaking- often all day long- seemed to keep me sane. It was ironic because half the time, I was talking to stuffed animals.

I didn't mind being alone during the day, even as weeks turned to months. That being said, I was getting "sick of being sick."

Election Day 2008 had finally arrived. Everyone seemed passionate about some political party. People were adamantly canvassing for this or that person, declaring our nation was doomed without their favorite candidate in office. I had my own preference, but I could do nothing but pray for the future.

"Next year you can vote," my phlebotomist Barb had told me at a lab visit in late October. "And in just four more years, it'll be the presidential election!"

While that was an exciting proposition, it also made me ponder some serious questions. What would my life look like during the 2012 Presidential Race? What medicines would I be taking? Could I be in remission? Would I be on dialysis or have a transplant? Would I even be alive on November 6, 2012?

It was around 3:00 in the afternoon, Central Standard Time, when the political "preshow" began.

"Please," a local news anchor pleaded. "This is a historic election. The polls are still open in all fifty states. Let your voice be heard."

I scoffed and looked at Pepper's inanimate face. "How can I let my voice be heard if all I do is sit around and write all day?"

"Our next president is the nation's decision," the television droned on.

Decisions, I thought. People make dozens of decisions daily without realizing it. All this thinking was making my brain hurt. I decided to pull up a PFA piece on my laptop and read what I had written earlier in the day.

Pick President Day- Belle's POV
Takes Place: November 4, 2008

"HAPPY PICK PRESIDENT DAY!"

I opened my eyes groggily. A small, gray fur ball with whiskers pounced into my bedroom. "HAPPY PICK PRESIDENT DAY!" It shouted.

"Pepper?" I asked hazily.

"It's Selection Day," the cat announced. "Has you picked your president yet?"

"What does Election Day have to do with you being in my bedroom at…?" I glanced at my alarm clock. "6:30 in the morning?"

"You no answered Pepper's question. Pepper repeat slowly. Has… you… picked… your… president… yet?"

"I'm too young to vote," I said, getting out of bed. "Even if I were eighteen, I'm an imaginary. No one in the Underground City can vote in the Presidential Election. The poll workers don't even know we exist."

"Oh." Pepper's glass eyes studied her front paws. "So Pepper never get to vote for real… EVER?"

"No. Sorry."

Her whiskers trembled, and she ran out of the room howling.

Great, I thought. *It's going to be one of those days.*

I got dressed and went downstairs. Pepper had already recovered from her grief and was in the kitchen devouring microwaved bacon. Dad and Kitti were nowhere in sight, but Tayoe and my niece Leah were at the table. Something was wrong. Since my sister Ariella had moved to a smaller apartment downstairs, Leah didn't usually come over before school.

"What are you doing here so early?" I asked Leah, hoping to lessen my concern.

"My mom and I came here last night because Auntie Kitti was sick," Leah replied. "Mommy went home to sleep, so grandpa kept me here for breakfast."

"What happened last night?" I asked Tay.

"Pepper had nightmare that she got picked as next president," the kitten asserted from across the table. "So many persons want Pepper's autograph that pizza delivery couldn't get to White Place. And then they threw a zillion-trillion quarters at Pepper's head, and she drowned-did."

"Hey Pepper, you and Leah can use my Game-Guy upstairs until it's time to go to school," Tayoe suggested, redirecting the kitten.

"FOR REALLY?"

"Yeah, sure," Tay confirmed. Before I could blink, Pepper was gone. Two seconds later, she was back in the room. She grabbed two strips of bacon with her mouth, said something about being a saber-tooth tiger, and left again. Leah followed.

"You didn't hear Kit throwing up all night?" Tay asked.

"She was throwing up all night?"

"Well, not all night. Just some."

"She's on an immune-system med, not chemo," I stated. Even after eleven months of watching my best friend be ravaged by severe side effects, I still couldn't grasp the concept that these medicines were treatment. In the past, when I'd heard the word "medicine," the words "all better" and "cure" came to mind. I knew of two "bad" treatments, chemo and radiation. I had no idea non-cancer medicines had harsh side effects, too.

"It doesn't seem to matter," Tayoe said, bringing my mind back to the present. "Chemo or not, this stuff makes her sick. Anyway, Kit thinks she's got too much of it in her system.

Every two weeks, she gets her cyclosporine levels checked to make sure she has the right amount in her blood."

"Cyclo-whatever never made Annie throw up," I recalled. "Is she sure it's that stuff and not something else?"

"Yeah, she had the shakes."

"Annie calls that 'tremors.'"

"Whatever you call it, her shoulders jumped like those super bounce balls I used to buy at the Dollar Mart. When I got up to go to the bathroom, dad was freaking out because he thought she was puking blood. She wasn't, her gums were just bleeding like Annie's used to, so..."

There went my appetite. I must have turned green.

"Sorry," Tayoe apologized. "I forgot gross stuff makes you sick."

"It's fine. I'm going to see how she's doing."

"Ask dad if she's okay before you go in there- if you can't handle me talking about it, you don't need to be seeing stuff like that."

"Thanks."

I jogged up the stairs and found dad spraying the hallways with disinfectant.

"Good morning, Belle," dad said, hugging me tightly. "Did you hear any of what happened last night?"

I shook my head. Apparently it had been traumatic. My dad, who had been through so many of life's hardest trials, seemed shaken.

"Is she okay?"

"She had tremors, her head hurt, and she vomited three times in two hours. When her gums started bleeding, I called the after-hours doctor. He guessed it was just the cyclosporine. She was able to drink fluids, so it wasn't severe enough for us to go the emergency room. We're going to the lab in a few hours to get her cyclosporine levels checked. It usually takes a few days to get the results back, but they're going to expedite it for us."

"Is she going to be okay?" I repeated.

"Yes, honey," dad answered. "They'll lower her dose, and she should feel better."

A scary thought crossed my mind. "What if it's not the cyclosporine?"

Dad put a hand on my shoulder. "We'll check her blood and go from there."

As dad went downstairs, I tiptoed to Kitti's room and opened the door.

"Belle?" Kit whispered.

"Hey," I said softly as I walked across the room and knelt beside her bed. "I heard you had a rough night."

"Did I wake you?" She whispered groggily and rolled to face me. "Belle, I'm sorry."

"Kit, that's not what I meant!" I scolded gently. "Sweetie, I was talking about you. Are you okay?"

"It was a rough night, but I'm better now. Is Tayoe okay?" She whispered as if her life depended on quietness.

"He's fine. Dad said you're heading to the clinic to get blood drawn in a few hours."

She nodded sleepily, her eyelids drooping from water weight and fatigue.

"Hang in there, alright?"

She smiled feebly but cheerfully. "I was going to say that to you!"

~~~

Kids were scattered throughout the school bus. Tayoe and Tomes sat in the back. Unfortunately, I had gotten stuck in front of Pepper and her circle of friends. She had regressed from talking about the actual election to shouting about literal donkeys and elephants. The bus driver and I sighed in relief when we finally unloaded at the elementary school. During the brief stop, Tay moved next to me.

"What are you thinking?" Tay asked quietly.

"About Kitti? I don't know."

We sat together, staring out the window on the way to the middle school. Tayoe was never this quiet. He was a sweet but goofy thirteen-year-old. He despised- or at least pretended to despise- any kind of human contact, unless it was frivolous roughhousing. I was surprised when he scooted close to me. Our arms touched slightly, and I knew it was intentional.

"Belle," he said tentatively. "I want to go home. I want to go home and cry."

I put my hand on his knee. For the first time, he didn't pull away or jokingly yell "cooties!" Instead, he looked at me with misty eyes.

"It's okay to cry," I told him.

"Not here," he whispered, his voice wavering. I couldn't blame him.

"Then think of something good, something funny."

"Can't. Not when Kitti's doing so terribly." He put his head on his backpack and pretended to sleep as the tears fell.

"It's okay," I said, putting my hand on his shoulder. "You know, I've seen guys cry. It's normal."

"Name one."

"Dad," I said. That got his attention. After a few minutes of sitting with his jacket positioned over his face, he sniffled and wiped his eyes. "Name another."

"Graham."

Tay squinted his eyes. "You've seen Graham cry?"

"Once or twice. He's tough, right?"

"Wow," Tay said, sitting up straight. A certain twinkle returned to his eyes. "He must really like you."

I elbowed him in the side. Two minutes later, we pulled up to the middle school. "You gonna be okay?" I asked.

"I don't have a choice," he replied.

"He's got us," Tomes said, moving up the aisles with his sister Tori trailing behind. "We'll take care of him."

There was no one in my building to take care of me, but somehow, I made it through. By the time we reunited after school, Tay had worried himself sick. Instead of bounding onto the bus with limitless energy, he boarded so quietly I didn't hear him coming.

"My head hurts," he complained as he sat beside me. "I think I might hurl."

His comment was contagious. Seconds later, my stomach seemed to twist into knots. I became more and more nervous as we got to the PFA housing complex. I could only hope that Kitti was okay, and I was terrified that she might be worse.

I didn't know what to expect when I opened the door to our apartment, but I didn't anticipate what I saw. Everything was normal… or as normal as a home can be while living with a chronically ill person. Kitti was sitting on the couch, doing homework on the computer. Dad was nowhere in sight.

"What happened?" Tay asked.

"My cyclosporine levels were high, just like we thought," Kitti said, barely looking up from the screen. "Dr. Emilie lowered my dose a bit. I didn't take the cyclosporine pills this morning, and they told me to skip tonight, too. I feel better."

"Really?" Tayoe asked, his face brightening.

Kitti set the laptop aside. "Yep!"

"So you don't have to go the hospital or take any new pills or do anything else that's bad?"

"No," she answered. "Dad even went to work after lunch. He doesn't want to use up all his sick days in case I end up in the hospital for albumin or something. We're going to do lab work every week now to make sure my levels are where they should be, but other than that, nothing's changed."

"Cool!" Tayoe shouted, running to the kitchen. "I'm going to get the cookie jar! Be right back!"

I suppose I should have felt more relieved, but I was ticked at the situation. This morning, Kit was so sick, she could hardly move. Now everything was "fine." How could this be, and why did dad just abandon her after such a rough night?

"I'm sorry," Kitti apologized suddenly.

"Why?" I asked.

"It was a little insensitive of us not to let you guys know I was okay," she apologized, practically reading my mind.

"We were worried," I admitted, sitting beside my swollen little sister.

"I know," Kitti replied sadly. "It's just... I'm so used to this. I live minute by minute, second by second. When I feel better, it's like nothing ever happened."

"But it did happen," I insisted. "He can't just leave you here alone afterwards."

"He had to work, Belle," Kitti explained. "Besides, he didn't just leave me alone. Rachel has been homeschooling Squeaky. They were here until just a few minutes ago. Squeaky had a swim meet at the pool."

Dad got home, but I was reluctant to talk to him; if he hadn't told me what was going on with Kitti all day, why should I share with him? I had spent eight awful hours stressed out, wondering whether we'd spend the night in the hospital's hotel. It was as if I'd wasted a whole day while Kitti rebounded without a problem. When Kitti's side effects started up again an hour later, I felt guilty, even though I knew it wasn't my fault.

After dinner, Rachel showed up to check on Kitti before she and Squeaky went home. The little penguin wore a bronze-colored ribbon around her neck.

"I came in third," Squeaky moaned.

"That's great!" I exclaimed.

"I'll do better when I'm in remission," she squawked, waving her wings. "It's hard to swim fast when you're weighed down by water... Kitti!" The aquatic bird suddenly spotted my sister lying silently. Squeaky's webbed feet looked like inflated water balloons, but she managed to waddle to the couch for a hug. When dad entered the room, I began to sprint up the stairs.

"Belle, I give up," dad admitted. "What did I do now?"

Kitti sighed. "We were insensitive," she said quietly. "Tay and Belle were worried about me. When they came home, I acted like it was no big deal."

"I can't blame you," I told Kitti as I rushed back down the stairs. "That cyclo-whatever stuff is messed up. I've seen what it's done to Annie."

"So it's my fault," my dad stated in a flustered tone. I didn't know what to say. It was his fault… or was it? If it was hard to be a chronically ill kid's sister, what would it be like to be the parent?

Rachel asked to speak with dad alone in the hallway. I heard bits and pieces of their conversation.

"At my old job, we used to call siblings 'the forgotten children,'," Rachel said. "Never underestimate what those kids go through. I know it's tough, but try to imagine what the other two are thinking."

After Rachel had taken Squeaky home, dad hugged me and Tayoe. "I'm sorry," he apologized. "I'll try to keep you better informed."

I looked up from my laptop. On the television, a reporter illustrated the political differences between our presidential choices. My mind drifted to my latest medical decision, which had been to give up on cyclosporine. While it had worked wonders at first, the strong medicine had failed to get me into remission. After eleven months, it had become less effective, and my kidney function was getting worse. Dr. Jones said it was time to switch to a new "FSGS fighter" in hopes of saving my native kidneys.

I was hesitant. Cyclosporine had bothersome side effects, but it was a relatively "safe" medication. My doctor's new proposal, mycophenolate, had risks I wasn't sure I was willing to take. There wasn't much FSGS research at the time. Since mycophenolate seemed to be my only option to avoid kidney failure, I decided to give it a try.

Within a day of stopping cyclosporine, its trademark negative effects began to disappear. Mycophenolate gave me moments of mild to moderate nausea, but I felt better than I had previously. I think I would have "liked" this drug if it hadn't been for the size of the pills.

Even after a year of battling kidney disease, I was no expert at taking pills. I could down small gel caps, but that was about it. After all, if eating made me sick, how was I supposed to swallow giant, solid tablets? Usually, chewing pills into pieces worked. Besides prednisone, nothing tasted too disgusting, and my pharmacist assured us that nothing needed to be taken whole.

Not until mycophenolate.

"It's not an absorption issue," the pharmacist told me. "It's a safety issue. Mycophenolate is a powerful drug. The tablets' coating is meant to keep the medicine from touching your body's tissues until it is deep within your intestines. From there, it can be absorbed into your blood. You *have* to swallow it whole. Do not take any pills that have broken open."

While the mycophenolate capsules weren't the biggest I'd seen, they were too big for me. Thankfully, the pharmacist suggested switching to the children's suspension form of mycophenolate. Reluctantly, Dr. Jones agreed. Life was better for a while.

Day by Day- Kitti's POV (Takes Place: November 2008)

I was sick of always feeling sick, but not everything about my illness was awful. Going to the hospital was kind of fun.

In the Underground City, almost every medical service was provided at the sprawling hospital. While there were a few outpatient practices elsewhere, almost every doctor and nurse worked on the Underground City Medical Center's campus. This being the case, I visited the children's building every week for blood work.

I wasn't known throughout the hospital- that honor seemed to be reserved for children fighting cancer. However, I was well known in the pediatric nephrology areas. Dr. Emilie said there was even talk about me on the adult kidney floors.

"You're a superstar," Dr. Emilie had once said while listening to my heart.

"What about me? What about me?" Squeaky wondered.

"Yes, you are, too."

Squeaky and I had similar clinic schedules. While dad came with me to any "official" appointments, Rachel usually took Squeaky and me together for routine outpatient lab visits.

Squeaky liked the children's hospital and called it her home-away-from-home. She loved all the kid-friendly details, from the accessible playground to the hospital classroom. While she certainly hated relapses, she didn't loathe having kidney disease most of the time. She endured biopsies, x-rays, medicines, and the other medical un-pleasantries with extraordinary patience.

Everything except blood draws. She handled them well and even made a "no screaming" rule for herself, but she hated venipunctures with a passion. She scrunched her face, closed her eyes, and held her breath until the needle was in the sharps container.

"I used to be afraid of needles," I told her once.

"I'm not scared of needles," Squeaky replied defensively. "Finger pricks, shots, stuff like that... those are okay. But venipunctures- when they use a needle to access a vein- I don't like those."

"They don't hurt too much," I reminded her.

"I know! I just don't like them! The phlebotomist- that's the lab man or lab lady that draws blood- is extremely important, you know."

I wasn't a hospital veteran like Squeaky, but I had quickly learned that a skilled phlebotomist made a huge difference when it came to making venipunctures more bearable. I did some "detective work" and quickly discovered that the ER and pediatric oncology units had the best phlebotomists. Michelle, one of the nephrology units' roving lab ladies, was the worst. She wasn't the nicest person in the world, either. One time, I overheard Dr. Emilie trying to get rid of her.

"That woman had a twelve-year-old transplant patient screaming. A transplant kid! Do you have any idea how tough those kids are? The least we could do is give them a decent tech…"

"Give it a rest, Ballard. It's not going to happen," the Nephrology Department Head said.

"Why not?" Dr. Emilie asked. "That could have been me! When I was twelve…"

"When you were twelve, you were one of the luckiest kids in this building."

"Yes, I was," Dr. Emilie agreed. "But remember, I still grew up in this hospital. Getting lucky after nine years of treatment makes me more sympathetic toward children who don't beat the odds."

I was confused. Dr. Emilie was at least thirty years old. As far as I knew, the Underground City of the Shramere Family Backyard had been built in 2000 or so. How could my doctor have 'grown up' here?

And more importantly, why in the world had she needed to grow up here? I didn't have time to ponder this question, because the department head- Dr. Flacon, as his lab coat read- handed a pager to Dr. Emilie.

"Adult dialysis needs you," he ordered.

"Of course they do," she muttered as she turned to leave.

"Dr. Ballard!" Dr. Flacon called after her. "We have different methods, but we are playing on the same team."

Dr. Emilie nodded courteously, but as she walked away, I heard her mumble, "We are playing on the same team, Flacon, but I'm not sure you know just how fearsome our opponent is."

Monday, November 10, 2008

Soon after the election, I began hating school. It was so different from what it had once been. Each day I attended, it was as if FSGS was in charge. Everything revolved around surviving another eight-hour day of waddling from class to class and sitting in uncomfortable chairs. I had to stop marching in band because the physical exertion was too much. I wanted to talk to my friends, but I usually ended up vomiting in the bathroom.

My parents and I discussed homeschooling. If I could finish my work at my own pace, I might still have enough energy to do the things I loved. I might even be able to have a social life of sorts.

Unfortunately, the legalities of homeschooling seemed overwhelming. In early November, I asked Dr. Jones to sign a waiver that allowed me to be legally "homebound," which freed me from the laws of missing only ten days of school per year. I went to school when I was able, but if I couldn't, I didn't have to try. It wasn't as liberating as homeschooling would have been, but it did help. Thank God for that document, because I don't think I would have survived without it.

Any Wish- Kitti's POV
Takes Place: November 2008

I hobbled into my English class and sat down. It was the beginning of second period, and I was exhausted already. The entire school day was ahead of me, and I was not looking forward to it. My jumbled mind bounced back and forth between different thoughts.

In August, dad had made sure someone he trusted was with me in every class, just in case something happened. Tomes happened to be my "buddy" in English.

"Young and in 'puppy love,'" Belle had teased me back in September, when second period had been one of my prednisone-euphoric talking points. (I'm glad I don't remember the monologues Belle describes, and it's good she's the only who heard them.)

"Hello?" A familiar voice called, bringing me back to present time. Tomes placed my books on my desk and sat behind me. "You're zoning again, Kit."

"Where are we?" I asked, not at all kidding.

"English," he answered. "Where are you?"

"Jupiter," I answered randomly, resting my head on my desk.

Our teacher entered the room and wrote our daily journal prompt on the board:

If you could have any wish, what would it be?

I glanced at Tomes. We had talked about this at church youth group a few weeks before. For most people, it's a daydreamy discussion question. Something that's commonly asked but rarely important. No one really gets that opportunity, unless they're a famous person... or a chronically ill child picked by a wish-granting organization. With a shaky hand, I began writing.

If I could have any wish, it would be a cure for all chronic diseases.

It's ironic because some seriously ill kids get chosen to have a wish granted through special organizations. It's one of the best things that can happen to you, besides remission. You can ask to go anywhere or do anything within reason. It's an amazing opportunity.

I know a penguin who might have a wish granted. She keeps getting denied because she's not sick enough.

This time, her guardian had two doctors sign the request. I hope it works. My nephrologist wants to refer me to Dreams Come True as well, but I won't let that happen. There's nothing I want. The things I long for are humanly impossible at the moment. A toy shopping spree won't cure me, and it would probably be more meaningful to some dying six-year-old boy than to me.

Most of my healthcare workers say I'm rare in this respect, but I don't think I am at all. I think all of us "sick kids"- children and teens with long term health problems- really wish for things social networking can't get and money can't buy.

We want to run without being tired. We want to stop taking medicines. We want to quit worrying about germs and special diets. We just want a cure.

~~~

Two days before Thanksgiving, a blood test revealed that I was sliding backwards.

"The protein in your urine has gone down," Dr. Emilie told me at another doctor's appointment. "That being said, it's not low enough, and your creatinine has risen quite a bit. I think we should switch treatments. There are several things we can try. Because you've responded to prednisone in the past, I suggest we try cyclophosphamide first."

My throat tightened. "Cyclophosphamide," I repeated hoarsely. "That's chemo, isn't it?"

"Yes," Dr. Emilie said gently. "But it's a lower dose than what is used to treat cancer, so the side effects aren't as intense."

My dad asked why we should try chemotherapy before any other immunosuppressive treatments; after all, didn't it have more risks than the medicines Annie had taken? Dr. Emilie agreed that there were dangers to using cyclophosphamide in nephrotic syndrome but that the other medications had downsides, too.

"In the real world, most nephrologists prescribe oral cyclophosphamide, but I think you might do better with a monthly IV dose. You will probably feel terrible for a few days after each treatment, and we'll have to monitor your blood counts closely."

We discussed all the different options for about thirty minutes before we agreed the benefits outweighed the risks.

"Will my hair fall out?" I asked. "And will I throw up all the time and..."

"Kit, I can't promise you one way or another at this dose. Some patients experience no side effects whatsoever while others have a lot. Your hair might thin out, but I doubt that you'll lose all of it. Even if that did happen, it will grow back. As far as stomach issues, those are more likely, but the other medicines can also cause them. Because this isn't an emergency, we can give you a break from cyclosporine before your first treatment."

"No more cyclosporine?" I asked.

"That's right," Dr. Emilie confirmed. "I'm scheduling you for IV cyclophosphamide on December 2nd. You'll be outpatient on Platypus Unit, where they give chemo to kids with cancer."

"What are the chances it will work?" Daddy asked.

"It's hard to say," Dr. Emilie admitted. "Basically, treatment for FSGS- and many other diseases- is trial and error. As of now, the real people have no FDA approved treatments for FSGS, and we follow those standards for the most part. Everything we do is an educated guess, almost like a clinical trial without the benefit of networking results. None of my nephrotic syndrome patients are enrolled in official clinical trials, but almost all of them are guinea pigs. That said, I wouldn't be advocating this move if I didn't believe it wouldn't help at least a little."

"Kit, let me borrow your arm." Dr. Emilie felt the insides of my elbows as well as tops of my hands. "Your poor veins," she commented. "You have teeny blood vessels and a lot of scar tissue. It might be a good idea to place a port in your chest. We can use it instead of venipunctures and IVs." She explained that a medical port is a device that is surgically implanted under a patient's skin. "We can access a port using a special needle. It slides right into the port and can give you intravenous drugs or draw blood. There is a slight risk of infection and clotting, but I think it'll protect your veins. We're going to be sticking you many times over the next few months, so it would be worth it."

We agreed. On the way home, I added fourteen colorful beads to my extraordinarily long strand and carried ten others in my purse for Belle and Tayoe.

Jobelle's POV-
Takes Place: Tuesday, November 25, 2008

"Do you understand what that means?" I shouted after dad told Tayoe and me about Kitti's next treatment. "You're letting them pump poison into that little girl's veins!"

"It's poison?" Tayoe asked.

"No," dad assured. "It's not poison. It's medicine."

"It's toxic," I countered. "When the nurses hook her up to the drip, they'll be decked out in protective gear because it's TOXIC."

"Stop," dad commanded sternly. I hadn't heard him speak so harshly in years. He took a deep breath before adding softly, "Tay, I'll talk to you soon. Kitti is going to be okay. Right now, why don't you hang out in your room?"

Tayoe obeyed. When he was gone, dad wiped his misty eyes. "Do you think this was an easy decision, Belle? Kitti's kidneys are severely damaged. Without aggressive treatments, her kidneys will fail. If that happens, the toxins in her bloodstream will build. She'll be poisoned every day by her own waste. She'll be dependent on machines to keep her alive, and even after a transplant, she'll be on harsh medicines for life. I will do anything to save her from that fate."

His reasoning made sense, but the whole situation was still scary.

~~~

In the living room, Kitti sat on the couch, watching reruns of a crime-solving drama.

"What's going on this time?" I asked. Without taking her eyes off the screen, she responded.

"Someone is poisoning people, so the FBI has hired a consultant to find out where the suspect lives."

"Dad lets you watch this stuff?"

She smiled. "Yes. It's more about math, science, and logic than crime."

I sat beside my little sister, who rested her head on my shoulder. We watched as a federal negotiator used the details of a person's house to describe personality traits.

"I'd love to be an FBI agent," Kitti mused. I looked down at her with a raised eyebrow. Kitti running around with a gun, even if she were healthy, was something I just couldn't picture.

"Why in the world would you want to do that?"

"I don't know," Kitti commented as the show went to its commercial break. "It's detective work- looking for details, profiling, and piecing real-life puzzles together."

"And toting a gun," I added.

"I'd be careful," she guaranteed.

"You're fearless," I told her, thinking more about her upcoming chemo treatments than her random ambitions.

"No," she whispered as if reading my mind. "I'm afraid of lots of things. I'm afraid of getting sicker. I'm afraid of nightmares. I'm afraid of losing my kidney friends, like Annie, Squeaky, and the kids I know from the hospital. I'm afraid of chemo. I'm afraid of losing my hair. I'm afraid of renal failure and dialysis. I'm afraid of having a transplant."

"You're afraid of having surgery?" I asked.

She shook her head. "I'm nervous about Monday."

"I thought you're starting chemo on Tuesday."

"Yes, but they have to place my port on Monday. It's an outpatient surgery. Dr. Emilie says they do it all the time."

"Surgery?" I exclaimed. "They're doing surgery?"

"Mild surgery," she said. I smiled. Kit had learned so many medical terms in the past few months, it was wonder I understood her at all. But now, my brilliant fourteen-year-old sister confused the word "minor" with "mild."

Or did she do that on purpose to calm me down?

"Anyway," she continued, "I used to be afraid of sedation, but then I had my biopsy. It wasn't bad. I'm not afraid of transplant surgery, although I never want to have to have one because of transplant after care," she clarified. "I'm afraid of the medicines and their side effects."

"You make my fears seem stupid," I admitted. "I only have one serious fear that matters."

"What?"

"Losing you."

She smiled. "I'm not going to die, Belle. I promise."

Her sincerity didn't make me feel any better.

~~~

Jobelle's POV Continued- Monday, December 1, 2008

"Come on, sweetheart! You don't have all day, you know!"

The sound of a woman's voice jolted me awake. Before I had time to freak out, I remembered that dad had taken Kitti to the hospital for her surgery early this morning. Our next door neighbor Rachel had come over at 5 AM to see us off to school.

"Is that how you wake Squeaky?"

"Yes, unless there's a reason I shouldn't."

"Like what?"

"Prednisone side effects or NS symptoms," she stopped. "That isn't anything you need to worry about."

"My sister has NS," I retorted. "It is something I need to worry about."

"You're right," she admitted. "And I'm truly sorry you have to deal with this. It's not fair. Even so, your sister is going to be okay."

"They're putting her on chemo!"

Rachel put a hand on my shoulder. "I know, Jobelle. I know this is scary, but I can't imagine her being as sick as she was that night she got too much cyclosporine. She's going to be alright."

On the school bus, Tay and Tomes sat in the back. I was in the front. Just before we came to the elementary school, an evil creature flew in front of the bus. Five months ago, everyone probably would have screamed, but life was different now. We had all become desensitized to the presence of roving "bad guys" passing through. I'd never been to a comic book city, but we had learned about that type of imaginary world at school. Super villains ran amuck through those places, and the superheroes saved the day.

The Underground City didn't have a lot of superheroes. We had one, the mysterious Chopper, but no one had ever seen him… or her… up close.

Anyway, no one was too alarmed by the freaky thing in front of the bus… until we hit it. There was a loud smash, high-pitched screams, and a low roar from Pepper.

"WE ALL GONNA DIIIIIIIIIIIIIIIIIIIIIIIIIIIIIIIIIIIIIIIIIEEEEEE!"

And then silence. The injured beast limped away. No one

was hurt, but the front fender of the school bus was crushed. We had to sit at the scene for close to three hours waiting for a replacement bus.

The only thing I had in my backpack was my English class journal. Out of boredom, I decided to complete my Monday writing assignment. Carelessly, I jotted down everything I could remember about the past few days.

What I Did Over Thanksgiving Break

Jobelle Newbrey

On Tuesday, I got home and played computer games with my brother. On "Thanksgiving Eve," I babysat some kids, watched TV, and found out my little sister would be starting chemo in less than a week. I got so mad at my dad. Kitti doesn't have cancer. Why should she have to take an anticancer drug if there are other options? But Kit's doctor says that this might work. She thinks that it's worth trying.

I can't believe Kitti agreed to chemotherapy. This time last year, she was scared of everything, and now she's okay with ~~cyclofomide~~ ~~cyclophosmide~~ whatever it's called! She's not afraid of chemo's trademark nausea and vomiting. She's been through that periodically with the cyclosporine. She's terrified of the possible hair loss. I don't blame her. At least they say the cyclophos-stuff alone doesn't usually cause baldness. At a low dose, it's possible her hair won't even thin. But she's lost plenty on cyclosporine, so I can't help but worry that she could get bald spots.

On Thanksgiving morning, Kitti and Tayoe went to Rachel's apartment to watch the Underground City parade. I slept in. In the afternoon, we had to go to the PFA Thanksgiving dinner. Unique is a respectful term to describe the celebration. Everybody in the Pretend Friend Association was there.

When you eat a fancy meal with a big group of people- especially when there are kids and people who don't like kids- usually there's a "baby table." Since Annie was with her own family, I was the youngest person eating with the "grownups." Graham and I sat together. No one paid attention to us, and I didn't even care. Unfortunately, Squeaky ran into the dining room and announced that Kitti had thrown up.

Dad and Kitti went home to our apartment upstairs. I stayed with Graham, but I felt guilty about it. I checked on Tayoe. He was fine, or at least distracted enough to appear fine at the moment. Graham walked me to my apartment, but by the time I got to the living room, I couldn't stay. Our "house" is big, but I could hear Kitti crying wherever I went. Graham stayed with me. We tried to talk and watch TV, but I couldn't focus.

There was a knock on the door. Tay, Rachel, and Squeaky came to the rescue. We went across the hall to Rachel's apartment, where we played board games and watched videos for several hours. Dad finally came over with Kitti because she wanted to see a movie on one of

Rachel's fancy channels. Of course, she fell asleep halfway through.

Before we went home for the night, Rachel invited me to go shopping with her on Black Friday. "It's more fun with friends," she said. "Your father is going to watch Squeaky at your house early that morning. Kitti plans on tagging along with me."

I couldn't imagine that. Kitti had just spent five hours crying and vomiting and couldn't even stay awake during a 90-minute movie! "I can do it," Kitti begged. "I have to get out once in a while."

I agreed to get up early and go along, mostly to take care of my sister, but I didn't say that. I woke up at three in the morning and got Kitti up thirty minutes later. She looked terrible- so pale, puffy, and weak. She seemed to feel me standing over her and opened her eyes. She said hi with a sweet but sad smile. I dressed her in warm clothes and crammed her swollen feet into her two-sizes-too-large shoes. At 3:45, Rachel met us at the front door with Squeaky in her arms. Dad was up long enough to carry the sleeping penguin to my bed.

I couldn't believe we were doing this- dragging my little sister out of bed in the middle of the night to go shopping. It seemed insane! I felt a little better when Rachel brought us to her apartment.

She handed me a mug of low-sodium hot chocolate and pulled a foldable wheelchair out of a storage closet. Kitti sat exhaustedly. Rachel covered her with a pink fleece blanket and put a pillow on one of the armrests. She gave Kitti a mug as well, but Kit only sipped it.

Black Friday was crazy. There weren't any fights like there are in the real world, but it was still insane. We saw Bubba and his parrot buddies snatch all the $1 computers at Doll-Mart by flying over the crowd and grabbing boxes from above.

We didn't buy much. I thought it was a waste of time, but Kitti loved it, so whatever.

"BEEP! BEEP! HONK! HONK!" Pepper's loud voice jolted me back to reality. "New school bus here!"

As the replacement vehicle pulled up to take us to school, I stopped writing and stashed my notebook into my backpack. Before the migration to the other bus began, Rachel entered the bus. Little Squeaky followed closely behind, wearing a mask over her beak to protect her from germs. Rachel signed Tayoe, Leah, Pepper, and me out of school. "Since you've already missed most of the morning anyway, I thought I'd take you all to see Kitti at the hospital," Rachel announced as we crammed into her car. "Your dad called me and said she did fabulously this morning. "They'll probably let her go home in a few hours."

A few minutes later, we trekked through the medical center's vast parking lot. I hated hospitals to begin with, but visiting the children's building always seemed especially awful. It wasn't a scary place. On the contrary, it was colorful and bright. The fact that so many sick kids stayed here upset me each time I was forced to come back... until I walked through the doors for the first time with Squeaky.

"Welcome to my home away from home," she squeaked, delighted to show Leah, Pepper, and me around "her" hospital. From the gift store to the themed units, I already knew where everything was, but I had never seen it through the eyes of an eight-year-old patient. She put a positive spin on everything, and suddenly this sad place became joyful. It's surprising how another perspective can change a situation.

"This is the gift shop," she pointed to her left as we walked by. "Dr. Emilie let me get jellybeans at the candy counter once when I wasn't eating enough. To your right is the accessible indoor-outdoor playground. Down the hall are pediatric admissions, where you get your wristband and start your adventure toward getting better."

When we got to my sister's room on Penguin Unit, they were getting her ready to go home. Kitti's IV had just been pulled, and she was sitting up in a wheelchair, wearing her normal clothes.

"Told you I'd be fine," she said dreamily.

"Why isn't she whacko?" Tay asked. "Didn't they put her to sleep?"

"Did not, that silly," Pepper commented. "They no euthanize her. If they put her to sleep she not wakes up until heaven."

Everyone ignored the comment, except for Squeaky, who laughed hysterically.

"She was under general anesthesia," dad confirmed. "It was a short procedure. She woke up a little loopy, but she's just sleepy now." Kitti nodded. Her eyes seemed a bit bigger than usual.

When we got home, Kit ate more than she had for a while and didn't fall asleep while we watched TV that night. Her port was just a little bump under her skin next to a tiny scar.

"Does it hurt?" I asked.

"A little," she answered, slipping into bed. "They said it shouldn't for long."

"You'll probably be asleep when I leave for school tomorrow. I don't know what to say, except... I love you, I guess."

She smiled. "I'm not going to die. It's just medicine."

"I know," I answered. "Sometimes, it's just hard to find the right words. That was the only thing I could think of."

"'I love you' or 'I'm praying for you' are always okay," she assured. "And I love you, too. Goodnight."

"Goodnight," I whispered, hoping she wouldn't be listless the next time we talked.

Kitti's POV- Takes Place: Tuesday, December 2, 2008

On the morning of my first chemotherapy treatment, dad decided to drive Belle and Tay to school rather than make them ride the bus. Once we dropped them off, I sprawled out in the backseat and recalled the fun I had on Black Friday. Rachel took Belle and me all over the Underground City. We mostly just got the freebies, but it was so much fun! On the way to our first shopping location, I had drifted in and out of sleep.

"Why are you doing this for us?" I had overheard Belle whisper.

"As a kid, my home life was a mess," Rachel had explained. "Both of my parents were mentally ill. Despite its stigma, mental illness is just as real and serious as any other chronic illness. It wasn't their fault, but I had a rough childhood because of their health. Long story short, I had no one to watch out for me in high school. I'm a nurse because my tenth grade biology teacher told me I should be in the medical field. I couldn't afford med school, so I became a nurse. I met my husband at college during my prerequisite year. He'd had liver disease since birth and had gotten a transplant as a child."

She recalled her husband's story. He'd died while waiting for his second liver transplant only months after the first rejected. They had one child who died from a rare congenital disease before his third birthday. Needing some relative stability, she had moved to the Underground City and worked in the ER.

"When I had an opportunity to be a personal nurse to a little girl, I jumped at it, especially considering I'd get a chance to be a mommy again. Then I found out my apartment was right across the hall from you guys. I was Kitti's nurse the night she was diagnosed; for some reason, I remembered her. Kitti and Squeaky have virtually the same disease. I see what this does to Squeaky every day, even when she's in remission. If I can help Squeaky, I figure that maybe I can help your sister, too. Because my parents were chronically ill, I know all about the anger, sadness, fear, confusion, and lack of stability you're facing. Since my son spent most of his life in the hospital, I can relate to your dad. I can help, so I should. It just makes sense."

Daddy parked the car. I opened my eyes. We were at the hospital.

"It's busy today," dad said as he helped me undo my seatbelt. We were in the lot farthest from the main entrance of the children's building. Thankfully, a security guard with a golf cart delivered us to the door. We checked in through admissions, just like we did when I had my port surgery. They sent us upstairs to the children's oncology clinic, where a nurse checked my vital signs and drew blood. It was the first time anyone had accessed my port. I was nervous that it would hurt more than a typical "poke," but I think it hurt a little less.

"That was the bravest first access I've ever seen!" The nurse bragged. She gave me a tour of Platypus Unit, one of the pediatric oncology areas on 3C. Everything seemed brand new, and you could tell a wealth of money and time had been poured into this part of the hospital. Platypus had several large playrooms and more resources than the Eagle, Penguin, Dialysis, and Transplant units combined.

"Why is this unit so new?" I asked my nurse.

"Have they taught you about building transplants yet in Imaginary-Reality Theory?" I shook my head.

"It's an imaginary technique to move a building… or even an entire city… from one place to another," my dad explained. "They can move mobile houses around in the real world, but this is on a much larger scale."

"This hospital was transplanted here when the Underground City was built. Platypus is one of the newest additions."

They brought me to the Treatment Room. It was a large room with recliners. I had my own curtained "zone" that reminded me of that night in the ER when I was diagnosed. A child life specialist came to talk to me. She was surprised by my medical knowledge and gave me a bag full of gifts. That seemed kind of weird because no one had done anything like that when I was diagnosed with kidney disease. Rachel had given me beads, but this was extreme, almost like an early Christmas.

When I had imagined getting chemotherapy, I anticipated a scary place where everyone spoke in hushed tones. It wasn't like that at all. In fact, it wasn't much different than any other place in the hospital. People were laughing. Kids were playing, reading books, and watching movies. The nurses were as friendly, calm, and cheerful as people anywhere else in the hospital. There were a few patients crying, and someone had thrown up, but that wasn't too unusual on the nephrology units, either.

A nurse brought me several pills- acetaminophen, diphenhydramine, and ondansetron. "These are your pre-meds," she told me. "They are mostly for fever and nausea prevention." She injected intravenous steroids into a tube connected to my port, like an IV push. She flushed my port by pushing a syringe of saline solution into my body before and after she injected the medicine. It didn't hurt, but I could taste it. It was like salt mixed with metal, but it wasn't too gross.

"Now, we're going to pre-hydrate you with this sodium chloride," the nurse explained, hooking my port's tube to a bag on my IV pole. "We infused mesna into this bag. Your chemotherapy treatment could hurt your bladder and kidney cells. This medicine will help protect your body's tissues. Even so, it's extremely important you drink lots of fluids in-between treatments. Because you're being treated for nephrotic syndrome, we're also adding furosemide and albumin."

I was still tired from Black Friday and yesterday's surgery, so I drifted off for about thirty minutes. I woke up as the nurse hung a second bag of clear liquid on my IV pole. She wore gloves, a gown, and a mask.

"Are those to protect you from the medicine?" Dad asked. He spoke coolly, but I could tell his eyes were scared.

"It's protocol," she answered sweetly. "Many of the agents we use in this room are highly toxic, and my coworkers and I handle many different kinds of potentially dangerous medicines every day. We don't need extended exposure."

She read my patient wristband several times before starting the drip of the chemo drug.

"Alright, sweetie, this is cyclophosphamide. It will start entering your body in a few minutes. You need to tell us how you're feeling. Some people get nauseous, but we can give you extra medicines to help you feel better."

I fell asleep before the medication got to my chest. When I woke up, the IV bag was almost empty. Dr. Emilie came to check on me.

"Hey," she whispered. "How're you doing?"

"I'm okay," I said dreamily.

"Yeah? No nausea?"

I thought for a moment and shook my head.

"Good. Your body is handling this exceptionally well." She looked toward a monitor. "Perfect blood pressure, good pulse, and no fever last time they checked." I noticed a blood pressure cuff on my arm and a pulse oximeter on my finger. When the infusion was over, Dr. Emilie signed my discharge papers.

I didn't throw up in the car. In fact, I ate a hamburger,

onion rings, and a milk shake without getting sick. At home, I slept most of the afternoon. I was exhausted and had a headache, but it wasn't as miserable as I had anticipated.

Jobelle's POV
Takes Place: Christmas Season 2008

I expected Advent Season 2008 to be a nightmare with my sister on "real chemo." I was pleasantly surprised. It wasn't that cyclophosphamide didn't affect Kitti, because it did. She was exhausted for a few days after each treatment, but it wasn't the torturous experience we had expected.

The worst part for her seemed to be the constant worry that her hair would fall out. She was afraid to brush or wash it. I didn't blame her, but it did get annoying.

"Early on, I was so afraid of needing chemo," Annie told me one day. "I was scared of throwing up and going bald. I still want to avoid cyclophosphamide if I can, but nausea doesn't freak me out anymore. I feel sick most of the time anyway on mycophenolate. Personally, I'd rather go bald from chemo than have a fat face from steroids. Bald is beautiful; you can wear a wig or a hat to cover it up, and people seem to understand it better. Most people know about chemotherapy, and they feel for those who have to go through it. Very few people know about prednisone."

As Annie, Kitti, and Squeaky fought kidney disease, the Underground City faced its own battles. Besides mythical creatures, attacks from super villains became more and more common. Super heroes rose up, and while they tried to help, the most efficient warriors were from the Fictional Alliance. The only non-Alliance hero loved by the population was Chopper.

No one knew who or what Chopper was. Confirmed "Chopper sightings" were judged by five criteria: a golden object hovering in the sky (considered to be Chopper itself), the sound

256

of a helicopter, a whoosh of wind, blinding light, and heat. The sound, light, and heat elements of Chopper sightings convinced me that Chopper was who- or what- had saved Graham and me back in March.

Even with Chopper flying around, the City's Fictional Alliance officials made "fight training" mandatory for certain citizens. Schools added "emergency safety" classes for children as young as six. (Pepper came home one day, trying to "disarm" Kitti of the television's remote control.) My twelfth grade Imaginary-Reality Theory (IRT) class required us to take weekly self-defense courses after school. Beating up a punching bag every Monday was kind of fun. With my dancing background, I did well physically, but I hated learning about different weapons.

Despite the city's dangerous circumstances, people seemed to adjust to their new normal. With Christmas approaching, everyone anxiously awaited the arrival of Santa Claus.

Except me. I had to write a thesis paper on him for IRT. It may not be a typical topic in any actual American high school classroom, but in the Underground City, it's a fascinating subject. In our world, unlike in Anna Grace's world, there's no question whatsoever- of course Santa is real. The security guards let him in every year. His mysterious methods and motives appear on our news channels and are as common as politics and cartoons. When I wrote my report, I was mad because I was having a terrible morning. I wrote that Santa Claus was evil for detracting from the real meaning of Christmas. My teacher thought it was unique and gave me an A.

Ten days before Christmas Eve, my family had our own holiday of sorts. Ariella was getting married to Tinarg, a Fictional Alliance civilian who worked as a meteorologist. After being best friends for two years, they had dated for three more. He had finally proposed.

Little Leah was thrilled to "be getting a daddy for Christmas." Tinarg "proposed" to Leah first, making sure she wouldn't mind him joining their small family. In response, she had asked what had taken him so long.

"I'm glad it's finally happening, but I wish Tinarg had waited just a little longer," dad told Kitti and me. "I already have my arms full with Christmas and chemo."

Kitti giggled. "Daddy, I'm fine. Besides, I think a winter wedding is a fun idea!" She was right. The snowflake-theme was gorgeous; even self-conscious Kitti felt beautiful in her junior bridesmaid dress. I was the Maid of Honor.

December 15th was a cold night, and I was glad the event was held inside. Afterwards, there was over an hour of family photography. In between shots, I kept playing with my dangling snowflake earrings. When it was finally over, someone tapped me on the shoulder. I spun around to see Graham. He looked so handsome in his rented tuxedo.

"Your ears are snowing," he said randomly.

"The snow thing's beautiful but weird," I whispered.

"So what would have you done?"

"At this time of year? Poinsettias," I answered. The red flowers were a staple of the Underground City holiday traditions. Along with American traditions, real-life Mexican holiday celebrations such as Las Posadas and Three Kings Day were prominent in our corner of the imaginary world.

"No Santa beards?" Graham teased. "Kitti told me about your IRT midterm. You think Santa's evil?"

"I don't know," I answered. "I was mad at kidney disease when I wrote it."

"So you took it out on Santa? Couldn't you wait until after you got over it?"

"No, it was due in an hour."

Graham rolled his eyes. "I should have known. Kit looks like she's doing okay under the circumstances. How are you with all of this?"

I sighed. "I'm alright. It's just..."

"What?"

I stopped. It was too embarrassing to say, even to Graham. "I don't know."

"Sure you do. You can tell me."

"Everyone is treating Kitti like royalty. It's nothing new from dad, Rachel, and Tay. I'm so grateful for that. But because she's on an actual chemotherapy drug now, even though it hasn't affected her too much yet, everyone's spoiling her. They even call her princess. It's just… it's great, but… I don't know, I'm so glad I'm not sick, but…"

"You're jealous," Graham correctly assessed.

"I hate myself for it."

"Don't. I'd say that's normal. Anyway, you look nice in white."

"Thanks," I gushed. "Dance with me?"

"Sure, princess," he said as he took my hand.

Monday, January 5, 2009

There's no "roadmap" for most chronic illnesses. Kidney diseases and other health problems come and go as they please, and more often than not, they stick around for a while.

For months, people had been asking when I would get better. In reality, I didn't know. I would tell people "a few months," but that uneducated estimate was often answered with "be positive!"

I am being positive, I usually thought. *The truth is probably "a few years at best!"*

After Christmas, I began getting random suggestions. Most people had admirable intentions. Even so, anyone who had never personally dealt with chronic illness or another *real* hardship didn't know what they were talking about. It was frustrating.

"Couldn't you just do a kidney flush?"

"Maybe if you became a vegetarian..."

"Take cranberry pills!"

"My friend has this drink that is beneficial for your immune system..."

Others just didn't know what to say. Trying to be kind, they would accidentally say something upsetting.

"I know just how you feel. I had a fever for two days last week."

"Wow! You're out and about! You must be feeling better!"

"Thank God it's not cancer!"

"Oh, you're on medicines? I'm glad everything's going so well!"

"But you don't look sick..."

I brushed off offensive phrases by telling myself that everyone was *trying* to help, even if they inadvertently did the opposite.

While the hurtful phrases were common and would echo in my mind for days, my prednisone brain never remembered who said what. Because I forgot, it was easy to forgive.

The good deeds and comments were rare but powerful. Somehow, I could recall the names of each individual who said and did "the right things." Those wonderful memories will last forever.

"My brother and I pray for you every night."

"Is there anything specific I can pray about?"

"How can I help?"

There was the boy who genuinely wanted to know how I felt. A high school teacher drove me home from school when I got sick in the middle of the day. Another teacher had her fifth grade students write notes to me. Several friends gave me get well cards or called to tell me that they missed me. Others kept their distance when they were sick, because they understood I was immunosuppressed. Supportive or not, most people had good intentions.

Sadly, there were some who actually implied kidney disease was my fault.

"If only you had more faith, you'd be healed."

"God doesn't want you to be sick! Have you done something wrong?"

"You obviously don't believe God can heal you."

I think those words were the hardest of all to hear.

It was difficult to make sense of the avalanche of advice that toppled around me. I attempted to sort out my feelings through writing.

The Guy in the Green Sweater- Jobelle's POV
Takes Place: Wednesday, December 24, 2008

The church was beautiful on Christmas Eve. At a party after the Candle Lighting service, I sat behind a face painting booth, doodling Christmas trees and stars onto little kids' faces.

"How's she doing?" Annie asked, putting a temporary tattoo on a kid.

I shrugged. "Today's been a good day."

"How're *you* doing?"

"About the same."

A loud commotion came from the giant, inflated bounce house next to us. Pepper came flying out of the door, followed closely by Leah, Tayoe, and Tomes. Graham emerged with Squeaky in his arms. The little penguin looked exhausted but was laughing happily. As the other kids ran off, Squeaky sat at an empty chair, and I etched a penguin onto her sleek feathers.

"Don't let them tell you penguins can't fly," Graham said, petting Squeaky on the head. "She bounced all by herself for close to five minutes."

"Pretty good for partial remission," Squeaky piped.

"Annie?" Kitti asked, approaching us from across the huge lobby.

"What's wrong, Kit?" Annie replied kindly, gently putting her arm around my little sister's swollen shoulders.

Kitti uneasily nodded her head toward several people standing a few yards away. "See the elderly man in the green sweater? He said... he said... that I got sick because I did something wrong and that I relapsed because I don't have enough faith."

I was about to go confront the ancient dummy, but Graham put his hand on my shoulder. Annie looked sad, but shook her head dismissively as if she hadn't been hurt by the man's comments. "He doesn't know anything about what you're fighting, Kitti. Come on, let's get some hot chocolate. Rachel found a low-sodium variety..."

Kitti stopped in her tracks. "Annie," she said timidly. "He had cancer once. He prayed, and he went into remission right after surgery. He didn't have to have chemo or radiation. He does know. He doesn't think about it anymore. He doesn't even go to the doctor anymore! He says he doesn't need to because he's trusting God. What if he's right?"

"That moronic lunatic..." I spouted, but Graham grabbed

my hand.

"Hey," he whispered soothingly. I tried to break away, but he put his arm around my shoulder and pulled me into a side-hug.

"Kitti," Annie said quietly. "This is not your fault. It isn't anyone's fault. We live in an imperfect world. Bad things are going to happen. I don't know why, but that's the way it is. Yes, we need to trust God, but His ways are not ours. He has a plan we can't comprehend, even when it seems like everything is out of control." Annie paused for a minute. "I know that's the most annoying thing in the world to hear, but I'm only saying it because I'm sick, too. You wouldn't have relapsed if that man was right. Heck, you never would have gotten NS, let alone FSGS. There's a story in the Bible about a blind man. Jesus healed him. Later, the teachers asked Jesus whose fault it was that he was born blind. Was it his or his parent's sin? Jesus said it was neither."

"Whose fault was it?" Kitti asked.

"It wasn't anyone's fault. God used it to show His power."

"But doesn't that make that guy correct? Not about me getting sick to begin with, I mean, but about me relapsing? I thought about relapsing a lot. I tried not to worry, but I had a plan, just in case. Maybe if I had told myself that God wouldn't let me relapse..."

"Alright," Annie interrupted. "God wants me to be happy, so I'm going to Orlando tomorrow."

Kitti laughed. Annie smiled and continued. "Just saying something doesn't make it happen... if it did, I think everyone would have a million dollars by now, don't you?"

"Sure, but if God wants to show His power, why doesn't He heal people who are sick, especially the ones who really believe He can?"

"I don't have a perfect answer for that, but God is a lot smarter than I am. In the Bible, Jesus' friend Lazarus got sick. Jesus could have dropped everything and rushed to his close friend's side. Jesus could have used His power and healed Lazarus immediately. That would have been an incredible miracle! Instead, Jesus didn't come, and Lazarus died. Who knew what kind of death it was? He might have suffered. His sisters didn't understand. It didn't seem right! Several days after Lazarus died, Jesus came and brought him back to life! Sure, a simple healing would have been cool, but the guy was as dead as a doornail, and he lived."

Kitti giggled again, and it was great to see her smile. Annie continued. "I don't want to have a kidney transplant. I want God to heal me. He made the universe, so fixing my kidneys would be a piece of cake. For over a year now, I've prayed and prayed. I want to go into remission and never take another pill in my life. If that's God's Will, it will happen."

"And if it's not?" I asked. Graham held me a little bit closer as Annie turned to face me.

"I have to trust God. He will take care of me, even when it seems otherwise. There is a purpose in this, even though we can't see it yet. No matter what happens, I will be okay; promise me you'll remember that?"

Kitti slipped her puffy arm around Annie's back. "I'll be okay, too." Her tired eyes glanced across the room suddenly.

"Be right back," Kitti said sweetly. Graham held out his other arm to Annie. She slid into his hug, and the three of us stood together, watching Kitti walk across the room.

"I'm proud of you," Graham said to Annie.

"I'm just doing what I have to do to survive."

"Yeah, but even so, it's gotta be tough." He planted a kiss on the top of her head. My heart leapt. I knew Graham and Annie's friendship was strictly that- a close friendship- but if he kissed her, maybe he'd kiss me, too.

"What is she doing?" I asked as Kitti approached the cruel man. She smiled brightly. It was impossible to hear everything said, but I could read her lips. "Merry Christmas," the precious girl said as she handed him a homemade card from her purse.

Wednesday, January 21, 2009

As I had learned during my hospital stay in March 2008, kidney disease causes anemia. Every week, I went to the lab for a hemoglobin check. The test procedure was identical to checking blood sugar with a pinprick and diabetic glucose meter, except with different results. If I was anemic, I was given a pre-prescribed shot of darbepoetin alfa. This injection replaced the levels of the blood-boosting hormone my sick kidneys couldn't create.

On this particular day, my hemoglobin was 8.1 on the glucometer-like device. Barb was instructed to draw blood into a vial and send it downstairs to be tested on the "million dollar machine." It came back at 9.0, so I was allowed to go home. On the following Tuesday, I would come back to make sure my blood levels were rising rather than falling.

Severe anemia was quite the experience. The fatigue was overwhelming. Anytime I was sitting up, I felt like lying down. When I managed to walk, I would get dizzy and out of breath. My heart felt like it was doing somersaults. At night, I couldn't sleep.

The next week, I came into Dr. Jones' office for my hemoglobin check.

"Your hemoglobin is 8.1," Barb said after reading the results. "Let me get Debbie."

Debbie walked into the room several minutes later. "Dr. Jones wants you to get blood tomorrow morning. You aren't an emergency case so it will be an outpatient procedure. It's too late to start today. It will take several hours to make sure the donated blood is compatible with your blood. The transfusion itself will probably take four to six hours since each unit lasts about two hours..."

"Two units?" I asked. "But last year, Dr. Wright didn't want to transfuse me because he didn't want to complicate a future kidney transplant."

"Without this blood transfusion, you might not make it to a transplant," Debbie said honestly. "We hold off on blood products as much as possible, but sometimes, there's nothing else we can do. Go home, take it easy, and maybe eat some beef. You're scheduled to be at Nectarwood General's admissions area tomorrow at 8:00."

When I got home, I rested on my bed because the couch wasn't comfortable enough for my achy body. I stared at my room's empty left wall, where the guinea pigs' cage had once been.

Nectar and Brownie had been our family pets since I was four. I loved our dog and cat, but they weren't exactly the most child-friendly animals. Brownie lived in our laundry room and preferred us to be friends at a distance. Nectar had a habit of jumping on me and knocking me over. I couldn't play with Nectar or Brownie without supervision, which was frustrating as a little girl. When I was six, I decided I wanted my own animal, something that I could take care of, play with, and hold anytime I wanted. My parents agreed, so I spent the summer between kindergarten and first grade "researching" rodents. On my seventh birthday in late autumn, my mom took me to a pet store, where I had adopted my first guinea pig.

Several weeks later, I had battled a case of walking pneumonia. No one had mentioned death, but I had wondered if pneumonia could kill me. While home sick from school one day, I'd held my guinea pig. It made me feel better.

My family had become 'guinea pig people' over the years. When one guinea pig died of old age or sickness, we bought another. At times, two or three little guys lived in my room. When the last pig had died around the time of my diagnosis, we hadn't replaced it.

"When you get into remission, we'll get a new one," my mom had promised.

So far, no new guinea pig.

Outside my window, Nectar barked. My thoughts turned to the old dog. Her fur had changed from black to gray to white, and she had to have been nearing death.

Exhaustedly, I headed to the backyard with my trusty camera. Nectar came trotting over, going as fast as her old legs would carry her. I patted her head and proceeded to take dozens of pictures.

Thinking of Debbie's words, I turned the camera and took several pictures of myself for my family, just in case.

That night, I was sitting with Todd on the couch when, suddenly, I noticed something that stunned me.

The "evil elbow brothers" were back.

Several years before, Todd had had a miserable school year. When he was nervous about something, he picked at the dry skin on his elbows. The "evil elbow brothers" were the two recurring scabs he would itch until raw.

They weren't half as noticeable as they had been when he was eight, but it still terrified me.

In the morning, Nectarwood General admitted me faster than I had expected. My outpatient room looked identical to those on the inpatient units. My mom and I settled into the familiar setting as a phlebotomist drew my blood and started my IV.

"We need this for a cross-matching test to make sure the donated unit is compatible with your blood," he explained.

"What's her blood type?" My mom asked.

The man flipped a page on my chart. "O positive," he answered. "It seems we've found a perfect match for you."

While I waited for the infusion to start, I pulled out my laptop, carefully positioned Pepper on my bedside table, and wrote.

Kitti's POV- Takes Place: Monday, February 16, 2009

"Please?" Tayoe begged as he followed my gurney.

"No, Tayoe," Dr. Emilie said breathlessly as she pushed my rolling bed out of the ambulance and into the UCMC's emergency entrance.

"But I'm really healthy," Tay promised. "Really!"

"I can see that," Dr. Emilie said kindly. "I can also see you're a courageous young man who would do anything to help his sister. I admire what you're willing to do, but the blood transfusion rules are extremely strict about a donor's age."

"Can't you at least test me? You know, see if we're the same blood type and everything?"

"I'm sorry, Tayoe."

"But… but she's my sister! And we're twins! I have to do something! She passed out at school because she needs blood, and I can't even give it to her!"

I looked over my shoulder. "Tay," I called. "In my mind, just volunteering to give me blood is as important as if you were the one who donated the unit."

"But I'm not the one who'll give it to you!" Tay exclaimed.

"There are people who need blood every day," Dr. Emilie said to Tay. "When you turn seventeen, you might be able to save someone else's sister. For now, I need to focus on Kitti." Dr. Emilie found a child life specialist to take Tayoe to the family room while she rolled my bed into a curtained "zone." Nurses immediately began to assess me and Dr. Emilie listened to my heart.

"What in the world were you doing at school today?" She asked.

"You said I could go to school when I felt like it…"

"Yes, but somehow, I don't think you should have been at school if you passed out within thirty minutes of arriving! It's not even 9AM right now!" A nurse pricked my finger in order to check my hemoglobin levels.

"Whoa," Dr. Emilie said as she saw the results. "When was your last chemo?"

"February 6, I think?"

"Ten days? Well, there you go. Your counts have pretty much bottomed-out."

"Is that supposed to happen?"

"It's not typical at nephrotic syndrome doses, but it isn't unheard of, either. Your dad is on his way. In the meantime, I'll order a unit or two of blood, and we'll go from there."

"Here it is!"

I shut my laptop as two nurses entered my room with the units of blood. Meticulously, they went through a precise routine to make sure I was getting the correct blood. The woman verified certain information from my patient wristband by reading identification numbers out loud. I waited nervously as the IV in my left hand was attached to a tube. A small bag of fluids hung next to the blood on my bedside pole. With the help of a pump, I watched a clear liquid flow from its bag, down the long tube, and into my hand. In minutes, the see-through line was continuously pushing the fluid into my body. If it weren't for the occasional, teeny air bubbles that moved down the tubing, I wouldn't be able to tell anything was entering my hand.

"We use saline first to flush the line," a nurse explained. She unsealed the blood bag and adjusted the medicine pump to a much slower setting. "We'll see how you do with the actual blood. If your temperature and blood pressure are acceptable, we can speed up the drip. If your blood pressure changes or if you spike a fever, we'll slow it down."

Over the next several minutes, red liquid streamed downward inside the tube, heading toward me. Before long, the clear fluid had emptied into my hand. As the new blood cells entered my body, I decided to try to write from different perspectives.

Tayoe's POV–
Takes Place Monday, February 16, 2009

I didn't want to be in the hospital playroom. It didn't matter that I had gotten out of school early, or that I was surrounded by the coolest gaming platforms in the world. It would have been okay if it was me who was sick, but it was Kitti.

I sat there for forever, trying to distract myself with once-awesome video games. They were lame. My dad showed up and took me to the cafeteria downstairs. He said I could have anything I wanted, including five ice cream sandwiches. It was the first time we had done anything alone together since Kit had started chemo. I didn't even care that we were mostly talking about my sister's sickness.

"She's O-negative," dad said. "Do you know what that means?"

"That she doesn't have any blood?"

"There are eight blood types- O, A, B, and AB. Each has a positive and negative variety: O+, O-, A+, A-, and so on. Recipients can only get blood from a compatible donor. For example, if you have positive blood, you can get positive or negative blood. If you are negative, you can only get negative blood."

"So Kitti can't get the positive kind?" I asked.

"That's right. And because people with O blood can only receive O blood..."

"She has to get O-negative?"

"Yes." He had a kind of funny look on his face.

"So... is that bad?"

"There's a blood shortage, especially in the imaginary world. Right now, the Underground City doesn't have any O-negative blood in its bank. They're widening their search, but..."

But what? A blood shortage?

"But she's gotta get blood! She got so sick, she passed out! If they don't give her blood, she'll die."

She'll die, I repeated in my head. That's one thing I hadn't thought of much. In the past, I was afraid for Kitti, but not because I thought she'd die. I didn't want her to be in pain, or feel sick all the time. I knew bad things could happen, but I never thought about her dying.

"What's your blood type?" I asked.

"I'm A-positive."

"Is Belle old enough?"

270

"Yes, but she and Ariella are also A-positive."

"Well, if it's an emergency, can't they give her a different kind?"

"No. It would make her very, very sick."

"But she's already very, very sick!"

"It would make her worse than she is now."

"What about me?" I asked. "Why can't I donate to her?"

"Tay, you're too young…"

"I don't care!" I said. "I don't care if it hurts me! I've got lots of blood, and because we're twins, we've gotta match, right?"

"You're fraternal twins, so it's possible but not definite. Even so, you're too young. You don't weigh enough, either."

"But it's not fair! She's dying, and I can't do anything to help her."

"I know. I feel the same way."

~~~

I got to hang out in Kit's room on Platypus Unit for a while. She wasn't doing so hot, but she still smiled. Her pale skin looked strange.

All these people came in to check on Kitti. The nurses took her blood pressure and temperature. Lab techs stole blood from her, which made me mad. Didn't every drop count at this point? There were lots of "gist" docs. You know, the oncologist who took care of chemo side effects, the cardiologist who wanted to make sure her heart was okay, and her regular nephrologist Dr. Emilie.

"Listen, we're checking everyone we can to find a donor," she promised Kitti. "Your hemoglobin is still 6.9. It's not dropping, so that's good."

"Why did it drop?" Kitti asked. It's like her brain wouldn't shut off… she was always thinking, even when her blood levels were crazy-low.

"At first I thought it was just the cyclophosphamide, but that was probably only part of it. The meds, your menstrual cycle, and the kidney disease itself seem to have hit you with a triple-whammy. You're going to make it through this, as long as we monitor you closely."

"Really?" I asked before I could stop myself.

Dr. Emilie turned around. "Yeah," she told me. "We're going to find her blood. It's just taking more time than I'd like."

I wished I had all the spy skills Kit had because I couldn't tell if Dr. Emilie was telling the truth or just trying to make me feel better. Her fancy doctor phone thing buzzed, and she looked at the screen.

"We found a unit," she sang twice in a sing-song voice.

"YES!" I shouted. "So where's the blood?"

"Well, it doesn't appear out of thin air," Kitti said.

"She's right," Dr. Emilie agreed. "We have to transport the unit and cross-match... it could take a while, several hours at least. The good news is that we should be able to transfuse sometime tonight. If all goes well, you should be out of here by this time tomorrow."

I didn't even care that meant that I'd probably have to go to school the next day.

Jobelle's POV– Takes Place: February 16, 2009

During second period, I got called to the office to take a phone call from dad. He told me about Kitti's predicament and promised to send someone to pick me up when school was out.

It was a rough day, at best. Thankfully, the "my sister is going to die if she doesn't get blood" card efficiently allowed me to space out in class without problem. I was surprised when Rachel picked me up right after lunch.

"Where's Squeaky?" I asked.

"She goes to a homeschool club twice a week. I have to pick her up in a few hours."

"Does my dad know about this?" I asked as we drove out of the high school parking lot.

"No, but I told him I'd take care of you, and that's what I'm doing. Besides, he needed me to pick you up and bring you to the hospital sometime this afternoon. I had to pick you up early so I could get to Squeaky in time. I figured how much earlier didn't matter." I was surprised when she made a turn at my favorite fast food spot on the way to the hospital.

"Your father told me you used to come here all the time to get cheese fries," Rachel stated, moving her car into the long drive-through line.

"I don't eat cheese fries anymore."

"No?" Rachel asked. "Why not?"

I closed my eyes. "Because Kitti can't."

"You're a better person than I ever was," Rachel confessed without taking her eyes off the parking lot. "Do you know what Kitti can have?" She asked rhetorically. "As long as her phosphorus doesn't start to climb, she can have ice cream."

I made the mistake of falling for the "so what are your favorite flavors" question while in line. Rather than buying a single scoop of rocky road as I had requested, Rachel ordered additional scoops of vanilla and chocolate chip cookie dough for me.

"Will you stop thanking me, sweetie?" Rachel insisted while we ate in the hospital parking lot several minutes later. "And don't tell your father about this. I don't need to be reimbursed."

As we started to walk toward the pediatric building, Rachel's cell phone buzzed. "It's a message from your dad." She opened her phone with a smile, but as her eyes scanned the screen, her face fell. I peeked over her shoulder and read the text.

They can't use the units for some reason. Her pulse is racing, but her hemoglobin is stable at 6.9. We are looking again.

A million questions ran through my mind. "Why can't

she get that blood? When will they find another unit? How long can she live with so little blood…?"

Rachel hugged me. "Sweetie, I don't have enough information. Right now, I just don't know."

"Can I donate?" I asked.

"For someone else, probably, but Kitti is O-. You're A+."

~~~

I got to see Kitti briefly before they moved her to PICU. She wasn't in critical condition, but with the blood shortage, we weren't sure how long she would have to wait. The hospital sent an alert throughout the city that they were looking for a blood donor. Things like this had happened before, but I had never paid attention to such announcements. I would from now on.

Tay and I stayed in the family waiting room. A child life specialist had us playing a board game, but it couldn't distract me. At 3:30, Rachel reappeared with Squeaky, a nurse, and Graham.

"Are you okay?" Graham asked as we hugged. I nodded.

"But you aren't," I noticed. "What's wrong?"

"Okay, come on," Rachel said urgently, tugging Graham's arm. "We don't have forever. Let's go!"

"Go where?" Tay asked before I could say anything.

"Graham's gonna give Kitti blood," Squeaky said with a smile.

"I'm O negative," Graham confirmed hoarsely.

"Alright," Rachel practically cheered. "I'll stay with Tay, Belle, and Squeaky. Now go!"

As I watched Graham and the nurse leave the room, my heart pounded. Ever since his mom had been diagnosed with cancer, Graham had been horrified of needles. I couldn't believe his selflessness or courage.

"A nervous hero," I said quietly, although the word in my head was 'terrified.' Rachel looked at me, intently studying my face.

"I'll be right back," she said, charging out of the room and calling toward Graham's nurse. "Hey, Miranda!"

Within a minute, Rachel returned. "Belle, come here," she called. I quickly walked across the room.

"You aren't squeamish, are you?" Rachel asked. I shook my head. "Good. You're Graham's moral support… if you don't mind, of course."

She took me out to the hallway, where I was introduced to Graham's nurse, Miranda. They had already done his paperwork and pre-donation mini physical. In the hospital's blood donation room, they had him lean back in a special recliner that looked like a dentist's chair. I sat next to him in a regular seat.

"You have great veins," a phlebotomist named Michelle said as she put a pressure cuff on his left arm. "But you're tensing up. Take some deep breaths."

I took his free hand. "I know I'm annoying, but look at me." He did so as Michelle cleaned his skin. Impulsively, he flinched.

"It's just Betadine," Miranda encouraged. "You're doing great."

Michelle pulled out a wide needle. I was thankful Graham was still facing me because the 16 gauge straight made me a little anxious. It was quite different from the teeny "butterflies" I had seen in the past.

"Graham, you don't need to see the needle," I said. Michelle scoffed. "I'm serious," I continued. "Don't make him look at it." Michelle glared at me, but I mouthed to Graham, "Don't look at it."

"Hold this stress release ball," Michelle ordered. Graham held his left palm open but didn't turn around. Nurse Miranda smiled, but Michelle seemed ticked. Grumpily, Michelle plopped it in his hand and picked up the needle.

"Thumb wrestle with me?" I thought, remembering one of

275

Kit's words of wisdom when it came to blood draws. "And don't let me win."

I lost within a second. I knew he was strong, but I never realized just how strong. Suddenly, Graham grimaced and closed his eyes. He squeezed my hand tightly as the needle slid into his vein. Michelle must have been a lousy phlebotomist because she seemed to readjust the needle more than I had seen before.

"Do you remember what I told you when I got mad at you on the school bus back when I was in ninth grade?" I asked, desperate to distract him.

"Yeah," he groaned. "'I hate you.'"

"'I hate you more,'" I quoted, and Graham actually smiled.

During my transfusion, the nurses frequently checked my blood pressure to make sure I wasn't having a reaction. The infusion didn't give me any side effects; if anything, I felt better as my hemoglobin slowly climbed. It was a little bit freaky to look up and see a bag of blood, but gradually, I got used to the idea.

About halfway through my second unit of blood, my mom went to the gift shop to buy a new stuffed animal friend for Pepper- a tradition started on the day of my renal biopsy. She came back with a pale-white stuffed kitten. I immediately named her Anemia. Taking a break from writing about Kitti's transfusion, I worked on a short Pepper piece.

Pepper's POV- Takes Place: February 16, 2009

Hello. This is Pepper. Guess what? Did you guess yet? You is slow guesser. Anyway, Pepper didn't have to go to school today! No school for Pepper, no school for Pepper, no school for Pepper! Instead, Pepper got to run around hospital and eat hospital food like chicken nugget (yum- don't let people say hospital food is bad). And then Pepper ride on up and downy bed and watch lots of cartoons and growl at mean nurse and purr at nice nurses.

Anyway, dinner is coming- yum- and grandma brought new friend. New friend is kitten named Anemia. She is younger kitten than Pepper. She is baby. So Pepper will show her how to be cool.

My monitor beeped, showing my infusion had finished. After a few minutes of observation, I was discharged. My mom went to get the car, and while I waited for a wheelchair ride to the parking lot, I finished my main PFA story of the day.

Jobelle's POV- Takes Place: February 16, 2009

Around 6:00, we were told Graham's unit would work for Kitti. It would take several more hours, but Dr. Emilie promised that Kitti would be transfused before midnight. Tay and I had missed only three days of the school year, so dad let us stay at the hospital overnight and "skip" the next day. When Graham announced he was going home, I walked with him to the parking garage. We talked about unimportant things until we got to his old green truck.

I had admired Graham from the moment I understood his background. He had always been heroic, but now, he was my hero. He had saved my sister's life.

Impulsively, I stood on my tiptoes and kissed his cheek.

All of a sudden, I was embarrassed. I had just kissed my best friend! It wouldn't have been a big deal, but I had a ginormous crush on him!

"What was that for?" Graham asked.

I didn't know what to say. "Thank you," I stammered. "Thank you for saving Kitti's life."

"You're welcome," he said, opening the door to his truck. "See you later, alright?"

I nodded. "Bye."

I expected him to get into his truck, but he didn't. "Thank you," he said instead. Hesitantly, he kissed me on the cheek.

277

"What was that for?" I asked.

"I couldn't have done it without you," he answered. "Dr. Emilie said that Michelle lady is the worst phlebotomist in the hospital."

I laughed and hugged him.

"Alright, Belle. Bye for real."

"Bye for real."

Wednesday, February 18, 2009

One of my biggest pre-FSGS fears had been throwing up. With each new prescription, I'd read the drug fact sheet anxiously, praying that frequent vomiting wouldn't appear on the side effect list.

Although mycophenolate isn't actually an anticancer agent, its side effects mirror those caused by chemotherapy. I battled nausea daily until noon. Although I had been fighting "mycophenolate morning sickness" for over a month, I'd never actually vomited until now. This had been the first time since before my diagnosis, and strangely, the experience was "fun" compared to taking prednisone.

Throwing up became almost as normal as urinating. Like clockwork, it happened at least once a day. It was restrictive, but it didn't stop me from going "out" with my mom for a few hours each Saturday morning. We carried gallon-sized zip bags in our purses. They came in handy much too often! To keep from getting too upset about this gross new side effect, I joked around. My mom and I would laugh when people avoided me like the plague after an 'episode.' Vomiting in stores became so commonplace that I could be looking at an item one minute, throwing up into a bag the next, and return to shopping as if nothing happened. When people told me I shouldn't be out with the stomach flu, I replied, "Oh, it's just the chemo."

Jobelle's POV- Life Goes On
Takes Place: Late February 2009

It was weird. In some ways, nothing was different. Then again, illness affected every aspect of Kitti's life and profoundly impacted our family. Our schedules were different, our budget was tighter, and the kitchen counter had transformed into a pharmacy!

The biggest change was the food. Sometimes it seemed we ate healthier, like when, to cut back on sodium, we switched from processed frozen foods to their homemade counterparts. (Breaded cod is better than fish sticks anyway!) We swapped potato chips with berries and got rid of the saltshakers. However, the renal diet isn't a typical "healthy" diet. Tayoe and I generally ate our bananas, potatoes, tomatoes, and other potassium-rich foods away from home and our sister.

Oftentimes, Kitti needed more calories. She had little appetite on chemo. Dr. Emilie said most "kidney kid's" weight loss is masked by swelling, but Kitti's wasn't. By her third cyclo infusion, the water weight began to melt off her. It was a great sign that the medicine was working, but at the same time, it was disturbing to see how underweight Kitti had become. A carton of whole milk joined our fat-free milk jug in the refrigerator. Nutrition drinks showed up in the cabinets. Candy seemed to flood into our house. It may sound strange, but Kitti relied on gummy bears to boost her calorie intake. Sometimes, she needed more water than she could drink. Rachel's apartment was equipped with plenty of medical supplies, so Kitti would often sleep over at Rachel's for intravenous fluids.

Meanwhile, Rachel had taken in another chronically ill child. This time, it was seven-year-old Spot, one of Todd Shramere's many stuffed animals. The little Fictional Alliance member was quite different from the many other Alliance characters, especially his rambunctious brother Bubba. A self-described "warrior," Spot was sweet, quiet, and a little bit on the clumsy side.

"But the poor little guy can't help it," Kitti explained to me after Spot had walked into a glass door. "He's actually pretty smart. It's just his illness- RATS- has shifted the stuffing around in his head."

Rip and Tear Syndrome- commonly known as RATS in the imaginary medical community- is an entirely pretend disease that affects plush animals. Rip and Tear Syndrome is exactly what its name suggests: affected stuffed animals' seams slowly rip and tear apart. RATS is different from an accidental fabric scratch. The syndrome is characterized by frequent tears in various parts of the body. It takes place on a molecular level, meaning stitches and patches are only temporary fixes. The disease is lifelong and often devastating, but surprisingly, it's rarely fatal.

Anyway, Spot was a cougar cub with moderate-grade RATS. He went undiagnosed for years, because… well, let's face it, Bubba and his buddies were rough on little kids. The kitten finally ended up in the hospital after the beans in his head began to pour out of a rip in his furry scalp. Spot underwent surgery after surgery, stitch after stitch, but he would never be entirely free of illness. Even so, he was such a phenomenal, happy little guy. He got along well with the PFA kids- especially Pepper- and gave Kitti a hint or two when it came to fighting illness. One of Spot's many medicines caused him to grow leopard-like patterns all over his fur. He never said a word about it. In fact, we didn't even think he noticed.

In late February, not long after her third chemo infusion, Kitti's hair began falling out in clumps. Her beautiful blonde hair had thinned significantly in the days after her first two treatments, but this time, it was obvious there wouldn't be any left by March. Kitti was horrified. She stopped brushing and washing her hair, but it didn't help.

One day, Tay and I came home from school to find dad holding Kitti on the couch. She was sobbing. I was afraid that her labs had been disappointing- that maybe her creatinine had risen or her albumin had plummeted once more. When she looked at us, I noticed the huge bald spot on the side of her head. Her hair was so thin I could practically see her scalp. I was about to say something- I'm not sure what- when I heard a growl from outside the apartment.

"MY FUR IS NONE OF YOUR BUSINESS!" A small voice shrieked. Tay opened the front door to see tiny Spot standing in the hallway, shouting at someone. "MY FUR IS NONE OF YOUR

BUSINESS!" Spot smiled contently as someone- Bubba, I'm guessing- went downstairs and left the building.

"Hi, guys," Spot said in his normal, lovable voice. "They were just making fun of me because I look like a leopard. I mean, there's nothing wrong about being a leopard. I like leopards. They're good. But it would be like someone saying you're a girl," he pointed to Tayoe.

"You told me you liked your new fur," Kitti said as she came to the door.

Spot shrugged. "It's okay. I miss my old fur, though. It was so smooth."

Kitti nodded. "I wish my hair was thick."

"It'll be thick again someday," Spot said.

"See?" Dad asked gently. "Spot's dealt with self-image problems, too."

"But people will laugh, stare, and think I have cancer," Kitti replied.

"Annie hates the prednisone moon-face and abdominal swelling," I added quietly. "Only one person has ever made fun of her, and her face is so puffy. Baldness is better understood than cushingoid symptoms," I said, using the term that described the appearance of people on corticosteroids. "Besides, what's so bad about people thinking you have cancer? Maybe they'll respect what you've been through for once."

"And you can always tell them your fur is none of their business," Spot added. "That's what I say, after all."

That conversation stuck with Kitti. She felt sad about her hair falling out but was no longer mortified. She often wore hats. With something covering her scalp, you'd guess that she had very thin hair, not that she was going bald.

About a week later, my family ate dinner at Rachel's house. The last of Kitti's hair kept falling into her macaroni and cheese. Everyone ignored it, although Spot looked at her sympathetically. Finally, Kitti got tired of it... and started giggling hysterically. Personally, I didn't think it was funny, but her laughter was contagious. Pepper snorted so hard she fell out of her chair.

The next day, we had a hair party as a child life specialist from the cancer unit had suggested. Dad, Tayoe, Tomes, Tinarg, Graham, and a bunch of other boys dyed their hair orange for nephrotic syndrome. I got orange highlights, and Rachel helped Kitti dye her hair pink. Dad, Tay, and Kitti had their hair shaved off. (I don't know whose idea it was to let Pepper do it, but she had a little too much fun making chainsaw noises with my dad and brother. Rachel did Kitti's hair to lessen the trauma.) I had my waist-long hair cut to just below my chin and donated it to a wig-making organization.

Kitti seemed upbeat the rest of the day, but that night, I heard her crying. "Kit?" I asked as I walked into her room. "Are you okay?"

"I know it's stupid," she whispered through tears. "I know it'll grow back, but Belle, I miss my hair."

I didn't say 'I know,' because I didn't. Instead, I scooted into bed beside her and pulled her close to me.

Thursday, February 26, 2009

Dr. Jones believed my frequent vomiting was caused by a stomach ulcer, a possible side effect of several of my medications. He referred me to a gastroenterologist, who ordered an upper gastrointestinal endoscopy.

An upper GI endoscopy is a test that examines the esophagus and stomach. It uses a small video camera attached to a tube. The doctor inserts the tube down the sedated patient's throat to see what's going on inside.

I don't remember agreeing to a colonoscopy, but loopy on sedatives after my upper GI endoscopy, I apparently had. A colonoscopy is performed the same way as an upper GI endoscopy, except it examines the large intestines.

Generally, people dread it, even though the test itself isn't terrible at all. The problem is the preparation.

For the first test, the pre-procedure instructions were to stop eating and drinking by midnight the day of the exam. Colonoscopy prep directions are detailed. I had to be on a clear liquid diet for over 24 hours before the procedure. I was prescribed a gallon-sized bottle of a solution designed to clean out my colon. The liquid wasn't as gross-tasting as you'd expect, but drinking so much of anything in a short period of time was difficult.

It's "normal" for patients to spend most of their colonoscopy prep time in the bathroom. Like usual, my body did nothing "normal." We discovered just how little I had been eating by how my liquid diet day went compared to the "typical" person.

I felt sick most of the day... even too sick to type. My mom stayed home to take care of me, and for the most part, we watched movies in-between my trips to the bathroom. When she left briefly to retrieve Todd from school, I looked through old PFA stories on my laptop. Before long, I ran into stories about Squeaky, my penguin with nephrotic syndrome. I thought about Squeaky's namesake, the little girl I had seen in the hospital over a year before.

"Do I have to drink that icky juice?" She had asked.

"She'd had a colonoscopy," I finally understood.

The next morning was the procedure, which wasn't too bad. In fact, as far as I could tell, it seemed identical to the upper GI endoscopy. The pre and post-procedural room was the same I had been in two weeks before. I even had the same nurses.

My results were normal. The gastroenterologist said I had the healthiest colon he had seen. With everything malicious ruled out, we finally were able to assume my constant nausea and frequent vomiting were caused by my medications. Dr. Jones prescribed Phenergan up to two times a day as needed. Because it's addictive, I had to take the smallest amount possible. The tiny pills worked wonders. On the day of my first dose, the debilitating nausea only lasted until about ten or so in the morning. This was the best thing that had happened to me in a long time! My mom and I carefully worked out a phenergan schedule that kept me from vomiting more than once or twice a day. Sometimes, I didn't throw up at all in 24 or even 48 hours!

Early one March morning, I awoke to news that Nectar had died. Dad found her collapsed on the grass, meaning the sweet old dog was probably enjoying a walk around the yard when her heart gave out.

Good, I thought. *She didn't suffer.*

I didn't feel sad. I would miss her, of course, but I had prepared for this. Every time I saw her, I had hugged her and said goodbye, knowing that it could be <u>the</u> goodbye. I talked to her and sang to her. I did all I could do to make her last months peaceful. There didn't seem to be a reason to be sad... at least, not for me. My family was poignant for several days, and I don't blame them. Mourning is an important and good thing. I just didn't feel like crying over Nectar's death. Unfortunately, I had seen worse things in the past few months.

Kitti's POV- Takes Place: March 2009

Nothing. Sometimes, when I didn't feel well, I stared blankly into space. Unlike most daydreamers, I wasn't thinking at all. Suddenly, daddy appeared out of nowhere; I had been so "zoned" I didn't even notice him approach.

"It's Dr. Emilie," he said. Usually, my mind would have gone into overtime, trying to decipher if my doctor had good or bad news. Instead, I simply put the phone to my ear.

"Hello?"

"Hey, Kitti. How are you feeling?"

"Really bad," I admitted sadly.

"That's because your BUN is 19," Dr. Emilie announced. "The protein in your urine is negative again. Your creatinine is on its way down, and everything is stabilizing. You know what that means: you're in remission!"

"Remission?" I repeated, not quite understanding. Remission... but how could that be? I was feeling so rotten! How could I be in...?

"Remission!" I exclaimed happily. "Then why do I feel so icky?"

"It's your BUN," Dr. Emilie explained. "You're so used to having toxins in your blood that your body doesn't know what to do now that your kidneys aren't 'leaking'. Also, your red blood cell count is low from the chemo. That could make you feel tired as well."

"So we can cancel tomorrow?"

"Sorry, sweetie, but I want you to get your last treatment. It'd be a shame if you relapse because we stopped the cyclophosphamide too early. We'll see what your blood counts are tomorrow."

Only one more chemo infusion! I squealed with delight. Both daddy and Dr. Emilie laughed.

"However you celebrated last time, upgrade!" Dr. Emilie said.

"Do you think I'll stay in remission this time?" I asked.

"I thought it would last last time," she admitted. "Just remember- one day at a time. I'll drop in to see you tomorrow on the oncology unit, but I just had to tell you and your father now."

I handed the phone to dad and ran (literally!) across the hall.

"Rachel!" I shouted gleefully, banging on her apartment's door. "We did it! I'm in remission!"

~~~

The next day, I headed to the hospital for my final treatment. My favorite nurse connected me to the IV and began my last cyclophosphamide drip.

"Looking good," Danielle said, checking my infusion pump after a few minutes went by. "Are you nauseous yet?"

I shook my head, sticking out my tongue to show the ginger hard candy in my mouth. "Maybe I won't need any extra anti-nausea meds this time." Nurse Danielle obviously doubted me and smiled sadly, but I was right. Somehow, I made it through most of the infusion without any reaction. Nurses gathered around me in excitement when I had only a few milliliters of medicine left in the bag. The IV pump finally beeped, announcing the last of the chemo had entered my veins. Everyone, including the other patients, applauded. The staff sang a song, showered me with confetti, and gave me presents.

Dr. Emilie showed up after the crowd had dispersed. She took me downstairs in a wheelchair after daddy went to the parking lot to get the car.

"It feels weird," I said quietly as we entered an elevator.

"Are you having side effects?" My doctor wondered, feeling my forehead.

"Not yet. I mean the party and getting presents feels weird. Last time I got into remission, no one thought it was a big deal but you, me, my family, and my very closest friends. I know this treatment was more intense than the prednisone, but it's still strange."

"I know," she agreed.

"Do you think it will last this time?" I asked. "Will I relapse?"

There was a pause. "That I don't know," she finally answered.

I closed my eyes, wishing I could say what was on my mind. I remembered overhearing a conversation between Dr. Emilie and the Nephrology Department Head back in November. It had left me with so many unanswered questions about my doctor's past. With a little detective work, I had unraveled the mystery.

"Did you relapse?" I asked Dr. Emilie.

"Eleven times in ten years," Dr. Emilie answered calmly.

"Was it minimal change?"

"No."

She walked slowly, as if deep in thought. We moved along the hallway at a snail's pace.

"Are you mad at me for asking?"

"No. I'm surprised you didn't ask sooner. I had FSGS once upon a time. Technically, I still have it, although I've been in remission for years now."

"You told me kidney disease ran in your family," I remembered.

"My mom had lupus nephritis. See, she was a patient in this hospital before it got transplanted here. She met my father when she was on dialysis. He was her transplant surgeon, and I was their miracle baby, or at least that's what mom always said. I was probably more of an accident than anything. Dad was afraid mom's pregnancy would kill her. Somehow, we both survived. Everybody sighed in relief. No one expected nephrotic syndrome, but that's what I developed. For the next ten years, I drifted in and out of remission. When I was twelve, the biopsy

288

showed tip-lesion FSGS. The last-ditch effort to save my kidneys was intravenous cyclophosphamide. Surprisingly, it worked. Of course, I didn't expect it to last forever, but time went by. A year, two years, five years, ten years… nothing happened."

"Can I ask you a patient-to-patient question?" I wondered. "When you were on cyclophosphamide, how long did it take for your hair to grow back?"

"It never fell out. Complete hair loss is very rare at such a low dose."

I made a face. "They need to make better-targeted medicines."

"From both patient and professional perspectives, I agree," Dr. Emilie said as we entered a glass elevator and rode to the floor level.

"How long have you been off the medications?" I asked.

"They took me off everything when I was fourteen or fifteen. I'm only on enalapril and aspirin now," she said. "My creatinine isn't exactly normal, but it's held steady for around two decades."

"You're an inspiration," I said.

"You are, too," Dr. Emilie mused. We got to the front door and waited for dad to pull up in the car. "Just remember: never give up. I'll see you in two weeks for a check-up."

I sprawled out in the backseat. As we drove home, I prayed that this remission would last forever. *If it continues to relapse, I'll be a child life specialist or nurse*, I told myself. *But if I can be completely normal, I'm going to be a doctor… or an FBI agent.*

Mid-March 2009

Time flies when you're fighting for your life. Before I knew it, spring had bloomed again in Arkansas. Sometimes, on warm days, I went outside to sit in the sunshine. Brownie had been lonely since Nectar's death, so she often let me hold her. With unusually careful supervision, I allowed her to play with Pepper.

My aunt came to visit during spring break. She hadn't seen me since before my diagnosis and was surprised I was so sick. She was very kind, but it scared me. I was doing wonderfully compared to how I felt in 2008. Exactly how sick had I been? Because, apparently, lying down in deserted aisles of the department store while my family shopped was alarming. (It seemed perfectly normal to me. In fact, I saw it as a step up from sleeping in the car during our previous shopping excursions!)

On one vacation day, we drove out to Hot Springs to visit their magnificent gardens. My aunt and mom paid a few extra dollars for a tour guide and, more importantly, her golf cart. I sat on the back seat with my mom. I held Pepper in one hand and my camera in the other as we watched the tulips roll by. While I wouldn't have found this exciting a few years before, I loved observing the stunning spring foliage. Mid-March was such a beautiful time to visit. The garden was blossoming; it was as if everything was awakening from the dead of winter into the new life of spring. If I could sum up this time of rebirth in one word, I think it would be hope.

As we rode around the grounds, the tour guide pointed out many optional adventures that were scattered throughout the garden. We could have spent an entire day exploring these breathtaking trails. Unfortunately, they could only be accessed by foot.

We opted to go home. That was the new story of my life.

But even so, I decided to never lose hope.